"Although this tale is about one of tne most risky and exhilarating sports of all, this book is rather quiet, gradual, and sweet."
— *VOYA*

"Lenz has written a wonderful and powerfully unique story."
— Jessie Ann Foley, author of *The Carnival at Bray*, a Printz Honor Book

"This is a richly layered story, visceral and thoughtful in equal parts."
— Tim Wynne-Jones, author of *The Emperor of Any Place*

"From dangling over a vertical rock face in Ecuador to navigating the rocky emotional terrain of friendship and love at home, Cara's journey totally captured my heart. Hold on tight to this book!"
— Vicky Alvear Shecter, author of *Cleopatra's Moon*, a Crystal Kite Award Winner

"A powerful, enveloping story about grief—the deep layers of heartbreak bubbling beneath the surface—and the ways relationships help us through our toughest times."
— Kelly Jensen, *Stacked Books*

"I loved this book. There's plenty of humor, romance, and great rock climbing scenes that will have you riveted."
— Anne Rouyer, New York Public Library

"This beautifully written YA novel details how difficult it can be to let go of the past, embrace the present, and make peace with an uncertain future." — *Bustle.com*

"This is a beautiful story of testing limits, a story of the bonds of friendship, family, and love."
— Lara Zielin, author of *The Implosion of Aggie Winchester* and *Waiting Sky*

"This novel will warm the hearts of both younger and older readers alike." — Laura Ellen, author of *Blind Spot*

"This is an intriguing story that brings something new to the table, something we've not seen before, and it does it incredibly well."
— Alice Reeds, blogger at *Alice Reeds* and author of *Petty Little Lives*

"Cara's story is about finding yourself, your family, and your center. Lenz encourages readers to think outside the pages, to find their own place in the world as Cara discovers hers."
— Meghan Dietsche Goel, BookPeople, Austin, Texas

"Lenz has shown me Cara's world and everything it involves, and I've come out on the other side with a different outlook than when I first started the novel." — Amy Delancey, *Crazy Book Obsessions!*

"*The Art of Holding On and Letting Go* will take you to new heights."
— Moriah Chavis, *A Leisure Moment*

THE ART OF
Holding On
AND
Letting Go

Kristin Bartley Lenz

ELEPHANT
ROCK
BOOKS
YA

Winner of the 2016 Helen Sheehan YA Book Prize

ISBN: 9780996864916

Library of Congress Control Number: 2016942722

Printed in the United States of America

Book Design by Amanda Schwarz,
Fisheye Graphic Services, Chicago

First Edition
10 9 8 7 6 5 4 3 2

Elephant Rock Books
Ashford, Connecticut

— for Maya

Mountains are giant, restful, absorbent. You can heave your spirit into a mountain and the mountain will keep it, folded, and not throw it back as some creeks will. The creeks are the world with all its stimulus and beauty; I live there. But the mountains are home.
　　　　　　　　　　　—Annie Dillard, *Pilgrim at Tinker Creek*

PART I: ECUADOR

I want to stand as close to the edge as I can without going over. Out on the edge you see all the kinds of things you can't see from the center.

—Kurt Vonnegut, *Piano Player*

1

The waiting was the worst. I gripped my worry stone from Uncle Max, turning it around and around in my hands. My fingers probed its golden grooves and contours. The sharp edges shimmered.

My teammate Becky sat next to me in the isolation tent examining her red, white, and blue–painted nails. It was the second day of qualifying rounds, and we'd been waiting two hours for our turns to climb. Tiny stars dotted her thumbs. I didn't understand why she bothered—the polish always chipped by the time she finished her climb.

My own nails were cut as short as possible, my fingers rough and calloused. A crosshatch of red lines spread across the back of my right hand where I had wedged it into a crack last week, the rock scraping my skin. I couldn't tell yet if it would leave a scar like the other white marks on my hands, the crooked gash on my thumb, my pitted palm.

"Ugh," Becky said. "I want my phone. Seriously, I'm, like, twitching. Look." She pointed to her eye.

"Maybe you got mascara in it." Her lashes were so clumped and coated, they looked fake.

She'd scrolled through her phone at breakfast, tilting it toward me so I could see the picture of her hand placed over her heart like she was reciting the Pledge of Allegiance. She'd managed to display our USA team logo, her cleavage, and her patriotic nails all in one close-up shot. Four hundred likes.

No phones allowed in the tent, and no checking out the routes before we climbed; the canvas walls blocked our view of the competition area. A collective groan came from the bleachers outside. Someone had fallen.

"Another one bites the dust." I tumbled the stone faster and faster in my hands. I swear I could feel its heat, its fire.

"It's pyrite. Fool's gold," Uncle Max had said. "Named after fire. It'll spark if you strike it against steel, so they say. Want to try?"

For the rest of the day, we struck it against anything metal we came across—tent poles, car rims—startling ourselves and giggling every time we saw the tiniest spark.

Becky nudged me with her elbow and nodded toward our teammate Zach. "Sleeping Beauty."

Zach was sprawled on his back, shirtless, his blue-and-white team tank top wadded under his head as a pillow. His eyes were closed, ear buds in. Zach always spent his isolation time listening to music on his iPod and snoozing.

"He climbs right before you," I said to Becky. "Make sure he's up after I leave."

"Oh, I will." Her slight southern drawl stretched out the word *will*, her lips curving into a sly grin.

I knew exactly how she'd wake him up, leaning in close so he'd open his eyes to her boobs in front of his face. I didn't understand how Becky could be so strong yet look so soft and curvy at the same time. I was all bone and muscle. My own chest looked like Zack's—two nipples sticking out of rippling, hard pecs.

A burst of laughter erupted from the other side of the tent. The French team lounged in a clump, girls and guys draped all over each other. They held hands, rested heads in laps, massaged each other's feet.

Becky had been eyeing them all morning. She rolled her eyes and laughed with me, but I knew she'd rather be hanging with them. In their cozy company, she'd have an excuse to hang all over Zach.

Becky sighed. "You're lucky your parents aren't here. Mine will be whistling and waving as soon as my name is announced. They make me so freaking nervous."

I glanced at the large digital clock over the tent's door. My name would be called soon. I set the chunk of pyrite next to my backpack and picked up my thermos of peppermint tea.

"Just don't look at them before you climb," I said.

"I can't help it. I always want to see who's in the crowd."

I sipped my lukewarm tea. The crowd made me nervous, not my parents. Knowing they were in the audience usually calmed me, but there was something freeing about being here by myself this time, as a serious competitor, not as the daughter of top mountaineers Mark and Lori Jenkins.

"At least your parents have a life," Becky said. "My mom would never leave me alone in a foreign country."

Mom hadn't been comfortable leaving me. We'd debated our plan for weeks, but in the end, I had insisted. Mom should go on the Chimborazo expedition with Dad and Uncle Max.

I shrugged. "They'll be back by the finals."

"What if you don't make it to finals?"

I arched an eyebrow at her. *I* would make it to finals.

A competition volunteer appeared at the tent entrance and motioned for me to follow. I handed Becky my thermos of tea and tugged on my well-worn, broken-in shoes. As long as the rubber soles were still grippy, I wasn't giving them up. Becky was still trying to decide which of the three shiny new pairs she'd brought looked best with her outfit.

I shook out my hands and cracked my knuckles. I rose up on my tiptoes and bounced. Up, down, up, down.

I nudged Zack's ribs with my toe on my way out, and he opened one eye.

"Send it!" he called out as I left the tent. I gave a thumbs-up without looking back and entered the competition area.

I squinted in the bright sunlight and slowly let my eyes adjust. The bleachers were a sea of color: parents and fans and climbers. The World Youth Championships banners covered the fencing that enclosed the outdoor venue. A gust of wind rippled the flags of all the countries. Russia, Australia, China, Mexico, Canada.

"Cara Jenkins," the announcer boomed, "age fifteen, from California, the United States of America, los Estados Unidos."

The crowd buzzed, a nest of bees, murmuring and shifting; I didn't look. Someone hooted. Another whistled. I took a deep breath, twinkled my fingers, and scanned the route. Sixty vertical feet of soaring artificial walls with exposed overhangs. I tied the rope to my harness and dipped my hands in my chalk bag. A puff of white dust floated in the air as I rubbed my palms together.

I nodded at the belayer. "Climbing."

"Climb on," he said with a Spanish accent. His face was neutral, all business, and made me long for a brief look of reassurance from my parents.

I reached for the first handhold and let everything else fade behind me. Steady breath, reach, grasp, pull, push, pivot, twist. My fingers wrapped around a doorknob bulge, pinched another shaped like a duck's bill. I slid my hands along a large diamond-shaped protrusion. The sandpapery surface scraped my calloused fingertips. My forearms quivered. My bruised toes jammed at the front of my climbing shoes, supporting my weight.

One handhold left, a tiny crimper. I balanced on the tip of my big toe, stretched, and inched myself up with the last bit of strength in my muscles. I teetered. I locked my eyes on the grooved nugget above my head. *Breathe.* My hand trembled as I reached upward, the nugget like the pyrite I had tumbled in my hands earlier. *Come on, Cara, you know how to do this.*

A final surge of energy erupted from my core, and I grasped the hold with two iron-claw fingers. Yes! I clipped the bolt, threw my head back, and grinned at the sky. My heart pounded all the way up to my ears. Over the top of the climbing wall, I searched the hazy distance for the snowcapped peaks of the Cordillera Occidental, the Avenue of Volcanoes. Yesterday, the mountains had been clearly visible, grand domes and jagged peaks against a backdrop of blue sky. But this morning, the Andes wore a mask of clouds. My parents were out there with Uncle Max, high on Mount Chimborazo.

The breeze swept across my face, ruffling my bangs and cooling the sweat on my forehead. I closed my eyes and sent a wish to my family, imagining my words traveling with the wind. They'd left four days ago. If all went as planned, they had reached the summit near dawn and were descending at this very moment.

The belayer lowered me back to the ground, and I untied from the rope with shaky hands. Heat pulsed through my body, from my blood to my muscles to my skin. I sneaked a sideways glance at the crowd of clapping, cheering spectators.

I never knew quite how to act when I finished a route. Usually, my gaze would connect with my parents. Mom's face would look relieved, and Dad would send signals with his expression, a nod or shake of his head, analyzing my performance. Uncle Max would cross his eyes or make some sort of goofy face, making me smile, releasing the tension. I'd really need them in two days, when I competed for my world ranking.

I spotted Coach Mel and my teammates who had climbed earlier. I grinned and waved, and left the stage to join them.

2

I was done climbing for the day, but I still felt jumpy. I always felt nervous for the other competitors, almost like I was climbing up there with them, and now it was Becky's turn. Just like she had said, her eyes swept over the crowd and her parents stood up, hollering and waving. Her dad held a camera with a huge lens, and her mom shook a glittery red, white, and blue pom-pom. She probably had patriotically painted nails too.

I tipped my head and squinted at Becky as she climbed. Something was off. She excelled at speed, much more than I, and she took risks, launching and leaping. It was her strength, but also her downfall; sometimes she miscalculated. She'd quickly launched over the first overhang, but now she kept pausing in position. Beautiful positions, her form was great, but she was going to burn herself out before she reached the top. At this rate, she wasn't going to make it over the crux.

"What is she doing?" Coach Mel muttered.

"Do you think she hurt herself?" I asked.

Coach Mel shook her head, her eyes still on the wall.

I knew exactly where Becky was going to have trouble, I could see the spot coming up. She didn't have enough momentum.

She paused on one tiptoe, her right leg trembling. Sewing machine leg, when your muscle fibers twitch uncontrollably from fatigue. Or Elvis leg, as Uncle Max liked to call it. She needed to drop her heel. Like right now.

My hands rose to my face as Becky soared off the wall, arms and legs spread wide.

The crowd groaned, and Coach Mel swore. I cringed. We'd have to wait for the scores later, but she must be out. I couldn't imagine coming all this way to be eliminated during the qualifying rounds.

I waited, but Becky didn't join our team in the stands. Climbing was a weird sport that way. Officially, we were the USA team, but we all had to compete individually. We lived and trained in different places, and we were all competing against each other.

I watched the rest of the competitors, my neck growing more and more stiff and cricked from looking up at the climbing wall. I rolled my head around to relax the muscles. I needed to stand and stretch, move.

"I'm going for a walk," I said to Coach Mel.

She nodded without turning to look at me, her eyes focused on a climber from Germany on the wall.

I went back to the isolation tent to get money from my backpack. A volunteer escorted me inside; they had to make sure I didn't talk to anyone who was still waiting to climb. My chunk of pyrite sat beside my pack where I had left it, and I zipped it into a pocket for safekeeping. I didn't see my thermos of peppermint tea, though. Thanks, Becky.

Back outside in the competition area, I spied Becky with her parents huddled in a corner. I expected to see them consoling her, but they looked at a phone and her dad's huge camera—talking and gesturing. Were they analyzing her climb, trying to strategize? I was curious, but I didn't join them. I still didn't know what to say to her. But if she wasn't crushed about her fall, I wasn't going to feel bad either. Finally, the jittery tension unwound from my muscles.

I darted through and around clumps of spectators, disappearing into the crowd. Outside the competition area, a colorful market lined the sidewalk. It wasn't as big as other markets I had been to in other countries; it seemed to have popped up just for tourists at the climbing event. Even with all of my traveling, this was my first time wandering off by myself. The freedom made me giddy; light and airy enough to skip. My parents must be feeling that way too. Way up high on the summit of Mount Chimborazo, the top of the world!

I wandered from one table to the next, gazing at hand-sewn purses, leather belts, and scarves. The alpaca wool blankets looked so soft, the colors vibrant, the patterns intricate, but I was afraid to stop and touch them. When I was in China with my parents last year, the rule was, "You touch it, you buy it." The vendors wouldn't leave us alone if we showed the slightest interest.

A man motioned to a tall stack of black fedoras as I passed his table. "Señorita?"

I smiled but kept moving. He didn't call after me, and the woman at the next table didn't even look up from her weaving. Not like in China where they followed us. "You likee, you likee? Big daddy have money. Big daddy buy." It had been so funny to see the little Chinese men and women herding my tall, burly Dad toward their stalls.

I smelled smoke and roasting meat, but I didn't see any food. I didn't seek it out, either, because I'd heard they ate guinea pigs, and that I did not want to see.

I finally gave in to my urge to touch the colorful wool, running my hand along a row of striped blankets, soft as cashmere. I hoped they were still here when my parents got back, so we could buy one to take home.

Up ahead, a woman sat on a bright red blanket, jewelry spread out at her feet. I wasn't one to wear much jewelry, I didn't even have my ears pierced, but I hovered over a row of beaded bracelets.

The woman wore a dark green fedora and a white peasant top. She had a baby wrapped in a rainbow-striped sling with a mass of dark hair peeking out. Even the baby had her ears pierced.

"Buena suerte," the woman said, lifting a bracelet and motioning for me to hold out my arm. I crouched at the edge of her blanket, and she slid the bracelet onto my wrist.

The beads were ivory with swirls of chocolate and caramel, weathered looking, and strung with an almost invisible elastic. They looked ancient, like maybe they really could bring good luck.

"Taguas," she said.

I squinted at her. *"Taguas?"*

She reached into a wooden box of beads and pulled up a handful, letting them slowly fall through her fingers. *"Taguas."*

"Taguas." I pointed and smiled. "Gracias. Uno mas, por favor," I said. "Para mi madre."

She nodded and handed me a second bracelet. This one was a rainbow of colored beads. Not quite pastels, but not bright either, they almost looked edible.

"Gracias," I said and handed over my money.

"Buena suerte," she said again.

I headed back to the competition, repeating taguas and buena suerte out loud, enjoying the sound of Spanish rolling off my tongue.

By early evening, the climbing judges announced the competitors who would advance to the semifinals. My stomach fluttered when my name was called, even though I expected it. I grinned and shrugged off my teammates' congrats. Four out of six of us were advancing, but I was the only girl.

I caught Becky's eye, still unsure what to say. "It was a really tricky route."

She shrugged. "I don't know how you do it, you climb like a freaking snail. At least Mama is off my back now. Daddy got the best shots of me climbing, wait until you see."

I half-laughed, half-snorted. Unbelievable. She'd altered her climbing style to pause long enough for good pictures! She held out her phone, and our teammates gathered to see. Instead of climbing, she'd been posing. She'd flown a gazillion miles from home just to enhance her brand. I shook my head, completely unable to relate.

Our team returned to the hostel for dinner, jostling and joking as we stomped through the entryway. Our host was an American expat, a mountaineer who came to Ecuador to climb twenty years ago and never left. My parents had shared adventure stories with him before leaving for their expedition. He had a salt-and-pepper beard and switched back and forth from English with us to rapid-fire Spanish with his staff. His last name was crazy long and Polish, but he told us to call him Mr. S.

He asked us about the competition, and Zach grabbed my wrist and thrust it up in the air.

"The championess!" he shouted.

Becky's eyes were laser beams. I jerked my arm out of Zach's grasp and elbowed him. I'd compete with Becky on the climbing wall but not over a boy. Zach was cute but like a brother to me. We'd climbed together at the same cliffs when I lived in Colorado years ago.

"Congratulations," Mr. S. said. "Ah, tagua nuts." He pointed to the bracelet on my wrist.

"Nuts?"

"Tagua nuts come from a palm tree that grows here. It's also called vegetable ivory. Much better than killing elephants for their tusks. It can be carved into all kinds of shapes for jewelry or buttons or figurines. Sometimes they're left natural, and sometimes they're dyed and polished."

Each of the small, round beads on my bracelet was slightly different in coloring. "Are they supposed to bring good luck?"

"Sure. Buena suerte." He laughed. "Why not?"

Becky leaned closer, and I held up my wrist for her to examine the bracelet. She snapped a picture with her phone.

"I have something special to show you," Mr. S. said. "A volcano began erupting today. Tungurahua has been belching since early morning. Don't worry, we're not in any danger—it's pretty far away. But come up to the deck and see."

We followed him to the deck and draped our arms over the railing, searching the distant horizon.

He pointed to the south. "The sky is filled with ash."

"I don't see any lava," Coach Mel said.

"No lava this time," Mr. S. explained, "just plumes of ash spewing everywhere."

"It looks like LA smog," I said. From the mountaintops near my home in the Angeles Forest, the city often appeared as a smudge in the distance.

"Tungurahua means Throat of Fire. We used to think these volcanoes were dormant, but Tungurahua came to life in 1999. Some days are quiet, but other days it puts on a show." Mr. S. turned to me. "Depending on the winds, climbers may need to turn away from their summit attempts on Mount Chimborazo and the other nearby peaks. The ash is blinding, like a snowstorm."

I froze, then leaned in closer to catch Mr. S.'s words.

"Too bad your parents might not be able to summit, but they'll be back early now, huh, to watch their *championess* climb."

I stared at Mr. S., but before I could fully process his words, my teammates whooped and hollered, jabbing my shoulder, slapping me on the back. I had been holding my breath, and now it came out as a gasp.

"Time for dinner," Coach Mel said, clapping her hands. "Fuel for tomorrow."

As my team filed back into the lodge, Mr. S. nodded at me. "I didn't mean to worry you. Your parents are experienced mountaineers; they know how to stay safe. Tungurahua's eruptions interfere with many climbs on the surrounding mountains. It's the chance you take here."

I looked back at the smoky sky. Climbers caught in any kind of storm was bad news, whether it was snow or volcanic ash, whether they were experienced or not.

"Your parents should be here watching you anyway," Mr. S. said. "Come on, let's eat. Our cook has prepared a special meal. Sea bass, fried plantains."

Later that night, I lay awake, listening to Coach Mel snore from her bed across the room. A lantern sat on the bedside table; she hadn't let me light the candle inside. Toxic fumes from Becky's manicure session hung in the air, stinging my nose. They were probably flammable.

Becky hadn't been happy with our rustic rooms. She lived in a big house near Atlanta, two hours away from rock-climbing mountains. Becky did most of her climbing in the gym. The wood-planked walls and floors of the hostel were comforting to me though, like my cabin in the mountains.

It wasn't like we were poor, but we really had to save and rely on sponsors for our gear and travel. Becky posted pictures from her first-class airplane seats, and her bedroom closet looked like a Lululemon store.

Becky sighed from the top bunk and rolled over, shaking the flimsy bed frame. "Zach likes you," she whispered.

"Me? You've got the boobs and fancy nails."

"You are blind."

Her accent made me smile. "I'm just one of the guys."

I wasn't here to find a boyfriend. Or become an Internet star.

"Sorry I lost your good-luck thermos," she said.

We had searched but hadn't found it. Someone must have picked it up; it wasn't like the isolation tent was that big.

"It's okay. I'll check the lost and found tomorrow." I spoke like it wasn't a big deal, but my stomach fluttered at the thought of climbing without my calming peppermint tea. "What really happened on the wall today?" I asked. "You weren't climbing like yourself."

"I knew I wasn't in the right position to make it over the crux. I was going to have to back down a few feet and start over, and then I would run out of time."

"So you just gave up?"

"I turned it into a better opportunity," she said. "I could feel my dad's camera zooming in."

"You might have been surprised at what you could do."

"I wasn't going to flail on the wall and get caught in all kinds of awful pictures. I had to let go before someone got footage of my sewing machine leg. If I was going to fall, I was going to look good doing it."

So she had let go and flew like Peter Pan. I clasped my hands behind my head. There had to be more to it. The springs of the bunk above me glimmered faintly in the dim light.

A deep snuffling snore erupted from Coach Mel, and Becky and I stifled our laughter.

"Who's that Max guy that's out with your parents?" she asked. "He's hot."

"Eww. Uncle Max is almost the same age as my dad."

Becky giggled. "He's still cute. Even my mom called him hunky."

I snorted. "He's not really my uncle. He and my dad have been best friends and climbing partners since they were teenagers." *Plus he's gay.* But I wasn't going to share that with Becky. Max was well known in the climbing world, but his private life was private.

Becky sighed again and was quiet.

At least I still had my worry stone from Uncle Max. He had lived with us on and off for as long as I could remember, especially in the winters when it was cold outside. It was like I had three parents. He'd followed us all around the country. Each time we moved, he'd be right behind us in his little VW van, sometimes the same day, sometimes a year later. But he always showed up eventually. I knew he'd had boyfriends over the years, but they never seemed to last long.

I twirled my new bracelet around my wrist. My mind was finally quiet enough to sort out the reality of the Tungurahua eruption and what Mr. S hadn't said. My parents and Uncle Max should have reached the summit of Mount Chimborazo early this morning. The volcanic ash storm may have prevented climbers from beginning their expeditions today, but what about the climbers who were already on the summit?

Six months before our Ecuador trip, a rock had crumbled in Dad's hand, and he'd taken a forty-foot whipper off the cliff, the rope stopping his fall barely ten feet from a giant boulder on the ground. I could picture my dad perched on the cliff like a great bird. Big and powerful, yet full of grace, like an eagle. Until he wasn't.

They'd be fine. Just like Mr. S. had said, they were experienced mountaineers. They knew how to stay safe.

3

A veil of dust obscured the mountains in the distance, but the sun burned bright for the rock climbing semifinals. I clung to the climbing wall twenty feet above the ground. Not a desperate cling, it was more like static electricity. I actually felt a magnetic power. My foot balanced on a dime-sized nub of faux rock. I pivoted, reached for the next hold, and pinched the thin flake. I inched my feet up the wall beneath me, rubber-soled climbing shoes gripping the vertical surface. My chest rose and fell with each slow, steady breath.

I coiled my body, forearms pulled, legs extended. I was weightless. Gravity had no power in this instant, this one second of free-momentum hovering in the air. I grasped the edge of a shallow bucket and swung my leg to the side, heel-hooking a curved edge. I clipped the bolt and breathed.

A droplet of sweat rolled down the back of my neck. The massive overhang loomed above my head. I reached up and curled two fingers over the lip of a tiny pocket carved into the wall.

A flash of heat washed over me like a wave. Blood pulsed in my temples. The ceiling of the overhang undulated in the glaring sunlight. A roar of darkness flooded my peripheral vision.

Down was up; sky was ground. Breath sucked out of my lungs. Throat parched. Core clenched. Biceps flexed. Knuckles whitening.

My fingers no longer belonged to my body. They slipped, skin scraping.

One millisecond of weightless freedom.

Gravity wrapped its hand around my ankle and yanked. My

stomach plummeted. The rope pulled taut, arresting my free-fall with a jerk. The crowd gasped below me. I swung and slammed into the climbing wall.

I sat on the ground, head lowered, knees pulled in to my chest. The sun beat down on the back of my neck.

Coach Mel plunked down beside me. "What happened?"

I didn't answer.

"After you pulled off that dyno, I thought you had it made."

I shook my head. My sweat-soaked top stuck to my back.

"How's your wrist? Did it give out on you?"

My left wrist was wrapped with white tape. I extended my arm and rotated my hand. "It feels fine." I flexed my fingers; the first two were bloody at the tips.

She winced. "Ouch."

My right wrist was bare. I had debated wearing the tagua bracelet that morning, but was afraid it would scrape on the climbing wall and break. I wasn't one to be superstitious, but now I wondered.

Coach Mel lifted her eyes to the top of the climbing wall as the crowd hooted and clapped, and I followed her gaze. A French climber had finished the route. She'd advance to the finals tomorrow.

"I'm afraid you're out of the running now, unless someone else falls," Coach Mel said. She turned to look at me. "It's like something spooked you up there. You sure you're feeling all right?"

I nodded, then shook my head.

Becky passed by and patted me on the head. "Sorry, I guess it happens to all of us."

I flinched. It hadn't been an ordinary fall. I hadn't miscalculated a move, my muscles weren't pushed to exhaustion. I had been balanced on the wall with a firm grip. And then it was like the earth tilted, and I wasn't even sure where I was. As if something had gone terribly wrong with the world; I felt it deep in my core.

"Keep drinking," Coach Mel said with a nod toward my water bottle. "Do you feel faint? Do you need to eat?"

I needed to sip my warm herbal tea, breathe the scent deep into my lungs, deep into my muscles. I had checked the lost and found and searched all around the competition area for my thermos, but it was still lost.

"You're worried about your parents."

I met her eyes, trying to read her expression. What did she know?

"They're not due back until later this evening, right? And they said not to worry if they were late." Her gaze was steady, confident. "I'm sure they're fine."

But deep down in some hidden, dark corner of my body, a raw fear was growing like nothing I had ever felt before, a physical sensation clawing through my veins.

The French climber waved and blew kisses to the crowd. I dropped my head onto my knees.

We were silent, watching the next competitors climb the route. A Japanese girl reached the overhang, looked up, and paused. My stomach quivered for her.

She crouched and tried to dyno over the crux. She soared off the wall.

Coach Mel whipped around to look at me. "That's the exact same hold you slipped off."

Incredibly, the next two climbers stopped and crouched beneath the overhang, then fell, swinging on the rope. My eyes were wide. That spot on the wall was cursed.

Coach Mel grinned. "I guess you're not out of the running after all."

I nodded, but I was climbing on Mount Chimborazo with my parents and Uncle Max, guiding them safely down the mountain. I was scanning the crowd, waiting for Mom and Dad to rush toward me with sweeping hugs. I wouldn't even feel embarrassed if Dad picked me up and swung me around. I wanted him to lead me back to that cursed spot on the wall, to help me understand what had happened.

My brain wouldn't let me sleep that night. It perked up at every creak and murmur, waiting for my parents to arrive. I crept out of bed and shuffled down the quiet halls of the hostel. The moon shone through the windows, and I slipped out the front door.

The breeze whispered over the silvery landscape, the mountains a hulking shadow in the distance. I sat on the porch steps and hugged my knees. The night felt wild, eerie and magical at the same time, like anything could happen, good or bad. The hair rose on my arms, and I shivered.

5

I joined my teammates at breakfast, but my churning stomach wouldn't allow any more than a few sips of tea. I couldn't even look at the bowls of ceviche, the fish soup that appeared at almost every meal. My head throbbed.

Zach picked up his bowl and drank the liquid with a loud slurp and smack, trying to be funny. Becky giggled. My other teammates gave me smiles, pats on the back; they thought I was nervous about my final climb. Tungurahua was silent again, leaving little more than a layer of ash on the neighboring hillsides.

I caught Mr. S. watching me. His eyebrows were drawn, his forehead creased, but he didn't approach me to say anything. He looked like he'd come to the same realization, that something might have gone wrong for my parents way up high on the mountain. I looked away.

Summit attempts need to take place near dawn. Mountaineers trek to a camp high on the mountain, then sleep until just before midnight. Rising in the deep darkness of night, they begin their final ascent. They need to reach the summit and descend before the mountain wakes up.

Chimborazo wakes up around nine a.m. The sun warms the snow to a sugar-like consistency, ice melts, and rocks tumble. Several years ago, an avalanche killed ten climbers on the upper slopes of the mountain.

My parents and Uncle Max were expert mountaineers; they respected the mountain's power. They had turned away from summit attempts in the past. But an expedition can go terribly wrong even when the climbers do everything right. Conditions on mountains are out of their control, and nature runs its course no matter what.

My tagua bracelet was back on my wrist again, along with the one I had bought for Mom. The bracelets tangled and entwined, the beads rubbing together. All I could do was wait.

And worry. In my room, I unzipped my backpack pocket and reached for my worry stone. I fished around, pulling out a Starburst, a quarter, lint. No golden nugget. I dug through the rest of the stuff in my pack, pulling everything out one by one. Fleece jacket, water bottle, phone, wallet. My trusty, beat-up copy of Thoreau's *Walden*.

I felt all around the inside of my pack. More lint and a penny. Buena suerte.

I dropped to my knees and looked under the bed and all around the floor. The chunk of pyrite was too big to have slipped through the cracks in the planks.

I sat on the edge of my bed and dropped my head into my hands. Think, Cara, when did you last have it? I had turned the stone around in my hands before my climb yesterday, just like I always did. But everything after that was a muddle.

I shook out my fleece jacket and fanned out the books, knowing it was useless. A postcard slipped out from the pages of *Walden*. "Greetings from Ecuador" was scrawled across a photo of a llama standing in front of a mountain range. It made it look like the llama was speaking.

Dad. I smiled and flipped it over, squinting to read his messy handwriting.

> I want to stand as close
> to the edge as I can
> without going over. Out on
> the edge you see all the
> kinds of things you can't
> see from the center.

Dad always sent me postcards from his expeditions with lines of poetry or quotes from books. I had an entire bulletin board full in my bedroom at home. As usual, I didn't know exactly what this quote meant or where it came from, but it made me feel better. I reread the lines out loud, tucked the postcard back into my book, and returned everything to my backpack. Mom and Dad and Uncle Max were climbing to their edges. Now it was time for me to climb to mine.

I waited by myself in the isolation area, the last of my teammates to climb. I didn't have my worry stone, I didn't have my thermos of peppermint tea. I closed my eyes and imagined the golden stone in my hands, the warm peppermint tea, relaxing my throat, calming my insides.

A woman entered the tent and gestured, and I followed her outside. I stood at the base of the competition wall and scanned the final route. I pantomimed the first few moves to focus my mind. There was a looming overhang to conquer on this route as well, and it was even higher up on the wall, at least fifty feet. I would need to conserve my energy.

"Buena suerte," I whispered.

I breathed deeply and climbed on. Slow and steady, just like my parents on their trek, step after step, one foot after the other, one hand after the other, until it became a meditation. I reached the overhang and focused my energy at my heart.

A loud grunt erupted from deep in my chest, and I launched over the ledge. My meditative pace continued and before I knew it, I was clipping the final bolt. I felt like I could keep going, just climbing and climbing. I peered over the top of the wall to the mountains in the distance and released a long sigh, sending my energy to Mount Chimborazo.

I was back on the ground before I noticed that my bracelets were gone. I touched my bare wrist. They must have scraped against a hold and snapped. I crouched at the base of the climb and searched, digging through the thick layer of shredded black rubber. Chalk dust scratched my throat, making me cough, but I couldn't find a single tagua bead. They had fallen through the cracks and empty spaces between the chips of rubber, buried below.

25

I sat on the grass and watched the last competitor in my age bracket, my back resting against the bleachers, legs splayed out in front of me. My knees and shins were dotted with fading bruises and new greenish purple ones from my slamming fall the day before. Was it simply dehydration? An attack of nerves? It didn't feel that way. It was like the universe had spoken to me. Was I being given a message? What was I missing?

Shouts and cheers jerked me back to attention. Coach Mel grabbed my hand and pulled me to standing.

"Third place. So close, Cara, so close."

My brain slowly registered what had happened. Third place was not what I came here to accomplish, but it didn't stop my teammates from dancing around me. Someone picked me up, the curse of being small. Zach swung me around in a hug; he'd placed third in his division, too.

Blood rushed to my cheeks, and I couldn't help but smile, my heart opening to the joy around me. The first-place French climber hugged me and planted a quick kiss, kiss on my cheeks. I laughed, kissing the air beside her face. I scanned the crowd for my parents.

Zach hammed it up with his bronze medal and pulled me into pics right and left. It wasn't long before the media realized my parents were absent. The rumors flew.

My smile became tighter and tighter. My throat closed as tears swelled. I escaped to the outer edges of the crowd and breathed deeply to calm my trembling insides. Some part of me had truly expected my parents to show up, as if I was capable of making them appear through the strength of my will.

I overheard a reporter from *Rock and Ice* magazine speaking into a microphone in front of a camera.

"We've been told the American climbers Mark and Lori Jenkins and Max O'Connor were planning to summit Mount Chimborazo by a rarely attempted and extremely dangerous route up the east face of the mountain. And now . . . they are missing."

The woman spied me and strutted my way. I was so stunned by her speed, I stood frozen.

"We're here with Cara Jenkins, daughter of the missing climbers Mark and Lori Jenkins. Cara, you must be very worried. What have you heard about your parents?"

I stepped backward, but the woman thrust the microphone closer to my face.

"I haven't heard anything yet," I stammered. I took another step backward, bumping into Becky, who had come up behind me.

Becky gave me a half hug and kept her arm draped over my shoulder. She flashed a sympathetic look at me, then at the camera. "It's just terrible," she said.

"We've heard reports of several avalanches on the mountain," the reporter continued. "Some are fearing the worst."

My eyes swept the competition area. Where were my teammates when I needed to be picked up and carried away? Becky's mother approached, smoothing her hair and smiling at the camera. Her diamond earrings flashed in the sunlight. I recognized my chance and sidestepped out of Becky's grasp. If those two wanted the spotlight, they could have it.

Coach Mel trotted toward me, but I didn't wait. I didn't make eye contact with anyone else. I bolted straight out of the competition area. I didn't need rumors. I needed answers.

Back at the hostel, I found Mr. S. leaning over a dining table covered with maps.

"Have you heard any more news from Mount Chimborazo?" I asked him.

Coach Mel burst through the door. Mr. S. motioned for her to join us. "Please sit," he said.

I scanned the maps of Ecuador spread in front of us, not knowing what I was looking for. My parents had shared their plans with me, but I had been only half-listening, too focused on my competition. I knew where they were going, but I didn't know their detailed route.

"I've been told that the American climbing group has not returned to base camp as expected," Mr. S. said, "but other climbers on the mountain have organized a search and rescue effort. They speculate that the volcanic ash from Tungurahua hindered the climbers' view of their planned route."

My parents! Not just any climbers, any American climbing group. Just say it already, my parents.

"It's possible they veered off course, which means coping with unexpected terrain." Mr. S. spread his fingers over the map, pointing out my parents' planned route. "If, for example, they ended up over here instead, they would encounter crevasses that they may have been unaware of."

I stared at the map; I knew how to read maps, but the scribble of foreign words, lines, and shadows bled into an incomprehensible blur. I didn't need a map to picture a crevasse and what it would mean to unexpectedly tumble into one during a blinding storm.

Mr. S. leaned back in his chair and stroked his beard. "But there's a good chance their descent is simply taking longer than expected. Most likely they are hunkered down somewhere on the mountain slopes waiting for Chimborazo to go back to sleep."

"So waiting for sundown?" Coach Mel asked.

"Right. For the temperature to drop back to freezing. Then there's less chance of falling rock," Mr. S. said.

"You think they might be waiting out the storm," I said. "Maybe tonight they'll be able to safely descend now that the ash has cleared. Or they might wait for sunrise."

"Like I said before, they know how to keep themselves safe." Mr. S. shrugged and held his hands open in front of him as if he was offering a gift, a gift of hope.

I rubbed my temples in circles.

I wanted to believe Mr. S. Expeditions became extended all the time when climbers needed to wait out the weather. My parents were gone an extra two weeks when they climbed Everest. But I was only ten years old then. I hadn't understood the degree of danger. All I knew then was that I would be staying with my grandparents for half the summer.

"What about avalanches?" I asked.

Mr. S. chewed the inside of his lip and drummed his fingertips on the table. "There have been reports of recent avalanches on the mountain. But this is common. Your parents knew this and were wearing avalanche transceivers."

I nodded. A transceiver could send or receive a radio signal if someone was buried in an avalanche, alerting others to their location. I searched Mr. S.'s face for more clues, but he was as difficult to read as the map spread before me. My legs wanted to run, but there was nowhere to go.

I shoved my chair back from the table and stood up. "I want to go to Mount Chimborazo. How can I get there?"

Coach Mel exchanged a look with Mr. S. "Cara, it's safer for you to stay here with us."

"The skies are clear now," Mr. S. said. "Your parents will find their way down the mountain."

"You said there's a search and rescue group. We could join them."

"We aren't prepared for that type of mountaineering," Coach Mel said. Her tone was slow and firm. "We'd only be in the way. We need to sit tight and hope for the best."

"She's right." Mr. S. nodded.

I just wanted to be home in California. I wanted to be back in the safety of our mountain cabin, curled up by the fire, engrossed in a book, Mom and Dad beside me. Uncle Max stomping through the front door, sniffing out dinner.

I walked out to the deck and searched the bruised sky, seeking the highest peak, the glacier-domed summit of Mount Chimborazo. *Please, please let them be all right.* My muscles felt twisted, wrung out like a sponge. I squinted into the evaporating daylight, through the layers of setting sun, but the distance was too great.

6

The next morning, Becky packed her suitcase for the return home. I folded my clothes and layered them in my bag, but no way was I leaving Ecuador. My teammates would drive to the Quito airport then scatter for flights to different states, Colorado, Oregon, Kentucky, Georgia. They didn't know what to say to me. I wouldn't have known either.

Becky fingered the tiny cross she wore on a delicate gold chain around her neck. The cross pointed down like an arrow toward her cleavage, which was pushed up out of her hot-pink tank top. Her patriotic fingernail polish had been changed to match.

"I'll pray for you," she said.

I clutched my copy of *Walden* to my chest, Dad's postcard tucked inside. I had been praying in my mind, over and over. *Please, please let them be safe.* It wasn't the type of prayer that Becky had in mind. I prayed to the earth, the sky, the wind, the trees, the mountains. My parents and Uncle Max were in the mountain's hands.

Coach Mel walked in. "The airport shuttle will be here in an hour."

I crossed my arms at my chest and stared at her. I wasn't going anywhere.

"I postponed our flights for one more day."

Despite her words, she looked like she wanted nothing more than to hop on her flight home that morning. She ran a hand through her short, spiky hair.

"And I called your grandparents in Michigan."

"Why?"

"They're who your parents listed in case of emergency."

Oh great. My parents would definitely *not* want my grandparents involved. Grandma had always been against our climbing life. Now there was going to be another fight for sure. My grandparents had thought Everest would be my parents' last expedition. What more was there to accomplish? But then Mom and Dad sent me back to Michigan a couple summers later while they climbed Denali, and the visit ended with a storm of angry words and Mom in tears. We hadn't been back in nearly four years.

I refused to believe this was the kind of emergency that would warrant a call to my grandparents. My grandparents were the last resort. I repeated my mantra, *please, please, let Mom and Dad be safe.*

I sat on the front steps of the hostel after my teammates left. My head jerked toward the sound of every passing car and truck, waiting for one to roll into the driveway. I saw my parents throwing open the doors, running toward me. Or maybe they'd been injured; they could be on their way to a hospital right now. It could be something as simple as a broken ankle, walking would be slow and difficult. Or altitude sickness, high altitude pulmonary edema; it could be deadly. My lungs constricted at the thought.

There was no cell reception high on Mount Chimborazo, maybe not even in the foothills. It'd be a while before they reached an area where they could call.

I wandered around the yard peering at flowers. Everything was different here. Plants that looked like artichokes but thick and spiky like cacti. Red bumblebees. Huge hummingbirds with pointy, long beaks and a plume of a tail. Foot-long yellow and orange flowers hanging upside down like tubular bells. The landscape was vibrant, full of life. This strange world where everything seemed possible in a magical yet frightening way. The pressure in my chest was unbearable; I wanted to jump right out of my skin. I couldn't sit around and wait any longer. I needed to go to Mount Chimborazo.

Mr. S. couldn't leave his work at the hostel, but he arranged a car for Coach Mel and me. He spread out the maps again and gave directions.

"Be careful. Mount Chimborazo is not like our national parks back home," he said. "There isn't a visitor center or park rangers to help you. It's true wilderness. Wildness."

He handed me a wool blanket like the ones I had seen in the market. "Keep this in the car just in case. It'll get colder and colder as you head up into the mountains. Don't underestimate the cold. You're not prepared to stay up there."

I nodded and hugged the soft blanket to my chest. "Thank you."

"Buena suerte," he said.

When I had first arrived in Ecuador and seen the Andes Mountains, I was awestruck, ready for adventure. Now I felt chilled. A tingle crept down the back of my neck, and I shuddered. The road wound through shades of green, pastures and fields carved into the slopes of the Andean highlands. Volcanic peaks rose up and disappeared into the clouds. Along the lower slopes of Mount Chimborazo, llamas scratched at the volcanic ash coating the ground. Or maybe they were alpacas; I couldn't remember how to tell the difference.

"Does this sound familiar?" I asked Coach Mel. "Something like 'I want to stand as close to the edge as I can without going over and see things you can't see from the center'?"

"I don't think I've heard that before, but it could be about climbing. Why?"

"It was written on a postcard from my dad. He always sends me something from his trips. If I was at home with Mom, we'd make it part of my schoolwork."

"How come you've never gotten into ice climbing like your parents?" Coach Mel asked.

"They said I complained about the cold too much, it was just easier to go without me."

"That's why you focused on sport climbing and not on mountaineering?"

I shrugged. "I like hiking way up high, just not when it turns to snow and ice. There's something freeing about just slipping on your shoes and heading out, not being weighed down by all that other gear. They have their thing, and I have mine."

"Well, your focus has paid off."

"I should have placed higher than third."

"Yep, you should have. You'll have other chances." She tapped my knee. "And your parents should be there to see it."

"What about you?" I asked. "You've had some great summits in your past. Why did you stop?"

She didn't answer right away. "The same reason you never started."

I was about to ask her what she meant, but she leaned forward, squinting out the windshield. "I think that's it." She pointed to a dirt and gravel road on our left.

We turned and headed up the steep, rutted road. Coach Mel braked around the switchbacks, and the car bumped and dipped in and out of the ruts. My ears popped. The temperature dropped as we drove higher and higher. I rubbed my arms.

"It's freezing." She fumbled with the dials for heat. Cold air blasted from the vents.

I pulled my knees into my chest and hugged myself against the cold.

She waved her hands in front of the vents and turned another dial. "Seriously? I think the heat is broken."

I reached into the backseat for the blanket from Mr. S. "Here, we can share." I spread the blanket across my lap and over to Coach Mel.

"It's okay. You can have it." She switched off the malfunctioning heat and veered around a giant pothole, only to dip into another. The car shuddered.

I pulled the blanket up to my chin.

Finally, we spied the Carrel Hut as Mr. S. had described, the first of two refuges where climbers could rest before their Chimborazo treks began. My parents had been here just a few days ago. Sorting their equipment—crampons, ice axes, ropes—before heading up the steep slopes beyond.

"I think that's their car." I leaned forward in my seat. My parents' rental car sat by itself at the edge of the dirt lot. A little Chevrolet something that I had never heard of before. We parked next to it, and I untangled myself from the blanket, leaving it in a heap on the floor. I couldn't get out of the car fast enough.

I peered into the Chevrolet's windows as if there'd be a message waiting for me. I lifted the driver's door handle. Locked. They were still on the mountain. Somewhere.

The cold wind blasted my face. I pulled my fleece jacket out of my backpack and slipped it on as I headed toward the hut. The fleece was all I had. I had only packed for the competition in the city where it was warmer, maybe some hiking in the foothills. I hadn't expected to go this high into the mountains. My parents had layers of fleece, down parkas, gloves, gaiters, helmets.

I stopped beside a pyramid-shaped cairn of boulders and rocks as tall as me. Cairns are often built to mark a trailhead. This one was different. *RIP* had been carved into the lowest, largest boulder. Back in California, I had built a small, simple cairn to mark the grave of my dog, Tahoe, a couple years ago. Three rocks balancing. The number of rocks in this pile made me light-headed.

I exchanged a look with Coach Mel. Neither of us spoke. We moved together toward the hut. But then I stopped and dropped to one knee, examining the stones and pebbles on the path.

I picked up a thin, oval stone the size of my thumb. Dark gray, almost black with a wavy line of copper running through it. I ran my fingers over its smooth edges and turned it around and around in my hand. So different from the pyrite with its deep grooves and sharp edges. A good luck token. *Buena suerte.*

I stood up, slipped the stone into my jacket pocket, and caught up to Coach Mel at the hut. The silence was eerie. My mind jumped to images of splattered blood, ghosts. I stepped back while she knocked on the door and peered inside.

"No one's here," she said.

My heart hammered. I didn't know if I should be relieved or disappointed. I peeked in the hut to see for myself. It was just an empty, rustic space with plank floors that looked like they'd been swept clean.

"Let's go to the next one," I said.

Mr. S. had told us the Whymper Hut could only be reached on foot. I tightened the laces of my hiking boots. This trail was too rough for my Converses; I'd roll an ankle for sure. And again I prayed for something simple like a sprained ankle to explain my parents' delay.

I zipped my jacket up to my chin against the biting wind and tugged the sleeves down over my hands, wishing I had gloves. We hiked for an hour up the steep path, picking our way over and around rocks and boulders. I didn't pause to take in the view. I was on a mission, one foot after the other.

John Muir wrote about the mountains. Dad had scrawled quite a few Muir quotes on postcards over the years.

> Sickness, pain, death — yet who could guess their existence in this fresh, abounding, overflowing life, this universal beauty?

But this mountain felt jagged, dark, and threatening, not like my California mountains. My California mountains were bright and safe; they were home.

The Whymper Hut was the refuge where most climbers stayed to eat and sleep before their midnight ascent. I heard voices as we approached, but I couldn't make out the words. The sound was muffled—it was coming from inside the hut, and the words weren't English. Spanish, Portuguese?

Beyond the hut, the trail disappeared into snow and ice. Fields of white with spires of gray granite, rising up, up, up. A moonscape lost in the clouds.

I rapped on the door, then opened it with a shaky hand. Were my parents here?

"Hola," Coach Mel called out.

Inside, three climbers were unloading their backpacks and rolled out sleeping bags on the bunks that lined the room. They nodded hello but continued their work. With our small packs and lack of gear, Coach Mel and I must have looked like tourists.

I knew it wasn't likely that we would simply find my parents sipping tea, but still my stomach dropped in disappointment. My ears stung as they warmed up from the cold wind outside. I slid my hands into my jacket pockets and fingered the smooth stone. I looked to Coach Mel, unsure what to do. She introduced us in halting Spanish, but the climbers answered in accented English.

"I am Marcus, a guide with Ecuador Treks. I am leading the others up the mountain tonight."

"Have you heard about the missing group of climbers?" Coach Mel asked.

"The American group?" Marcus said. "I heard a search and rescue effort was organized the other day."

I strained to understand his accented words.

"Mark and Lori Jenkins. Max O'Connor," he said.

At the sound of their names, my heartbeat quickened. The other climbers nodded their heads. They'd heard these names before.

Marcus continued. "They're big-time pros. They were on the other side of the mountain. Arista del Sol, the Sun Ridge route. We're heading up the Whymper route. This is a novice group, we're taking a much safer path to the summit." He nodded at the other climbers as if to reassure them.

"But people are still searching, right?" I asked. My voice sounded squeaky, like the words didn't want to come out. Coach Mel was gripping my upper arm; she squeezed tighter. I turned the stone over and over in my pocket.

"Other expedition parties will, of course, be on the lookout for their—"

Marcus stopped his sentence abruptly, eyeing me. He looked at the other climbers and said softly, "La hija." Daughter.

Coach Mel's nails dug into my arm. A quiver began in my stomach and moved to my lips. I knew what he had been about to say. Bodies. They'll be on the lookout for their bodies.

7

Mr. S. had arranged for Coach Mel and me to spend the night at an inn in the foothills of Mount Chimborazo. I didn't remember the drive there. I didn't even remember getting off the mountain.

I followed Coach Mel into the room and curled up on the bed. She rubbed my back in slow circles but didn't say anything.

I thought I would somehow know if my parents had been seriously hurt. I would feel it, some sort of intuition, a sharp fracturing of my heart. But instead I felt a heaviness surrounding me, smothering. I couldn't catch my breath. I thought about the day I fell off the climbing wall, the air sucked out of my lungs. The world was suddenly all wrong. Could that have been my parents reaching out to me?

Coach Mel made phone calls, and I heard random words, *police, missing,* that jumped, *presumed dead,* and faded, *lawyer, grandparents,* in and out of my thoughts.

I remembered a story Dad told me during the flight to Ecuador.

"In October 2002, climbers found the remains of an aircraft and its passengers on the mountain. Guess how long the plane had been missing?" he asked.

"No idea," I said.

"Come on, guess, how long could a huge airplane stay missing?"

"A week, a month?"

"The plane disappeared in 1976. It took twenty-six years to find it!"

I awoke at dawn. My legs were like jelly, as if I'd been walking all night. Indeed, I'd been hiking and scrambling, combing the craggy hills and valleys of the mountains, peering over rugged cliffs and down into snowy crevasses all night long in my dreams.

I tugged my arms through the sleeves of my jacket, but even wrapped in cozy fleece, I felt chilled. The wood floor creaked as I crossed the room. Coach Mel was still asleep. I stepped outside into the damp air. The thick fog was like a wall, blocking off the rest of the world. It seeped inside the collar of my jacket. But it was the brightest fog I'd ever seen, like it was lit from within.

Falling rocks tumbled in the distance, breaking the eerie calm. I stood perfectly still. I listened. Ice melted and cracked. The quiver returned to my lips, tears puddled in my eyes and spilled, warm against my chilled skin. I folded my arms, hugging myself. My parents could be anywhere.

Coach Mel drove slowly around the twisting mountain curves, peering through the white mist. I rested my head against the side window, feeling the moist coolness against my forehead. I scanned the milky hillsides in search of movement, a spot of color. Up, up, up to the glacier bowls and peaks, the heavy clouds. The scenery blurred, my eyelids drooped.

I woke up with a start and cracked my head against the window.

"You okay over there?" Coach Mel asked.

"Ow." I rubbed my head.

"You must be hungry. Me too. Look in the glove box, I stashed some energy bars."

I grabbed two bars and unwrapped Coach Mel's for her. She took it from me without looking away from the road. I tried a bite, my favorite kind, oatmeal chocolate chip, but it might as well have been cardboard. I chewed and chewed, unable to swallow.

"You heard me talking on the phone last night, right?" Coach Mel asked.

I nodded.

"I wanted to talk to you about everything last night, but by the time I made all the calls you had fallen asleep. That's good, you needed to rest."

I swallowed the cardboard in my mouth, slivers stuck in my throat.

"I talked to the Ecuadorian officials, and there doesn't appear to be anything else we can do. They have helicopters for emergency evacuations if your parents are found injured. Like that climbing guide said, other groups will continue looking, but your parents were on a rarely traveled route. Few people are skilled enough to even go there."

The road straightened out, and Coach Mel pressed on the gas.

"Now is the time for you to be with family. I've spoken to your grandparents. More guests have arrived at Mr. S.'s hostel, but he has one small room still available. We can stay there tonight and wait for more news, but then we need to fly home. I can fly with you from Quito to Miami," Coach Mel continued, "but we need to take separate flights from there."

I nodded, an automatic response. I was only half-listening. The world was muted around me. Urgency had been replaced with numbness. The fog had dissipated, and we traveled through valleys and villages, but I was color-blind. Even the brilliant hues of the flowers and markets looked dull.

"Your grandpa will meet us in Miami, and you'll fly with him back to Detroit."

I nodded again. Then, wait. Detroit. For a second, the word held no meaning, then it clicked. "What?"

Coach Mel continued with a forced brightness in her voice. "I understand your grandma doesn't travel well, but your grandpa was ready to fly all the way to Quito to come get you."

"Detroit?" I blurted. "I'm not going to Detroit. I'm going home to California."

"I'm sorry, Cara," Coach Mel said. Her voice became soft, gentle. "You can't just go home by yourself, back to an empty house."

I stared at her face. What was she talking about?

"They had a will that designates guardians for you in case something ever happened to them. Your Uncle Max is listed as the first guardian, and your grandparents are next."

Coach Mel's eyes finally left the road for a second. They were intense, urging me to understand.

I knew about the will. My parents had had it done before they climbed Denali. But it had never seemed real. It was just a formality, part of the planning for a trip that could be dangerous. Accidents could happen anytime to anyone, a car crash, a freak heart attack. I never imagined I'd have to go live with my grandparents for real.

"But . . ." I sputtered. "I have to go home first. I want to wait there for Mom and Dad and Uncle Max. No, I want to wait here. What if there's more news? I need to be here for them."

My brain tumbled, trying to latch on to something solid.

"I'm so sorry, Cara. We'll contact friends in California to pack up some of your things and send them to Michigan for you. You need to be with family now. They'll take care of you."

Coach Mel returned her gaze to the road, both hands gripping the steering wheel. I continued to stare at her, dumbfounded. This could not be happening. How could she just give up? We still had time. My parents were going to show up, stumbling down off the mountain tonight, tomorrow, the next day. It was gonna happen.

A raw helpless rage erupted from a dark, hidden corner of my body. I squeezed my eyes shut, opened my throat, and screamed like I'd never screamed before.

Coach Mel slammed on the brakes and veered off the road. The car bumped and slid, spitting gravel. I opened the passenger door.

"Cara!" she barked.

I stepped out onto moving dirt and stumbled to my knees. Rough, sharp, tearing my skin. I fell forward onto my hands and heaved.

I tumbled out of bed face first, opening my mouth to scream, but my lungs had no air. A strangled cry escaped from the back of my throat. I landed with a thump. Where was I? Crinkly fabric, a knobby lump. I struggled to open my puffy eyes. Sunlight flooded the room, and I recognized the plank walls of Mr. S.'s hostel.

I'd landed on a sleeping bag, cool and slick against my hands and feet. A body squirmed inside, and a head of mussed up hair emerged.

"Mom!" I squeaked, my voice hoarse.

She opened her arms, and I scampered into her embrace. "Cara." She kissed the top of my head, her arms squeezing me tight.

I tried to speak, but it came out as a whimper.

"It's okay. I'm here. You've been asleep for twelve hours." She tucked a strand of hair behind my ear. "How do you feel?"

I felt like the world was moving in slow motion, like there was a time delay after every sentence, every thought. "My knees hurt." I picked at the bandage covering one of my knees, remembering the gravel biting into my skin.

"It'll probably sting for a while. Pretty bad scrapes," Mom said. "But your hands don't look too bad."

I examined my hands, tough and calloused. I lifted my eyes to my mom's face, her arms, her hands, tough and calloused like my own.

"You're okay?" I said. "You aren't hurt?"

She nodded. "I'm fine." And sensing my next question, she added, "So is your dad."

"He's here?"

Mom shook her head. "No. I have a lot to explain to you, but you should eat first. Okay? And I want you to tell me all about the competition. Let's get some breakfast."

"No," I said, louder than I expected, then softer, "tell me. Where's Dad? What happened?"

Mom sighed. "You must have been so scared, not knowing what happened and why we didn't show up. I'm so sorry."

She took my hands in hers. "I really didn't anticipate we'd get delayed that long. I thought we had built in enough extra time to still get back by your finals. We knew that Tungurahua was active, but the weather was clear when we set off for the summit.

"The glaciers had receded even more than we had heard. There was a lot of mixed rock and ice, very technical stuff. But we were doing fine; it just took us longer. Then the ashes blew in, just like a sudden storm."

"Before you reached the summit?" I asked.

She nodded. "We all agreed. We needed to descend."

Mom's eyes misted.

"The storm worsened, and we needed to find shelter. The ash was blinding, and we got lost. We were afraid to keep moving, not knowing if we'd come upon a crevasse. So we hunkered down and waited. It felt like ages."

It had felt like ages to me too.

"When the skies began to clear, we argued. Max wanted another attempt at the summit. But we were already delayed, and off course. It was midmorning, not a safe time to climb higher up the mountain.

"So we headed down. Max was in the lead. We were roped together since we were off route and unsure of the terrain. We hoped to cross paths with another group, get our bearings, and maybe Max could join them to the summit while your dad and I came back for you."

Mom's grip tightened over my hands.

"There was a sound. This deep rumbling, trembling. Like a hunger coming from far within the earth. I saw the crack forming, as if it was in slow motion. This massive ledge of snow, like an iceberg breaking free. It was in front of your dad, right behind Max. Then a thundering, a deafening roar."

My fingers were crushed by Mom's grasp, but I didn't move.

"Your dad and I were knocked to the ground, thrown into the snow." Her voice quivered. "But Max . . . he was just gone."

She finished in a whisper. "I've never felt so helpless in my whole life."

I squeezed my eyes tight against the heat of tears and folded myself into Mom's arms.

9

Mom was safe. Dad was still on the mountain. Uncle Max was missing. I stared at the breakfast foods spread across the table. Ceviche with octopus, shrimp, and scallops, guanábana juice, and a bowl of popcorn, which strangely accompanied every meal here. Uncle Max was a mastermind of popcorn concoctions. He'd introduced me to his ultimate trail mix: a blend of caramel and cheddar popcorn with peanut M&M's. Mom had not approved. And Uncle Max would not approve of the unsalted stuff here.

The last food I'd eaten was the cardboard energy bar the morning before. It didn't feel right to be hungry, yet saliva flooded my mouth. My stomach roiled with half hunger, half nausea.

"Eat," Mom said.

"You too." I slowly slurped the ceviche, the lime juice tingling my tongue, and I remembered Zach draining his bowl, lips smacking, Becky giggling. It seemed like so long ago.

Despite the food on her plate, Mom only sipped tea. She needed food even more than me after her struggle down the mountain.

She met my gaze. "Mr. S. gave me a meal last night when I got here."

"Where's Coach Mel?" I asked

"She left this morning for her flight home. We didn't want to wake you. She told me to give you a big hug from her."

I nodded. I knew she must have been more than relieved to turn me over to my mom.

I ate a few kernels of popcorn and sipped some juice, until my questions could wait no longer.

"Is Dad hurt?"

"No, not that he'll admit, anyway, just bruised. Both of us." Mom winced and readjusted her position. "I couldn't get him to leave."

"He's looking for Uncle Max?"

Mom nodded and sipped her tea.

"What about the avalanche transceiver?" I asked.

"No signal." Mom's face was pained, her voice faint.

"Do you think Dad can find him?"

She set her cup on the table and shook her head. "I don't know, but he's not giving up. He's determined to find him, either way."

Either way. Dead or alive. I shoved the bowl of ceviche away from me. The liquid sloshed over the rim.

Mr. S. appeared behind me and mussed up my hair like I was a little kid. We smiled grimly at him, and he nodded back. He moved on to clear dirty dishes from the other tables.

"Mr. S. and Coach Mel told me you finished in third place," Mom said. "I'm proud of you."

I shrugged. The competition felt far away and insignificant now, but one moment remained raw in my mind. "I fell," I said.

"It happens."

"This was different." I described my fall, how I felt like the earth had tilted.

"It was during the semifinals?"

I nodded. "It's seems like so long ago, but it's only been five days." I remembered how it had felt as though the universe was speaking to me. "When was the avalanche?"

Mom placed her fingers on her temples and closed her eyes. "It's been hard to keep track of time, it feels like much longer to me too."

She opened her eyes and met my gaze. "It was five days ago."

We sat in silence. I looked out the window at the mountains in the distance, blurred by tears. I didn't say it aloud, but I knew. My dad wasn't going to find Uncle Max alive. Max had already said good-bye.

10

"Let's try to do something normal for a couple hours," Mom suggested.

We headed to town and wandered down the cobblestone streets. We admired the beautiful churches and haciendas, but there were areas with leaning shacks, cardboard walls, straw or rusted metal roofs, a shantytown. I felt so far from home. A cloud passed over the sun, and I folded my arms against the harshness of this country.

The competition climbing wall was still up in the center of the village. It'd been turned into an attraction for local kids and tourists, and the children scampered up the artificial holds and swung on the ropes. The clamor of the market reached us, and we headed that way.

A group of children flocked to us, poking and tugging at our clothes. One grabbed my hand, and I jerked away reflexively. Then I felt bad, seeing her dusty bare feet, her stained clothes. I didn't have any candy or gum to give her. Coins? But I didn't have enough for all of them. The children hadn't swarmed like this when I was here before. Maybe the security from the climbing competition had kept them away. Merchants shouted and held up their goods, beckoning us toward their tables.

This was the real market, not the makeshift one that had appeared for tourists during the competition. The vendors were more organized, with tents for shade and coatracks to display their ponchos on hangers. The tables extended down the side streets too; you could weave your way through here for hours. The smell of roasting meat was stronger, and we passed a table with dark-pink pig heads. A cage of live guinea pigs sat on the ground.

I met my mom's eyes. "Yes, I think they do," she said. She put her arm around my shoulder and steered me through the crowds.

"Wait," I said, turning back. We had just passed a bright-red blanket on the ground, spread with jewelry. It was harder to see this time, tucked behind two tables stacked high with colorful blankets and scarves. The same woman greeted us, but her baby was awake this time. The baby gazed at us with enormous brown eyes and gave a burbling grin.

The woman nodded and smiled like maybe she remembered me.

"Mi madre," I said, gesturing to my mom. I held out my bare wrist. "I lost our bracelets."

The woman nodded again, then chose a tagua nut bracelet similar to the one I had before, with ivory and chocolate and caramel–swirled beads. She slipped it on my wrist, then studied Mom for a moment.

Her hands hovered over the colorful beads then settled on a bracelet nearly identical to mine. "Buena suerte para una madre y su hija. Ustedes deben permanecer unidas."

I slowly translated the words in my head. *Good luck for a mother and daughter.* I looked to Mom to see if she understood the rest and was startled to see tears in her eyes. She fingered the beads on her bracelet.

"Don't they look old and weathered, like they really could bring good luck?" I said.

She sniffed and smiled at me and squeezed my hand. "We better get back. Mr. S. will have dinner ready soon, and I want to study his maps of Mount Chimborazo."

"Gracias," we said to the woman. The word didn't feel so carefree rolling off my tongue anymore. It felt foreign and heavy.

Mom lit the lantern in our room. The candle flickered and cast a warm glow around us. It almost felt like we were back at home, safe and snug in our cabin in the woods.

I offered the bed to Mom. "I'll sleep in your sleeping bag."

"Thanks. My back could use a nice mattress for a change."

She took off her shirt to sleep in a tank top; bruises covered her arms and back. Much worse than she'd ever had from her climbing falls.

"Mom!"

She twisted to examine her back. "I know. I hit the snow hard and slid quite a ways. But nothing's broken."

I stared at the large, mottled brown and purple bruises.

"Don't worry, it looks worse than it feels."

I snuggled in the down bag, glad I had offered Mom the bed. She lay on her side, propped up on her elbow, and looked down at me.

"I need to go back to Chimborazo tomorrow and meet your dad," she said.

I began to think of what I'd need to go with her. If we stayed in one of the huts, I'd need my own sleeping bag. If I needed to trek farther up the mountain, I'd need a warmer coat, waterproof gloves. I already had my harness, but I'd need ice crampons, an ice ax. We didn't have extra money to buy a bunch of new gear for me, but maybe Mr. S. had some things I could borrow.

"Mom, didn't you say you and Dad and Max were roped together?"

She nodded.

"So what happened when the avalanche hit? Did you all get pulled down together?"

"We did. And that's how I got all these bruises, but I tried to stop myself with my ice ax, a self-arrest. Your dad too."

"But what about Max? If he was struck by the avalanche and couldn't stop himself, wouldn't the rope have pulled you and Dad with him?"

"I don't know exactly what happened, just that at some point my ax dug in, and I was able to stop."

Mom was quiet for a moment. "The rope was still attached to me and your dad, but it was severed after that. The other length of rope had disappeared."

A horrifying thought crept into my mind.

"Maybe it severed over a rock or something?" I asked.

"You're not even thinking in a moment like that, it's pure panic and reflex, you're sliding and twisting, caught in a roiling monster . . . the rope—"

"Dad might have chopped the rope with his ice ax?"

Mom gazed at the flickering lantern. Shadows lurked on the wall.

"He won't leave the mountain. He blames himself for letting Max go. He's determined to find him."

"But if he hadn't cut the rope," I said, "you and dad would have disappeared too."

"But we'll never know for sure. And that's what's killing your dad."

Because he blames himself for killing Uncle Max. But he saved himself and Mom.

"Or Max severed the rope himself, to save us. I need to go back and help your dad," Mom said. "And I need you to go stay with Grandma and Grandpa while your dad and I figure all this out. I rescheduled your flight to Detroit for tomorrow morning."

I sat up in the sleeping bag. "What? I'm not leaving now. I'm going with you!"

"I know you want to be with us, and I don't want to leave you again. But you don't have the experience for Mount Chimborazo. Not where we need to go."

"Fine, then I'll stay in one of the huts and wait for you."

"Cara." Mom said in her warning voice.

"Or I'll stay here with Mr. S. I could help him with the other guests. I'll do dishes, whatever."

My voice rose higher, but Mom's remained low, steady.

"Cara, I'm really worried about your dad. He's not himself. We've lost other friends before, but not like this, not like Max. Max is like his brother. Mine too. I need you to be safe and taken care of, so I can focus on getting him home."

"You just want me out of the way!"

"That's not what I said."

"Just like when you went to Denali. You shipped me off to Michigan then too."

"That was a different situation. You were younger then, and you didn't seem to mind going to Grandma and Grandpa's."

"Well I did," I snapped.

Mom sighed. "I didn't expect you to be upset about this. I thought you would understand."

"I understand that you almost died, and now you're going back on that mountain without me. What if something happens to you!"

The candlelight waned, and the shadows on the wall grew bigger, darker. I burrowed deeper into the sleeping bag. Uncle Max was like my second dad. That massive, cold mountain had swallowed him alive.

"I just survived one of the worst possible accidents," she said. "I'm not taking any chances with my life, or your dad's. I want to go home as much as you."

"Promise?" I whispered.

"I promise." She opened her arms, and I crawled into bed next to her. "We'll all be home soon."

11

I curled up in the window seat, hugging my knees to my chest, and gazed out at a sea of clouds. The pilot announced we were at an altitude of twenty thousand feet and climbing. Almost as high as the summit of Mount Chimborazo.

Everest may be the tallest mountain in the world, but the summit of Mount Chimborazo is the highest point on Earth through which the equator passes, the farthest from the Earth's center.

"See, the Earth is spherical," my dad had explained once. "An oblate spheroid. It's squashed at the poles like a beach ball that someone sat on, bulging at the equator. So, a mountain rising up out of that bulge is higher and closer to outer space, closer to the Moon, closer to the Sun."

What would it be like at the top of the mountain, the thin air squeezing your lungs, the lack of oxygen suffocating your brain cells, the wind clawing at your clothes? To be at the top of the mountain, looking down at the clouds. The earth hidden below, your only view the snowcapped peaks of other mountains wreathed with clouds. Would this new land be so startling, so dazzlingly surreal, so consuming that you'd forget about the earth below? Was the power and freedom so transforming that you could forget how to descend back to the life you lived before?

Was that what compelled Mom and Dad and Uncle Max to climb higher and higher peaks? And now that we'd lost Uncle Max, could my parents come back down to earth and stay there? Could I?

PART II: MICHIGAN

Not till we are lost, in other words, not till we have lost the world, do we begin to find ourselves, and realize where we are and the infinite extent of our relations.

—Henry David Thoreau, *Walden*

12

A folded note fell out of my locker, and I bent down to pick it up. White notebook paper, slanted messy writing, in pencil.

Why haven't you been to Planet Granite?

Then another note three days later.

We're waiting for you.

Now it was a Friday, my second week of school. The bell rang for lunch, and I drifted along the river of students toward my locker. I spun the dials on the combination lock and popped open the door. This time I was ready. I snatched the third note midfall.

I unfolded the paper, my pulse quickening with each square after square after square. Same messy scrawl, but this time written in blue ink.

Still waiting.

I glanced around the hallway, expecting someone to be watching. The river flowed toward the cafeteria, shouting, jostling, giggling. I turned back to my locker and stared at Dad's postcard of the llama that I'd hung on the inside of the flimsy gray metal door. If only I could step right through into another world. Back into my own world, back to the mountains.

My parents had made up their minds. Uncle Max was gone, the official search was over, but still my parents hadn't returned. And they wanted me to stay with my grandparents.

In Detroit. Motor City Ugly. No mountains, no rock climbing, no life. It didn't matter that I had rarely attended school before, or that I wanted to be anywhere but here.

I didn't think anyone at school knew about me, that I was a rock climber, or what had happened in Ecuador. Why would people in Detroit keep up with climbing news? The climbing blogs had followed our story, but the national news didn't care about a mountaineering accident on a remote South American volcano. I hadn't even heard of Mount Chimborazo before my parents began to plan the trip. Yet someone here knew who I was. Either that, or some sci-fi freak was stalking me. *Planet Granite?*

The river trickled to a stream. A guy and a girl each dressed all in black swept past me.

"I could *kill* you," the girl said, playfully shoving the guy.

He mock-stumbled, careening off a locker. They rounded the corner and disappeared.

I grabbed my lunch and headed for the front doors. I jogged down the hallway, rounded the corner, and stopped. It was raining. Pouring. I had been cooped up in this cinder-block prison all morning, waiting for my lunchtime escape. Now what was I going to do? Thunder rumbled in the distance, rain pounded the sidewalk.

So far, I had managed to avoid the cafeteria. It made no sense that I could scale cliffs without an ounce of fear, yet one glace at the lunchroom filled me with dread. For a moment, I considered marching right out into the downpour. I'd stomp through puddles all the way back to my grandparents' house. Maybe Grandma would say I looked like a drowned rat, take pity on me, and let me stay home the rest of the day. Yeah right.

Lightning cracked the sky. Thunder boomed. I sighed and trudged toward the cafeteria. I took a deep breath and paused just inside the doors, scoping it out. I didn't recognize anyone. The faces blurred together, one massive group. Their voices roared and echoed in my head. Finally, I spied an empty table and beelined smack into a lanky guy wearing basketball shorts. I let out an embarrassingly loud *oomph* as his elbow squashed my lunch bag against my chest. It fell to the ground, and we both crouched at the same time to retrieve it.

Crack. Our skulls collided. *Oh my God!* I clutched my forehead, the pain stinging my eyes. I squeezed them shut and sunk to one knee.

"Ow, ow, shit, oh man, sorry, ow, are you okay?" He dropped to one knee too, clutching his own forehead.

I met his gaze, but I couldn't speak. Heat rushed to my cheeks.

His mouth curved into a lopsided grin, and he half-laughed. "I'm such a klutz. Seriously, are you okay?" He touched my shoulder.

I nodded and tried to half-laugh with him, but it sounded more like a whimper. *Oh my God.* The contents of my lunch were dumped onto the floor, and I started stuffing everything back into the torn paper sack. Sandwich, apple, carrots, cookies, and yes, even a juice box. Grandma was a very thorough lunch packer.

"You're in my Algebra II class," he said.

I recognized him, too. He played basketball; I'd overheard some girls whispering about him, but I didn't know his name. He was average tall, not basketball tall. Brown wavy hair and hazel eyes.

"Mmm, Oreos. Can I have one?" He shook the baggie of cookies and grinned. His cheeks were flushed with two pink splashes.

"Um, sure?"

"Awesome." He took one, popped it into his mouth, and helped me gather the rest of my lunch.

He dipped and knocked his shoulder into mine as we stood up. "Nice running into ya, Cara."

"Yeah." I opened my mouth to say something else, but he was already gone.

The roar of the cafeteria came rushing back at me. I clutched the torn paper sack with both hands to stop it from spilling open again. The empty table I had seen before was now full. Figures. Thanks a lot, Basketball Guy. I forced myself to walk among the tables until I spied another empty spot.

I sat down and pulled everything back out of my lunch bag. Grandma packed it for me every day, and every day until now I had carried it back home to eat during my lunch hour. It was a protest of sorts. A way to show Grandma and Grandpa that I didn't want to be here. I didn't belong here.

Three Oreos minus one. He knew my name. My face flushed as I pictured our crash, and I caught myself wincing then grinning, sitting at this table all by myself. I glanced around, but he was nowhere to be seen.

I stared out the window at the curtain of rain, twirling my ponytail, wishing I had brought a book. I pulled out my phone; only a sliver of red battery left. I usually didn't care that I had an old crummy phone, but now I wished I could scroll through posts and pictures like everyone else.

Dark shadows fell across the table. One minute I was all alone with my bologna on white, the next I was surrounded by vampire kids dressed all in black. A glob of gluey bread stuck in my throat.

They swooped down on the chairs around me, stared for a never-ending minute, then dug into their food and chattered away as if I didn't exist. I was bug eyed. My faded jeans and forest green T-shirt were all wrong for hiding in this jungle.

One of them smiled at me. The same girl who had passed my locker earlier. Bright white teeth through lips painted purple black. She wore a long black sweater over a floor-length black skirt. She looked like a witch wearing combat boots, minus the tall pointy hat. Her hair was the same deep purple black as her lips, and her eyes were rimmed with a heavy black line that tilted up at the corners.

"You're Cara, right?" she asked.

How did everyone know my name? I nodded and tried to smile, but I couldn't stop staring at her hair. It was actually a really pretty color.

The guy she had wanted to kill in the hallway had squeezed onto the bench next to me. "What's the matter? They don't have goths in California?"

He used the same hair dye as the smiling witch. Was that eyeliner? A dimple flashed in each cheek as he spoke, softening the vampire effect.

"Shut up, Nick." The girl pegged him with a grape straight to his chest. "I'm Kaitlyn," she said.

"Kaitlyn, you are such a sophisticate," Nick said with a fake English accent.

Kaitlyn wrinkled her nose at him and said to me, "Everyone used to call me Katie. Now I go by my real name, Kaitlyn."

I had twirled my ponytail into a knot. I tugged, and untangled my fingers.

"So what do you think of the Motor City, California Cara?" Nick asked.

I shrugged and nibbled on a carrot stick. I was sure he didn't want to know what I really thought.

"You're a long way from the mountains, baby. But you've got rock climbing right in your own backyard."

I inhaled a carrot chunk, gasped and coughed. Mystery note writer revealed? I could understand how word had spread that the new girl was from California, but how did he know I was a rock climber?

"Leave her alone, Nick." This time Kaitlyn's grape dinged him on the cheek. And that's when I noticed her hand. She had a thumb and a half of one finger, maybe two? But the rest of her hand was deformed. It was almost hidden by the long sleeve of her sweater.

Don't stare. Don't stare.

"Hey, watch it." Nick brandished a french fry at Kaitlyn like a sword.

Another grape zoomed past his ear. He reached across the table and snatched a stem of grapes. "Bring it on!"

Nicks's first throw barely missed Kaitlyn's forehead. She yelped and ducked and then scooted off the bench as Nick jumped up and hit her square in the back. Kaitlyn tossed another grape over her shoulder, and it bounced off the table into my lap.

"Sorry Cara!" she yelled, laughing, as Nick raced after her.

My first cafeteria food fight. I picked up the grape and popped it into my mouth. Kaitlyn and Nick ran up another aisle of tables, and there was my basketball player. Tall and smiley, carrying a tray loaded with food. I held my breath for a second, thinking that Kaitlyn or Nick were about to crash into him. He held his tray higher as they darted past, then slid onto a bench next to his friends, unaware of my eyes burning a hole in his back. I flushed and couldn't help smiling. Just a little.

13

The rain had stopped by the time school was out. The sun was shining, but the air was humid, heavy and thick. It coated my hair, clogged my lungs. Twigs and broken branches littered the sidewalk. Soggy leaves had been plucked from their trees and washed toward the street.

Up ahead, I spotted Kaitlyn and Nick in an old station wagon, waiting to pull out of the student parking lot. As a canary-yellow Hummer passed by, Nick's arm shot out of the passenger window, middle finger raised. They turned in the opposite direction, not noticing me, and were gone.

What was that all about? There was something rebellious and defiant about Nick flipping off the Hummer that matched my mood. Hell yeah, screw you, gas guzzler.

I continued on my walk home, passed the pin oak, the shaggy hickory, the locust, and a new friend with elephant-ear leaves and dangling seedpods like giant green beans. Last week, I had carried one of the leaves home to ask Grandpa what it was.

"A catalpa tree. And it will be loaded with the sweetest smelling blossoms next summer," he had said.

I passed under a maple with brilliant red leaves on only one limb. The rest of the leaves held on to their summer green. I felt kind of like that tree. One small part of me was pushed into this new life, but the rest of me, most of me, was stuck in the past, trying to hold on to my old life.

I took my time getting home, wandering around the neighborhood, wishing I was hiking in the mountains. I remembered my mom's words.

There's a difference in being alone in the woods and being alone in the city. In the woods, I feel like I'm meant to be alone. In the city, I just feel lonely. Mom had left suburban Detroit for good when she was nineteen, and she rarely came back. I just couldn't believe she wanted this for me.

My grandparents lived in a dollhouse with shutters painted sky blue and plastic flowers in the window boxes. Grandma's ceramic goose waited for me on the front porch. She gave me her usual glassy stare. She was still dressed in her Fourth of July star-spangled outfit. I had discovered the rest of her outfits down in the basement the other day. I thought they were old baby clothes, which was weird enough, hanging neatly in the cedar closet, enclosed in plastic. Is this what happened to people when they got old?

I patted the goose on her head and opened the front door. The smell of mothballs settled in my nose.

Grandma and Grandpa began their daily chorus of questions about my school day. I shrugged off my backpack; school was okay, my day was okay. Grandma continued to buzz around me, as pesky as the Michigan mosquitoes.

"Isn't there a game tonight?" she hinted.

For a second I thought of the basketball guy at school, but then I remembered it was football season.

Grandpa sat in his recliner, tucked away in the corner, nose back in his book.

"Cara should go, don't you think? Norman? Norman!"

Grandpa's eyebrows lifted, eyes peered over the top of his reading glasses.

"That's okay," I said.

"We could go with you, if you'd like," Grandpa offered.

"You know I can't get up those rickety bleachers," Grandma said. "We don't need to go. Cara needs to go with her friends."

Friends. Ha. My friends were clear across the country.

I passed through the cluttered living room. Grandma was particularly fond of porcelain angel figurines. Round cheeked and iridescent glazed, they sat on end tables and shelves, in a curio cabinet and on the mantel. She tickled them clean with a feather duster practically every day. I didn't remember seeing all the knickknacks during my last visit. Grandma must have been steadily accumulating the stuff since then.

I headed toward my room. "I've got lots of homework to do."

I actually did have a lot of homework. Not that I was going to do it. Going to high school was a heck of a lot different than being homeschooled. And I didn't plan on sticking around long enough for it to matter.

"Homework on a Friday night? Girl her age shouldn't be sitting home on a Friday night." Grandma's words followed me into my room.

"Let her be, Margaret, let her be."

"Well, I suppose it's better than going around with some boy, smoking dope. Who knows what she's done with Mark and Lori and that rat pack they hang out with."

Grandma's words prickled my skin. Scaling cliffs was enough of a high for my parents; they didn't smoke pot. Maybe some of their climbing friends did, but not Mom and Dad.

I shut the bedroom door, plugged my dead phone into the charger, and flopped onto the bed. I grabbed a book off the nightstand. Agatha Christie. My mom loved mysteries, and I had found the hardcover Agatha Christies lined up on a shelf in the closet.

I flipped to the folded-corner page where I had left off last night. I read the words and turned the pages, but my thoughts veered. Grandma had ruffled my feathers. That's what Mom always called it when I got angry or annoyed at a competition. "Don't let your feathers get all ruffled."

I was surprised that my mom, such a tough tomboy, had grown up in this fluffy girly-girl room. The dresser was painted white, the wallpaper had red stripes and roses. There was even a vanity with a cushioned stool that I'd been using as a dumping ground for my clothes. I flipped onto my stomach and inched up toward the headboard. There it was, in the corner, almost hidden by the mattress. *LB + MJ* carved into the headboard, enclosed by a heart.

Mom met Dad right after her freshman year of college. They had summer jobs as camp counselors in the mountains in North Carolina.

Mom taught arts and crafts, and Dad worked as a river guide, guiding kayakers and rafters through rapids. The mountains were Dad's home, but it was the first time for my mom, who had never been outside of Detroit. She fell in love twice that summer, first with the mountains, then with Mark Jenkins. I traced the carved heart with my finger.

My phone chimed. Back to life. A message from Coach Mel. *How's your training going?*

I deleted the message and tossed the phone on my clothes heap. Now that my parents had been found, everyone assumed I was fine. No need for special care and attention. Uncle Max was gone, but no one really understood how important he was in my life, what a gaping hole his death had left.

Becky and Zach and my other teammates continued on with their normal lives. Back at home, going to school, training. That's what my parents expected of me. What Coach Mel expected. New home, new school, find a climbing gym to train. Planet Granite. Right in my own backyard, according to Nick, yeah right. Some plastic wall in a converted warehouse, not the real rocks in my own backyard, in the mountains.

I spun the beads on my bracelet from Ecuador. Was Mom still wearing hers? Out the window the moonflowers beamed from a tangle of overgrown ivy in the backyard. Brown crinkled leaves were clumped along the chain-link fence. The streets would be a blaze of color in a few weeks. No matter where we lived, North Carolina, Colorado, Oregon, California, autumn was my favorite time of year. The crisp air sparked my energy, the rocks felt cool to my touch, my fingers searching for the next handhold, a groove, a tiny pocket, anything to cling to.

Tears swelled behind my eyes, and I rolled off the bed, opened the closet door, and dragged out the heavy cardboard box stuffed in the corner. I blinked away the tears and dug past the stack of climbing magazines on top until I reached my books.

The cover of Thoreau's *Walden* was hanging on by a thread. I gingerly thumbed through the yellowed pages, searching for passages I had highlighted and the ones my dad had underlined. This was the type of homework I did with Mom and Dad, not the boring textbooks

I'd been assigned here. When you're homeschooled, you can spend days immersed in a book, dissecting and discussing, hiking and thinking. Here, I changed classes every fifty minutes. My brain didn't work that way. I needed time to study, think, absorb. By the time I settled in and concentrated on what we were doing, class was over. And everything had gone straight through my head like a breeze through an open window.

I read the underlined words silently, then aloud, whispering, trying to make sense of them. " 'Not till we are lost, in other words, not till we have lost the world, do we begin to find ourselves, and realize where we are and the infinite extent of our relations.' "

The cover released its final hold and fell off. Figures. Thoreau's words made sense when I read them outside in the woods, but they were meaningless sitting on the floor of a suburban closet.

I didn't want to climb in Michigan. Another protest of sorts. *Fine, send me away from the mountains, then I won't climb. I'll get rusty and flub my next competition, just like I had the last one, and what will you think about that, Mom and Dad?*

I picked up an old copy of *Climbing Magazine* and flipped to the back where there was a list of climbing gyms around the country. Under Michigan, it said Planet Granite, Pontiac. I didn't know where Pontiac was. Maybe I didn't even care. I just wanted to go back to California. I needed to go home.

The phone rang from the kitchen, and I raced out of my room and down the hall. Grandpa beat me by three seconds and picked it up with a grin.

"It's your mother. Would you like to talk first?" he asked.

I nodded and took the phone.

"Mom?"

"Hi sweetie." Static cut through Mom's voice. She sounded small and far away.

I took the phone into my room and shut the door. "Where are you?"

"We're still in Ecuador," Mom said. "But we've left Mount Chimborazo. Your dad is—"

Static took over her words.

"You disappeared for a second," I said. "Is Dad okay?"

"He's fine—Max—taking it very—" Mom's voice disappeared every few words.

"He needs to come home," I said. "I need to go home too."

"I wish it were that easy."

"What's so hard about it?"

"Your dad doesn't think he can handle going back to the cabin now."

Mom's voice came through clearly for a moment, then static drowned her out again. Dad and Uncle Max had restored our cabin in California themselves. It was a run down, abandoned shack when we first found it, and they spent an entire year turning it into a cozy home. But I had helped too. I had pounded nails and grouted tile right alongside them.

I stepped out of my room, trying to get better reception, but the problem was on Mom's end of the line. She had given up calling my cell, but now it was just as bad on the landline. It sounded like someone was crinkling wrapping paper in my ear.

"He feels like he owes Max. If he can't give Max his life back, he's going to live his life for him. Something like that, but more complicated. It's hard to explain."

"What about me? Our cabin is even more special because of Uncle Max. We can't leave it."

"I know. I agree. But—Dad's—ready yet. And we've—talk—what's best for you. —want you to stay—school. —best place—with Grandma and Grandpa."

"Mom!" I shouted. "I can hardly hear you!"

"Max's dream—K2. —first—head south—Peru, then—"

The phone was silent.

"Mom? Are you there?"

Silence.

"Oh come on!" I smacked the phone against the wall. I dialed Mom's cell. Busy signal. I waited a few seconds and dialed again. Still busy.

My parents and I had been arguing about school for years. They kept saying it was time for me to have a real education. They said I couldn't count on a climbing career; I needed something to fall back on. Like accounting or something. They wanted me to go to college, and their version of homeschooling wasn't going to cut it. They said I needed a real school with real homework, real tests, and real grades. They said I needed a real life. I told *them* to get real.

"You've made a life out of climbing—you don't think I'm good enough?"

"Get off it, Miss Junior National Champion," Dad had answered.

Mom had given her spiel about having choices. About how she and Dad didn't have an education to fall back on if climbing didn't work out, like if she or Dad got injured.

We were still arguing about it on the plane ride to Ecuador. "I'm confident you can handle school and climbing," Mom had said, "and we'll plan our trips around the school holidays."

But I was supposed to be attending school back in California, not in Michigan. And what was she talking about when she mentioned K2? K2 was in the Himalayas, not South America. And Peru? Was that where they were headed next? Seriously, they were going to Peru and leaving me in Detroit?

I gripped the phone tighter and willed it to ring. Nothing. I punched in Mom's number one more time, but it immediately went to voice mail. I didn't bother leaving a message.

"You're done already?" Grandpa said.

"We got cut off." I sighed and dropped the phone into its holder. "I wanted to talk to her too. Maybe she'll be able to call back."

I shrugged and twisted the beaded bracelet on my wrist.

"What did she say?" Grandpa asked.

"Nothing." I trudged back to my room.

14

On Monday morning, I paused outside of the kitchen when I heard the bitterness in Grandma's voice.

"What kind of parents just go off and leave their child? Lori never would have done this by herself," Grandma said.

"I know, I know," Grandpa muttered.

"Mark was trouble from day one. You remember I told you that when she first brought him home."

"I know, I know."

I entered the kitchen with barely a creak of the floor. If I surprised Grandma, she didn't show it.

"Good morning," she sang. "Tea?"

"Thanks." I sat down across from Grandpa.

"Here's your sports," he said, passing me a section of the newspaper.

Grandpa thought that since I was into rock climbing, I must be some kind of jock and therefore must like all kinds of sports. I didn't mind. It was nice that he was trying to understand me. I looked down at the paper, not even seeing it, and cupped my hands around the steaming mug of tea.

Tea has always brought me comfort. Both Mom and Dad drank tea instead of coffee, not the average Joe Lipton in a bag like my grandparents but exotic greens and oolongs we'd brought back from China, steeped loose in a pot. Herbal teas we saved for cool nights around the campfire or for when we curled up on the couch, reading, in the evening. And always before a climbing competition. It was a ritual.

My nerves were like earthquake tremors, but give me a warm mug of peppermint tea and I became a different person. I breathed in the scent, and the warm liquid relaxed my muscles one by one. I focused on the route I was about to climb, and everything else disappeared. By the time my feet left the ground, I was alone in the world. Handhold to handhold, foothold to foothold. Slow and steady, like a snake slithering, just me and the rocks. The world disappeared until I reached the top of the cliff, clipped the last bolt, and looked down at my belayer.

I glanced up to see Grandma nudge Grandpa. She sent him signals with her eyebrows. I wasn't interested in decoding the message. Grandma was clueless about my parents, my life; I didn't need to hear her theories.

I shoved my chair back. "I gotta go."

My sack lunch waited on the counter as usual. I knew I should appreciate that Grandma made it for me, but she was ruffling my feathers again. I grabbed the lunch, hoisted my backpack, and headed out the door.

I was almost looking forward to school; Grandma and her knickknack clutter were suffocating. I probably smelled like mothballs. Outside, the sun was brilliant; a giant sponge sopping up yesterday's humidity. I gobbled up the clean air. Bloomfield High had hardly any windows. It was a giant, rectangular, two-story brick building. You know what kind of building has no windows? A prison.

In California, the local high school was like a sprawling villa tucked in the hills. Whitewashed stucco, open corridors. You left your classroom and walked outside under a veranda to get to your next classroom. Not that I ever went there, but when my parents talked about me going to "real" school, that was what I pictured.

I took one last deep breath of fresh air and entered to serve my time. The door hissed shut behind me. Four hours until I could escape at lunchtime. I touched the bruised bump on my forehead from Friday's crash with Basketball Guy. At least it was mostly hidden by my bangs. I was steering clear of the cafeteria today.

Something was on my desk in Algebra II. I slid into my seat and picked up the little blue and white package. Snack-size Oreos.

Basketball Guy was at the front of the room, leaning over the pencil sharpener at the teacher's desk.

I pushed the package of cookies to the corner of my desk and took out my notebook and pencil. The lead point was broken. Okay then. I headed to the sharpener and waited my turn.

"Regular or the super special?"

Basketball Guy was asking me a question. His shoulders hunched to come down to my size. Since I was only five-foot-three, he had a long way to go. I gave him a blank look. Was he asking me about cookies? He flashed his lopsided grin and held out his hand, waiting for . . .

My pencil. Duh. He took it and said, "Just a regular sharpening today, okeydokey."

What a goof! But cute. His cheeks were still flushed with those two pink splashes. A faint scar cut into his upper lip, and I wondered what had gashed his skin once upon a time. That thick wavy hair. What ethnicity was he? Italian? Maybe some Latino blood? A curly lock fell over one eye as he bent down to sharpen my pencil.

"Thanks for the Oreos." I tipped my head in the direction of my desk.

"I owed you." He squinted at my forehead. "You have a goose egg!"

I raised my hand to the bump on my forehead and smoothed my bangs.

"I'm so sorry!" he said. "Does it hurt?"

I shook my head. "No, it's fine. Really. What about you?"

He rapped his knuckles against his skull. "Hard as a rock."

He gave my pencil back to me and nodded at the bracelet on my wrist. "Are those acai beads?"

"Um, no, tagua nuts. From Ecuador." I held out my wrist for him to see.

"Cool. My dad brought my mom a bracelet like that from Brazil." He touched the beads on my wrist. "But it's made from acai seeds."

He gave me another grin, I smiled back, and we returned to our seats.

A guy gave him a fist bump as he passed. "Triple T."

A basketball nickname? Tim, Trent, Trevor? How was I going to find out this guy's name?

I fiddled with my bracelet. My nails had grown out into a ragged mess, and the crosshatch of scratches on the back of my hand had healed into raised red scars. I hoped he hadn't noticed.

The teacher's scribbles on the whiteboard might as well have been written in Chinese. I twirled my ponytail, squirmed in my seat; my legs twitched. How could long-legged people like Triple T tolerate being cramped in these uncomfortable chairs? His profile from across the room was much more interesting than the mess of quadratic equations on my desk. He didn't seem to be having any trouble with his problems. He hunched over his desk, pencil moving smoothly across the page, working out the answers.

He looked up and busted me. I looked away, then back. He was still looking at me, and of course my fingers were stuck in my twirled ponytail. His grin grew wider as I tugged and disentangled my gnarly hand. I made a funny grimace; what else could I do?

Lunchtime came, and another note fell out of my locker.

How long are you going to make us wait?

What the hell? I shoved the note in my pocket, grabbed my lunch, and slammed my locker door. The sun beckoned, and I was about to bypass the cafeteria and head home when Kaitlyn and Nick appeared, one on each side.

"California Cara," Nick said.

"You gonna sit with us again?" Kaitlyn asked.

"Uh . . . I was just—"

My words fell away as I spotted Triple T up ahead, flanked by two girls. Their arms were linked with his.

"Come on." Kaitlyn and Nick steered me toward their group. The rest of the vampires had beaten us to the table by the window. That morning I had put on a black T-shirt, just in case. There was something appealing about melting into their somberness. But in this crowd, my blond ponytail stood out like a crescent moon in a midnight sky.

"Scooch over," Kaitlyn said to Nick, who made room for her at the end of the table. The guy across from her had piercings in his eyebrow, nose, and lip. He looked at me sideways and moved over an inch. I squeezed onto the bench with one butt cheek, while he turned toward the girl on his other side. Fine by me. I gazed longingly out the window, then opened my lunch.

More Oreos from Grandma. I had left the snack pack gift in my locker. My eyes drifted up the next aisle; he sat at the same table as Friday, laughing with the two girls he'd been walking with. Maybe I just hadn't noticed them before. Why did I care? I didn't even know his name. And Triple T sounded like a Kentucky Derby racehorse.

I pulled the crust off my sandwich. Kaitlyn picked seeds out of her sandwich's bread, keeping her hand without fingers mostly hidden in her long sleeve. I tried to peek at it, but I didn't want her to notice. If I was embarrassed about my wrecked hands, how must she feel? The pierced-face guy kept bumping me with his elbow. I told myself to just stand up and go outside while I still had a chance for fresh air, but instead I watched Nick use four napkins to soak up the grease on his slice of pizza.

"He's afraid of zits marring his perfect skin," Kaitlyn said.

"Very funny," Nick muttered. His dimples flashed.

He ate the pepperonis first, then devoured the rest of his pizza in three bites. The greasy napkins sat in a gray lump on the corner of the cafeteria tray.

With his mouth half-full, he turned to me and said, "So what gives." Chomp, chomp, gulp. "You moved here before school started, right? How come you haven't been to the climbing gym yet?"

How long are you going to make us wait?

Pierced-face guy shifted, almost shoving me off the bench. A lightning bolt of anger flashed inside me. I yanked the folded note out of my pocket, shoving pierced-face in the process, and slapped it on the table in front of Nick.

"It's none of your business. And stop leaving these notes in my locker."

"Whoa!" Nick held up his hands. "Don't look at me."

Kaitlyn read the note aloud. "I don't get it."

"It's about the climbing gym," I said. "Planet Granite. Apparently *someone* thinks I should be going there. This is the fourth note."

"I didn't write them," Nick said.

Yeah right. I raised my eyebrows at him. Kaitlyn did the same.

Nick looked back and forth from me to Kaitlyn. "Why would I do that?"

"Because you know I'm a climber," I said. "How do you even know that?"

"Go on, explain." Kaitlyn nodded at him.

"Look at her hands." Nick reached across the table and grabbed my hand. "She's either a climber or a car mechanic."

I snatched my hand back.

"Nick!" Kaitlyn said.

"What? Okay, fine. I climb there sometimes. Everyone there knows you're here."

"What? How?"

"Are you kidding me? Have you been living under a rock?"

Kaitlyn elbowed him.

Nick sighed, pulled his phone out of his pocket, and tapped away. He handed it to me.

The *Rock and Ice* magazine website. "Juniors Rock!" was the heading in bold print, then "Tragedy Looms." Below was a close-up shot of me holding my third-place medal, followed by an older photo of Mom, Dad, and Uncle Max.

"The magazine is on a rack right at the counter at the gym. Everyone who climbs there knows who you are."

I zoomed in on the photo of my parents and Uncle Max, wanting it to be bigger, clearer. My body stilled, my mind went blank, all of my anger draining away.

"So how come you haven't been there yet?" Nick said.

Kaitlyn elbowed him again. "Leave her alone."

What was I supposed to say? *Well, Nick, let's see, my uncle is frozen and buried on a glacier in the middle of nowhere and my parents are traipsing all over South America while I'm stuck in high school hell.*

The clamor of the cafeteria was suddenly too much to bear. I stood up, muttered, "I gotta go," and flew out of the cafeteria, leaving my lunch behind.

I found my lunch sitting in front of my locker at the end of the school day. Kaitlyn? I peeked inside the bag; it looked like everything was still in there, even my sandwich with the crusts pulled off. My stomach growled.

"Cara?"

Kaitlyn leaned against the locker next to mine.

"You okay?"

"Yeah." I held up my lunch. "Thanks."

"Nick can be really thoughtless sometimes."

I shook my head. "He wasn't . . . I just . . . It's hard to explain."

"You don't have to, not to me."

I fiddled with the beads on my bracelet, unsure what to say.

"Nick keeps trying to get me to try climbing, but hello?" She held up her misshapen hand. "Not the best sport for me."

I smiled. "Most people think climbing is all about your hands, but your legs are just as important, maybe more so."

"Really?"

"For sure." I nodded at her hand. It was the first time I was seeing it fully exposed, the contorted shape and smooth skin where fingers would normally be. "Can you use it, I mean, like, does it hurt?"

"No, it doesn't hurt, and I'm actually pretty lucky to have a strong pincer grasp." She demonstrated by holding her backpack with her thumb and first finger—her only finger, and it was half-formed.

"How did it happen?"

"Just born this way."

"Sorry to keep asking."

"Whatever. A lot of people are freaked out by it. Which makes me kind of freaked out by it." She pulled her long sleeve over her hand again.

"I know a climber with missing fingers," I said. "An accident with ropes and frostbite. He still climbs though."

Kaitlyn was quiet a minute, and I busied myself pulling books out of my locker and putting them in my backpack.

"Well, maybe I'll try it someday," she said.

"You should, definitely."

There was something about Kaitlyn's face, her big blue eyes, a genuineness that couldn't be covered up by her dark makeup. An offer to teach her to climb was on the tip of my tongue, but I kept it to myself. I didn't plan on venturing to Planet Granite anytime soon.

I ate my sandwich on the walk home from school. For once, Grandma and Grandpa weren't waiting for me when I walked in the front door. A clatter came from the kitchen, and I breathed in deep. Mmm, freshly baked cookies. Even better, the rich, buttery scent had conquered the usual mothball odor.

The door to the curio cabinet stood open in the living room. Weird. I peered at the shelves full of angel figurines. Grandma never let me touch them when I was younger, but I had studied all of them through the glass. My favorites were the five baby angels. One sat in a baby carriage, another in a bubble bath, and three more in cradles. I pulled out the one in a bubble bath and ran a finger over the iridescent bubbles.

I had never thought to ask her why she started collecting all of these figurines. The cookie scent grew stronger, and I returned the angel to the cabinet and followed my gurgling stomach to the kitchen.

Grandpa was helping himself to a cookie right off the pan. "Ooh, ah, hot, hot." He pulled the cookie apart and a drop of chocolate plopped onto his shirt.

Grandma huffed. "You couldn't wait just one minute for them to cool off?"

"Oops." Grandpa grinned at me and tried to lick the chocolate off his shirt.

Grandma huffed even louder, but I couldn't help laughing.

"Do you have a lot of homework today?" Grandpa asked me.

I shook my head. Of course I had a lot of homework, but I had no plans of actually doing it. Agatha Christie was calling my name. I helped myself to a cookie.

"Good. I thought we could go for a little drive and check out the rock climbing gym."

I paused with the cookie half in my mouth, the chocolate burning my tongue. Grandma poured milk into a glass, but she paused too, raising her eyes to Grandpa.

"I figured you must be missing climbing after all these weeks," he said.

I swallowed the bite of cookie, scorching my throat. Grandma pushed the glass of cold milk toward me, and I chugged.

"Did my mom tell you to do that?"

"No, there was a flyer at the library. There's even an after-school club that meets there."

I almost snorted, but I knew Grandpa was only trying to help. An after-school club, *right*.

"I don't think that's a good idea—" Grandma pointed a spatula at Grandpa.

"Don't worry, Margaret. We'll be careful," he said.

"You want to try climbing too?" I asked him. He was old, but he was pretty spry.

"Ha! I can hardly move my arm from the darn flu shot I got yesterday."

"Nice excuse," I said.

"We should probably get you one too."

I shook my head and rubbed my arm. "Ugh, no way. I never get sick."

Grandma pointed the spatula at me and looked like she was about to lecture, but Grandpa was already grabbing his wallet and keys. "Let's go!"

15

We headed out to Grandpa's vintage car. I really could care less about cars, but his Mustang was pretty sharp. He had taught my mom how to drive on it, and it was still in great shape. I could picture my mom and dad on a date, cruising around town before I was born. But that would have never happened because I was born two years after they met down south. And my mom never came back to Detroit to live. Just a quick trip to pack up some of her belongings. She was a girl in the mountains from then on.

It turned out that Pontiac was only about a ten-minute drive from Bloomfield. Nick was right. There was rock climbing right in my own backyard. The plastic kind. I had been to climbing gyms all over the country for competitions, but never Planet Granite.

My stomach convulsed as we walked up to the industrial-looking building. Why was I so nervous? I wasn't going to climb. I purposefully hadn't even brought my gear. Grandpa walked his grandpa pace, and I slowed down to match his stride.

I paused just inside the gym. The guy behind the check-in counter gave the other employee a shove. Subtle.

"Hey, you here to climb?" he asked.

"Maybe. I'm not sure yet."

The guy stared at me for a second, then asked, "Aren't you Cara Jenkins?"

Was this my stalker? "You go to Bloomfield High?" I asked.

The guy smirked. "Uh, no. I graduated two years ago."

And then I noticed the rack of climbing magazines, just like Nick had said. *Everyone who climbs there knows who you are.*

"You're telling me you're not here to climb?" The guy's smirk was permanent. His arms were covered with tattoos—sleeves. The piercing in his tongue flashed when he talked. Why did I keep running into all these punks and goths?

"I'm just going to look around for a minute."

"What? You need to see if we're good enough for you?"

My scalp prickled. Who did this guy think he was? I wanted to tell him off, but tears threatened. I knew I shouldn't have come here. I could feel Grandpa moving closer to me. *Breathe.*

"Do you have a brochure with prices?" Grandpa asked. "Something about the after-school club?"

Oh my God, Grandpa. The other employee stared at us. He was the clean-cut opposite of the guy talking to us. Tall and fit with super short hair, almost a buzz cut. A spray of tiny pimples dotted his forehead.

"You have to take a class your first time here," Tattoo Guy said. If it was possible for his face to turn even more mocking, he accomplished it.

I gave him my best *Don't be an idiot* look. "Obviously I don't need a class."

"Well, you gotta pass the belay test before you're allowed to climb."

"Whatever." I hoped he would snag his lip on his tongue piercing.

"You should take their test now," Grandpa said. "Then you'll be all set to climb whenever you want."

I shook my head. "I didn't even bring my harness. Let's just look around."

The buzz-cut guy smiled. "No worries. We'll loan you a harness. I'm Blake. Follow me."

Grandpa nodded and nudged me forward. Tattoo Guy's sneer burned into my back.

We entered the climbing area, and the soaring walls and dusty smell of chalk hit me like a punch to the stomach. I couldn't help but think that Mom, Dad, and Uncle Max were going to walk up any minute. Choosing not to climb had seemed like a protest at first, but now I felt the full force of the fear behind my decision.

Grandpa gave my shoulder a squeeze.

Blake led us over to a corner wall and handed me a rope. "Sorry about this. It's just policy, you know, liability."

"It's okay. I get it." At least this guy was nice. I would have walked out for sure if Tattoo Guy was the one giving the belay test.

I ran my fingers over the tightly woven strands of rope—red, yellow, and green swirled together like the colorful market in Ecuador. I thought of my parents and Max roped together on the mountain, the rope severed, the end frayed and unraveling.

"This is how Mom taught me when I was little," I said to Grandpa. "You make a loop, then take the end of the rope. It's a rabbit. He runs around the tree and down into the hole. See, that makes a figure eight. Then I thread this through my harness and follow the figure eight all the way around to make it double."

"Okay, so what's the belay part?"

"I'm getting there." I untied the figure eight knot and clipped the belay device to my harness.

"Now Blake's the climber, and he's going to tie the figure eight onto his harness. I'm going to pinch the other end of the rope through my belay device. When he climbs up the wall and slips and falls, all I have to do is hold the rope back like this and it will stop his fall. He'll just be hanging there, and I can slowly lower him down."

A whoosh and a shout echoed from the other side of the gym. Laughter. A girl swung on the rope near the ceiling.

Blake laughed. "Just like that."

"Climb on," I said to him.

"Nah, it's okay. I know you know how to belay. Obviously. Um, if you want to climb, we can find you a belayer, or uh I can do it, like, you know, for you."

His face turned a darker shade of pink with each word, and heat flushed my face too.

"Thanks," I said with a smile. "Maybe next time."

What was up with me? Nervous about climbing, blushing over a belay offer? I was just one of the guys.

"That's it?" Grandpa asked. "You passed the test?"

"That's it."

"But you don't want to climb today?"

"Nope."

He stood with his hands on his hips, looking up and around. "What's over there?"

I followed his gaze to a cave-like structure. "It's for bouldering. The walls are shorter, so you can climb without a rope."

"Show me."

"Grandpa . . ."

"Oh come on, just give me a little demonstration."

"I didn't bring my climbing shoes."

He raised his eyebrows at me.

I sighed and headed over to the bouldering area and climbed on. I traversed part of the wall and maneuvered under and over a ledge. I felt the silence and a half dozen eyes on me as I jumped down. I was used to people watching me climb. I knew how to tune them out. But this was different. I didn't want anyone watching me now.

Grandpa grinned. "Reminds me of your mom when she was little. She used to climb the fence in the backyard, back and forth, until her hands were red and smarting. It was a game, how long she could last without her feet touching the ground."

Huh. Even here in Michigan, my mom had found a way to climb before she even knew it was a sport. Before she'd ever seen a mountain.

I could feel the smirking tattooed guy staring at me as we left, but I didn't meet his eyes. Buzz-cut Blake called out just as we reached the door.

"See you soon!"

Probably not, I thought, and gave a little wave.

16

Ever since I left Ecuador, I had been dreaming the same dream.

Falling, falling in a tumble of white. I'm curled into a tight ball, rolling, then flat on my stomach sliding face first like swimming underwater in an icy pool. A hard slam against my shoulder, my knee. A deep rumbling voice. Uncle Max. I can't see. The whiteness is blinding.

I woke up twisted in my sheets, sweaty but chilled. I straightened the covers and pulled the quilt up to my ears. Even when my heartbeat returned to its normal rhythm, I couldn't fall back asleep. The green numbers on the clock glowed 5:30 a.m. At 6:00, I got up and wandered into the kitchen.

Grandpa sat at the kitchen table, drinking tea and reading the newspaper. No sign of Grandma. He looked up and paused a moment, glancing back down at the paper, then back at me.

"Morning," he said. "Water's probably still hot in the kettle."

Did I imagine the look, that moment of hesitation?

I glanced at the paper over Grandpa's shoulder as I headed for the stove. "California Wildfire Blazes."

Wildfires were annual news in California. No big deal. I guessed Grandpa wasn't sure if it would upset me or not. I sat down with my mug of tea across the table from him.

"You're up early." He said it like a question.

"Yeah, couldn't sleep so good."

"Me neither. Your grandma snores like a freight train."

I laughed. "I thought that was you."

"Don't you believe it." Grandpa looked back down at the newspaper. "Looks like this wildfire business is getting out of hand back in your part of the world." He slid the paper over to me. "Must be scary."

The story was about several wildfires that had cropped up in the past week around California. The biggest one was in Southern California. It was being contained, but the authorities were cautious. They warned that once the seasonal Santa Ana winds started blowing the hot dry air off the desert, it could fuel the flames.

"It is a little scary when you see those fires popping up. We never had to evacuate, but there was almost always a fire nearby every year. The firefighters used to do controlled burns in the Angeles Forest near where we lived, trying to clear the brush. Even seeing the smoke and blackened ground from those fires made me nervous."

"Well, we don't have wildfires here, thank goodness, or earthquakes. But maybe you'll get to experience a tornado drill." Grandpa grinned.

"You're kidding."

"Oh no. You'll probably have to do one at school. They'll make you sit down in the hallways with your head between your knees. At least that's what they used to make us do. And if it's a real tornado warning, you'll have to hide under a desk or in the bathroom or someplace like that. Last year, those sirens went off when your grandma was in the bathtub. The sky had turned an eerie green. Oh boy, you should have heard her hollering! What to do? Stay in the tub? Run down to the basement? She was in a tizzy."

Grandma shuffled into the kitchen, her slippers slapping on the linoleum. "What are you saying about me?"

"I was just telling Cara about you leaping out of the tub naked as a jaybird and running down to the basement when that tornado siren went off last year."

"I did no such thing," Grandma snapped. "There you go again, putting ideas in her head."

Grandpa gave me a look and suppressed a grin before focusing on the newspaper again. I didn't know how he did it. The woman drove me nuts, but Grandpa just didn't seem to let it get to him.

Grandma was still griping as I left the kitchen.

"Putting ideas into her head. She hasn't said anything about climbing since she got here, and then you go encouraging it. Climbing is what got her in this mess in the first place."

I paused in the living room, waiting to hear Grandpa's response.

"You've seen the way she looks, Margaret. She's like a lost bird, fluttering around here, away from her own environment. She hardly talks, she hardly eats. Climbing is part of her identity. It's who she is. Besides, she won't climb until she's good and ready. I just wanted to open up the doors for her."

I drifted down the hall to my room, mulling over Grandpa's words. On an impulse, I jumped up and grabbed hold of the molding above my door. I held on with my fingertips as long as I could. It felt good to feel their strength again. It felt good to hold on to something after being forced to let go of everything. I dropped back down, grabbed my backpack, and left for school.

The humidity had disappeared during the night. I breathed in the sharp, crisp air. Goose bumps popped up on my arms, but I didn't go back for a jacket. I'd warm up as I walked. I took my time, crunching fallen leaves and helicopter seeds with my feet. For the next seven hours, I'd be stuck squirming on a hard, plastic chair, trapped at a desk.

Back in California, I'd be wandering the woods, one eye always alert for sour grass. When I was little, Uncle Max had once plucked a few stalks. He'd chewed a blade and handed one to me.

"Try some, Cara, it's fairy food."

I'd taken a nibble, my eyes widening at the yummy, sour taste. "Fairies live here?"

Uncle Max had shrugged. "I don't know. Keep an eye out."

And I had. I'd scanned every flower petal and tree trunk. I'd peered underneath leaves and inside hollow logs. And then I'd found it—a fairy wing, delicate and iridescent. In reality, it must have belonged to a dragonfly, but Uncle Max never let on. He'd acted just as surprised and enchanted as I was.

Nick and Kaitlyn were waiting in front of my locker when I got to school.

"Nick has something to tell you," Kaitlyn said.

"Isn't it supposed to be innocent until proven guilty?" he asked.

"Just tell her." Kaitlyn elbowed him.

"Okay, already. I didn't write those notes. I swear. See?" He held up the note I had left in the cafeteria yesterday and another piece of paper. "The handwriting is totally different. No way could I write slanted like that. It's probably someone left-handed."

What was I supposed to say? It didn't make him any less of a jerk. I opened my locker. Another note fell out.

The three of us stood there looking at it for a second, then Kaitlyn snatched it up.

"Can I see?" she asked, pausing before unfolding the note.

"Go ahead. I don't want it."

She opened it up and read.

You finally graced us with your presence.
Don't be a stranger.

"What the hell does that mean?" Kaitlyn asked.

"She was at the climbing gym yesterday," Nick said.

Kaitlyn and I pierced him with an accusing look.

"What? My brother works there. He came home talking about her. I didn't write the frickin' note, already."

His brother. Tattooed, pierced-tongue guy. Now I saw the resemblance.

"So your brother has been writing the notes?"

"He already graduated."

"And you've been playing mailman?"

Nick opened his mouth in indignation, then looked at Kaitlyn.

She was grinning. "You deserve it."

"What did I do? What did I do?"

"He's so clueless." Kaitlyn smiled at me and patted Nick on the shoulder. "Poor guy. I think he's too simple to have pulled this off."

The first bell rang, and we scattered for our classes, leaving Nick shaking his head.

The conversation resumed at lunch. The rest of the group sat the slightest distance away from the three of us. It was barely noticeable at first glance. It was like Kaitlyn and Nick were fringe goths. And I don't know what I was. Too blond and au naturel to be part of the goth crowd, that's for sure.

"So who is it then? Who else climbs there?" Kaitlyn asked Nick.

"Hardly anyone from school, not regularly anyway. There're these two freshmen that I see there a lot, but I can't imagine they'd have the balls to keep sending the notes."

"Why not? It doesn't take guts to send anonymous notes. They're wimps. We need to confront them."

I listened to their conversation ping-pong back and forth. Kaitlyn and Nick sat with their heads tipped toward each other, and I wondered if they liked each other as more than friends. I thought about Becky and Zach and my other teammates, and how they were all back home and training like usual. Once, I had asked Becky how she got into climbing in the first place. She said it was something different from all the preppy sports like tennis and field hockey at her private school. Her mom was devoted to Becky's training and competition schedule, and her dad loved to brag to his colleagues about her. Climbing made her interesting. Especially to guys.

I had never thought about climbing that way. It was just who I was. The wilderness, the mountains, the rocks, they were part of me. Part of my family.

I glanced down the aisle to Triple T's table. There was yet another girl sitting next to him. Whatever.

Back at my locker, the llama greeted me from the Ecuador postcard. I rested my forehead against it, the metal door hard and cool against my skin. Whoever was dropping the notes in my locker, they didn't know me. They probably thought I was like Becky, climbing for sport, a way to get attention, not as a way of life. I wanted to know who was writing the notes, but solving that mystery wasn't going to get me back home.

17

Kaitlyn asked me to come home with her after school. We had a physics test the next day, and she was stumped.

"You know, I can drive you home anytime, even pick you up in the mornings so you don't have to walk," she said as we pulled out of the student parking lot.

"Thanks, that'd be great. Sometimes I kind of like walking, though, fresh air and all."

"Yeah, well, pretty soon it's going to be kick-you-in-the-butt freezing air."

I grinned. "It gets cold in California too, up in the mountains."

"Just you wait."

Kaitlyn's station wagon was ancient and absolutely hideous, with fake wood paneling on the side and everything.

"Thanks to my brother, I inherited this boat. Parallel parking's a bitch, but other than that I love it," Kaitlyn said. "It's my beast. I feel totally safe in it, even driving next to monster SUVs."

I sank into the seat and lowered the window. Speaking of monster SUVs (and flipping them off), there had been no sign of Nick after school. "Did Nick drive himself today?"

"Oh no, Nick doesn't drive unless he's desperate. He's got a swim meet, and someone will give him a ride home afterwards. He's saving up to buy an electric car. His parents are loaded and own at least four cars, maybe five, of which Nick has his pick, but he refuses."

I breathed deeply out the window, but inhaled a lungful of exhaust. "Your beast must be quite a gas guzzler. Nick doesn't mind?"

Kaitlyn shrugged. "He rides his bike a lot. Besides, can't complain about a free ride."

Kaitlyn's parents were both at work. The silence of the house settled around me like a quilt. No TV blaring, no grandma sniping and griping, no knickknack clutter. Just neat, orderly quietness. It seemed like the whole house was cream colored, soft like a pillow.

"Welcome to the cream-puff house, utterly lacking of the tiniest smidgen of character."

"No, I like it. It's . . . it's warm and soft and . . ." I almost said "fuzzy."

"Ha. You don't have to live here."

I called my grandparents before they would start to worry. Grandma sounded downright gleeful. Oh goody, Cara made a friend!

Kaitlyn grabbed two Cokes and a bag of Doritos from the kitchen, and I followed her into her room. The walls were painted midnight blue, almost black but not quite. It was like walking into a cave after the cream puff rest of the house.

"It used to be cream, too. But I finally snapped last spring and painted the walls. They wouldn't let me get new carpet though. So, I just pretend that I'm floating on a cloud up in the nighttime sky, or walking across desert sand."

"I used to pretend our cabin in California was a tree house. I'd look out the window at the birds and imagine I was sitting way up high on a tree limb overlooking the mountains."

"Ha. Like that butterfly chick camping out in a giant redwood," Kaitlyn said.

I laughed and licked the tasty orange dust off my fingers. "These are amazing!"

"What? You've never had Doritos? You really have been living in the middle of nowhere."

"I guess. My mom's a major health nut, so we just never had this stuff around."

"You've been missing out."

Kaitlyn picked up a pile of black clothes from her bed, opened her closet door, and dumped them in a laundry basket. The front of her closet was full of every shade of black and gray, but shoved in the back corner, colors peeked out, red, pink, turquoise blue. How long had they been back there?

I could have stayed in Kaitlyn's room all afternoon. Her bookcase was full of fantasy and mystery novels, even old Agatha Christies like I'd been reading.

"They were my grandma's," she said. "She died a few years ago, and all the grandkids got to pick something from her house to remember her by."

Kaitlyn picked up one of the books, *Three Blind Mice*. "She used this huge magnifying glass to read. I would visit sometimes and read to her, so she could rest her eyes."

"I have that one too. My mom has a whole collection."

Kaitlyn returned the book to her shelf. "I haven't read one in years, they seem so old-fashioned now, but I remember Grandma and I would take bets on who was the murderer. She liked the Miss Marple stories best. Supposedly Agatha Christie got tired of Hercule Poirot and called him an insufferable, egocentric creep."

I laughed, and Kaitlyn continued, "I know, isn't that great? So she created Miss Marple based on her grandmother. My grandma told me that story over and over again. She would crochet blankets the whole time I read to her. She made this one for me."

I smoothed my hand over the purple afghan on her bed. "It's so soft."

"She was teaching me how to crochet right before she died. I made half of a red scarf but never finished it."

I tried not to look at Kaitlyn's misshapen hand, but I couldn't help it. Most of her clothes seemed to have long, floppy sleeves, and she kept her hand tucked away most of the time. She held the can of Coke and grabbed a book with that hand just fine, as if she wasn't missing three and a half fingers. Still, crocheting was pretty impressive.

"Do you still have the scarf? You could keep working on it."

She shrugged. "I know, but it's not the same without my grandma."

I scanned a row of her CDs, some older bands and some I hadn't heard of, probably indie groups. I loved the Van Gogh poster over her bed and the purple lava lamp. Her room was just so her. A comfortable cave.

"I work at a music store. They have a ton of records for collectors, but I haven't really gotten into those. They cost a lot, even with my discount. Most of the CDs are my parents' and my brother's. He gave them to me when he left for college."

"That's cool."

"Not really." She half-laughed. "Who listens to CDs anymore? He just needed somewhere to dump them. Actually, I kind of like listening to them, though, and opening up the cases, looking at the pictures, reading the lyrics . . ."

"You're so lucky. Wait until you see my room. It's my mom's from when she was my age. Hardly anything's been changed."

Kaitlyn's face softened as she looked at me.

"It doesn't even feel like my mom's room because now she's different from how she must have been then. It just feels like another part of my grandparents' house."

"Would they let you decorate it? I could help."

"I don't know. I guess I just haven't felt like I was really staying here. Like I'll be going back home to California, so why bother, you know?"

Kaitlyn had questions in her eyes. She looked like she wanted to ask me about my parents and was trying to judge whether or not I wanted to open up. I hadn't shared anything about my family so far. For all practical purposes, they'd abandoned me. How was I supposed to explain that?

"Well, we should probably take a look at our physics stuff," I said. "But take these things away from me," I added, handing her the Doritos. "I can't control myself."

Later, Kaitlyn dropped me off in front of my grandparents' house.

"Don't forget Miss Marple," she said, handing over two Agatha Christie mysteries for me to borrow.

"Are you sure? They were your grandma's," I said.

She nodded and smiled. "I trust you."

I waved good-bye and sat down on the front steps next to the ceramic goose. I wasn't ready to go inside.

I flipped through the mystery novels. I had been racing through my mom's books every evening. There was something so completely satisfying about all the clues coming together to solve the crime. Everything happened for a reason. Everything made sense. At least for a little while. Then the clutter started accumulating in my brain again, and I reached for another mystery. I was becoming an addict.

Were my parents addicted to mountaineering? I had always thought of climbing as a way of life for my family, but maybe somewhere along the line, it turned into an obsession, especially for Dad and Uncle Max. And now Dad had gone all Ahab.

Until now, there had been a numb, empty void when I thought of Uncle Max, like I had never really left the fog of that last morning in Ecuador. I could even trick myself into thinking he was simply traveling with my parents, away on an expedition. How could he be suddenly gone, just wiped off the face of the earth? The void was beginning to fill up, with memories and sadness. I could see more clearly, like a camera coming into focus.

Dad had always been a hard-core climber, a true adventurer, but Mom had balanced him out to some degree. People always gave her a hard time. Like, how can you pursue such a risky sport when you have a kid? What if something happens to you? It's bad enough your husband is climbing mountains, at least you should stay home for your daughter. And a lot of the time, Mom gave in to the pressure. She stayed with me while Dad and Uncle Max tackled the most challenging mountains, the riskiest climbs.

Sometimes we traveled with them but stayed close to base camp. Other times, we waited at home. Those were the times Mom said she wished we could live a normal, white-picket-fence kind of life. But then, she'd go home to Detroit for a visit, and suburbia would propel her straight back to the mountains. No matter what anyone said, she'd be ready to climb right alongside Dad. Just like Everest, and Denali, and Chimborazo. And wherever they were headed now.

And I knew what I had to do. I had to find a way to get back home to the mountains. I couldn't stay in Detroit anymore than my mom had been able to stay here. Just like Mom, just like Dad, I needed the wilderness to feel alive. I needed the wilderness to know who I was.

18

"Cara? It's eleven o'clock. Are you feeling all right?"

"Mmmhmm," I mumbled. I was stuck in that half-asleep, half-awake realm where I could hear everything going on around me but couldn't seem to open my eyes.

"Maybe you should get up now. Grandpa and I have something to show you. And you have mail."

I slowly opened one eyelid. Grandma waved a postcard in the air and set it on my nightstand.

She shut the door, and I curled up on my side. No use. I was awake now. I rolled onto my back, stretched my arms and legs as far as they would go, and rubbed my sleepy eyes. Sunlight spilled through the slats of the window blinds and peeked around the edges.

I slid the postcard off my nightstand. Peru. Machu Picchu.

Happy birthday, Cara!
Sweet Sixteen - how can that be?!
xoxo Mom

My birthday, of course, October 12. My parents had remembered, and they sent me a postcard. Big whooping deal.

I'm touching the Void.
The mountains are holding
me in their thrall.

I knew exactly what Dad was referring to. *Touching the Void* was Joe Simpson's memoir about a horrific expedition in the Andes in Peru.

99

Joe fell down a crevasse, breaking his leg. It was this whole big ordeal where his climbing partner tried to help him, but then had to cut the rope to save himself. He was racked with guilt afterward, knowing that Joe didn't have a chance.

But Joe survived. He crawled for three days, starving and in excruciating pain, all the way down the icy, rocky mountain back to their base camp.

I hated that book.

My parents went to Machu frickin' Picchu without me. I was spending my birthday alone not because Dad thought Max was alive but because of his guilt. The mountains held him in their thrall. Sure Dad, blame it on the mountains.

"Cara?"

God. "I know!"

I shuffled out to find my grandparents fluffing the cushion on a huge, round wicker chair in the middle of the living room. It looked like a giant bird's nest.

"What do you think?" Grandma asked. "Have a seat."

I sank into the cushion. "It's comfortable. But where are you going to put it?"

"That's for you to decide," Grandpa said. "Happy birthday!"

They grinned at me and beamed at each other. Tears swelled behind my eyes. In a backward way, I had almost wanted them to forget my birthday. Then I'd have another reason to feel sorry for myself.

I smiled and blinked away the tears.

"You look like a bird in a nest!" Grandpa said.

Grandma chortled. "She does!"

My smile grew, and I tucked my hands into my armpits to make little wings. Flap, flap. "Chirp, chirp."

"It's called a papasan chair. The people at the store said they're all the rage among you teenagers," Grandma said.

"We know how much you like to read, and this looked like the perfect spot for you to curl up with a good book," Grandpa said. "We'll find room in here if you want, or we can move it to your room. You could even have it outside on the deck for a while."

"Grandpa wanted to get you a hammock for outside, but we agreed you'd get more use out of this one."

"And we have another surprise for you, too," Grandpa said. "Unless you already have something planned with your friend."

I noticed that Grandpa had said *friend*, as in singular. He knew I wasn't becoming the social butterfly Grandma expected. "No. But really, we don't have to do anything. It's not a big deal."

"You see, Norman? She doesn't want to go," Grandma said. "Why don't we just stay home and celebrate."

"No, no, no. You two need to get out of the house. I've been ready for this little trip for weeks now."

"Maybe just you and Cara should go. I'll stay home. I still need to make Cara's birthday cake."

Yum, Grandma was a great baker. Not that I didn't want her to join us, but I could already taste that cake.

"And it's chilly out today."

"That's what jackets are for."

I looked back and forth between Grandma and Grandpa. They were having a tug of war. Pull, pull. Grandpa won.

"You'll feel better once we get there, Margaret. And Cara, you're going to love this place."

I grabbed my fleece jacket from my room. I hadn't worn it since Ecuador. I pulled it on and slipped my hand into the pockets, rediscovering the smooth oval stone from that day on Mount Chimborazo. I pulled it out and traced the wavy coppery line running through it.

Mom and Dad always got me a birthday gift, carabiners or quickdraws, a new pair of jeans, a book, but Max had even less money than they did. He was the one who started my rock collection. I never knew when or where he found the rocks; he always waited until my birthday to give me one. Shiny quartz crystals, a geode, fossils. I had them all lined up on my bedroom windowsill at the cabin. The golden nugget of pyrite had been a special gift just for the competition in Ecuador. How could I have lost it?

After their Everest expedition, Max had strung Tibetan prayer flags from our cabin to his little VW bus parked in front. "Make some birthday wishes, Cara." I don't remember what I wished for. Everything was right in my world at the time. I just remember the brightly colored little cloth squares, flapping and floating in the wind.

I know what I'd wish for now.

Uncle Max handing me a dandelion stem, white fluff ready to blow. Skipping stones into the river. Opening his cupped hands to reveal a ladybug. *Make a wish, Cara.*

I squeezed the stone in my fist, dropped it back into my pocket, and joined Grandma and Grandpa. Once we got in the car, I realized it was the first time I'd ever gone anywhere in the car with Grandma. Usually, I sat in the front passenger seat next to Grandpa. Now that was Grandma's seat. She was unusually quiet, her eyes fixed straight ahead. From my spot in the back, I could see her left hand clutching the edge of her seat. I leaned forward and it looked like her right hand was gripping the other side of the seat. Like we were drag racing or something.

Grandpa weaved the car through gently rolling suburbs that melted into one another. Smaller cookie cutter homes gave way to larger houses with expansive lawns. These cities and subdivisions cracked me up, Forest Ridge, Bloomfield Hills, Farmington Hills. These people didn't know what hills were.

"Here we are," Grandpa called out as we pulled into a crowded parking lot.

A red barnlike building was set back off the road, and a line of people waited to get in the side door. A hand-painted sign above the door read Mason's Cider Mill, est. 1952. We walked across the lawn full of families at picnic tables and took a place in line. Even from outside, the smell was intoxicating.

Grandpa was as giddy as a little kid. "Fresh apple cider and cinnamon-sugar donuts. I can taste it already." He rubbed his hands together.

Grandma, on the other hand, looked like she was about to puke. Or pass out. Maybe both.

Grandpa put his arm around her shoulder. "Once you get some food in you, you'll feel better. Do you need to sit down? You could wait out here, save us a picnic table."

Grandma shook her head and clutched a fistful of Grandpa's shirt.

"Are you carsick?" I asked. Mom got carsick, too. Unless she was driving. She had to drive every time we were on mountain roads, which was practically every day since that's where we lived.

Grandma nodded, breathing in and out of her nose, lips clamped.

When it was our turn at the counter, Grandpa ordered a sack of donuts and a jug of cider. We grabbed plastic cups and napkins and took our goodies outside to nab a picnic table.

First Doritos, now cinnamon-sugar donuts. I really had been missing out. They were heavenly. Crispy on the outside, warm and melt-in-your mouth squishy on the inside. My fingers were coated in cinnamon-sugar grease, and I licked every last one.

Grandpa was licking his fingers, too. Grandma had taken one bite, then began swatting at the bees that buzzed around our table.

"You're just going to make them mad," Grandpa said, as a bee dived into Grandma's cup of apple cider.

"I swear, will you look at that! Damn bees," Grandma swatted some more. Guess she was feeling better. Car sickness replaced by her usual orneriness.

"Let's take a walk," Grandpa suggested. "Let the little buggers enjoy their cider."

We headed to the back of the lot where it was wooded. Behind the barn, a waterwheel churned. The sound of rushing water drowned out the noise from the picnic area.

"You can pick apples from the orchards at some cider mills, but not this one," Grandpa said. "Those are farther away, and the drive would have been hard on your grandma."

We followed the small river, a creek really, walking quietly. It was the most peaceful I had felt since leaving my home in California.

"Did you ever come here with my mom?"

"Every year," Grandpa answered.

I thought so. I fingered the stone in my pocket and glanced at Grandma, hoping the quiet and fresh air was doing her some good.

"These damn gnats," Grandma said, waving her hands in front of her face.

Too much to ask for.

We drove home in silence except for the powerful purr of the Mustang's engine. Grandma gripped the sides of her seat again; I was glad I hadn't inherited the family car sickness gene.

As he pulled into the driveway, Grandpa turned to look at me in the backseat and said, "How about you and I go for another spin. I need to fill her up with gas, but I knew Grandma wanted to get straight home."

Grandma sat in the front seat and waited for Grandpa to get out of the car and open her door. Then she waited for him to walk up to the front door of the house, unlock it, and hold it open for her.

They were so old-fashioned! I hopped into the front seat, and we roared away. Grandpa's driving was much zippier without Grandma in the car.

"Does Grandma freak like that every time you go out?"

"Well, I wouldn't say 'freak,' but she does get quite nervous. It depends on where we're going. Your grandma . . . It's hard to explain. She's having some difficulties. It's not just that she gets carsick. The doctors think she's having panic attacks, or that she has an anxiety disorder, maybe even agoraphobia. Often it starts with panic attacks, and then you become so anxious you're afraid to go anywhere, especially out in crowds, where you might feel trapped. When she has these anxiety attacks, she feels very frightened. At first, we were afraid she was having a heart attack."

Grandpa slowed for a red light and glanced at me. The Mustang's engine rumbled.

"She likes to stay home. It's not that she's antisocial or anything. You've seen how much she talks on the phone. She likes when her friends visit. She just feels safe at home."

I was quiet, processing his words. I didn't especially like crowds either. One of my favorite quotes was from the man who started the company Patagonia. He said something like, "I don't like people. I like trees." I thought it was my personality and the way I was raised. I never thought of it as a sickness.

"Did she get her heart checked?" I asked.

"Oh definitely. Her heart's ticking just fine. Mine too. Let's hope you inherited those genes from our side of the family and not your dad's."

The light turned green, the Mustang roared and shot forward, pressing me backward into the seat.

My other grandparents had both died of heart attacks. Dad's dad had his first one at forty, then the one that killed him when he was only forty-five. I overheard Mom talking to her friend Susan about it once. Susan was suggesting that my dad was such a risk-taker because he knew he might die young, like his dad, and he was determined to live as much as possible while he could. That was one of the arguments with Grandma that left Mom in tears years ago. Grandma had said, "Mark may have a death wish, but he doesn't need to drag you and Cara along for the ride."

Grandpa continued talking about Grandma's anxiety problems. "It didn't used to be that bad. She never liked driving on the highway, and she's vowed to never set foot on an airplane." He glanced at me. "We would have come to visit you more often if your grandma wasn't so afraid to fly."

Grandma and Grandpa always drove down to see us when we lived in Tennessee, even though it was a ten-hour drive. Even so, how did Grandma manage that long of a drive?

As if Grandpa read my mind, he said, "She never liked the drive down South, but she slept much of the way and it was worth it to her to see you and your mom." After a second he added, "And your dad.

"Then a couple years ago, she threw her back out. It was the beginning of winter and she slipped on an icy patch getting out of the car one day. I felt so bad that I didn't catch her in time. Bruised her tailbone good, but luckily she didn't break anything. Oh, she was miserable. And cooped up in the house for months. Afraid to go out even when her back was better, afraid to slip and fall again. Even when spring arrived, she was afraid to plant flowers. Afraid to bend over wrong and twist her back."

Grandpa pulled into the gas station and aligned the car with one of the pumps. He shut off the engine, but sat with his hands resting on the steering wheel.

"I think that was the real start of her illness, that little accident. And then when your parents and Mr. O'Connor . . ." He paused, then cleared his throat. "Well, she's just had a real hard time dealing with it." His voice grew thick. "Everyone deals with loss in their own way, I suppose."

Loss. That was what I had been feeling. Like a wildflower dug up out of the woods and transplanted into a pot. I hadn't really thought about my grandparents feeling sad about my parents and Uncle Max. I just thought Grandma was crabby and angry that I got dumped on her.

Fear. Grandma was afraid to go out. I was afraid, too. Afraid for Uncle Max and what he must have gone through high up on the mountain. Afraid for my parents, who were still out there, tackling more dangerous climbs. Afraid for myself, unsure of what to do next, how to get back to my home. Afraid to climb again, to touch the rocks and have all of these fears spring to life, the earth tilting again.

"Well now." Grandpa turned toward me. "It's time for part three of your birthday present."

"What do you mean?"

"You're sixteen. It's time you learned to drive."

I raised my eyebrows. "Now?"

"You missed the summer program, but I found a class that starts on Monday after school. No need to waste any time. Better to get some practice in before the winter weather hits."

He handed me a brochure about the driver's ed class. The company was called Road Rules.

"But I can give you your first lesson right now," he said. "How to pump gas."

I laughed. It was true. I had never pumped gas before.

Monday after school, Grandpa drove me to the driver's ed class. He said he'd be back in two hours to pick me up.

I expected to get in a dorky car with an instructor and practice driving around. But I was stuck in a classroom with a small group of students, all teenagers except for two older, grandma-looking women.

So much for my private lesson. I slumped in a seat at the back of the class and spotted him in a seat near the front—Basketball Guy, Triple T.

I leaned forward and craned my neck to see better. He was scrolling on his phone and hadn't noticed me. It was definitely him. I sat up straighter. My knee bobbed up and down. When the instructor came in, he asked us to introduce ourselves. The two older women were sisters. And then it was his turn.

"Hey, I'm Tom Torres." He half-turned around in his seat and spotted me. He raised his eyebrows, surprised, then flashed his lopsided grin.

I smiled back. Maybe this group lesson wouldn't be so bad after all. And finally, I knew his name! My knee bounced even faster.

19

The notes stopped coming for a couple weeks, but on the last Monday in October, a tightly folded square of notebook paper fell out of my locker again. I opened it, square after square after square.

One visit is all we get? Why? Why?

A guy's voice rang out in the hallway. "You think you're hot stuff, don't you? Big-time climber, California girl."

And another guy, "What, you think you're too good to talk to me?"

They were gone before I could even pick them out of the crowd.

Two days later. *Thou shalt not climb again?*

And on Friday. *I'll be your belayer.*

At lunch, Kaitlyn's french fries smelled much better than my bologna sandwich from Grandma. She pushed her tray toward me to share. I grinned and dunked a fry in ketchup.

"So, let's see them," Kaitlyn said.

I pulled the notes from my pocket and tossed them onto the table. Kaitlyn and I unfolded the squares.

Nick nibbled his nails; he probably thought we were going to accuse him again.

"There's only one thing to do," Kaitlyn said.

"What?"

"You're going to have to go back to the climbing gym."

I crossed my arms over my chest. "Not happening."

"Why?"

I met her gaze and shook my head but didn't answer. There was no answer. Half of me was itching to climb, but the other half wanted to run away.

Kaitlyn's eyebrows drew together in concern, and I could still feel her questioning eyes on my face even when I looked away. Even Nick was looking at me without his usual smirk, no dimples.

I didn't know how to explain. I just knew I wasn't going to climb. It didn't even make sense to me. That my fall in Ecuador was different from all my previous falls. That Uncle Max's soul had reached out and left an imprint on mine. That one person leaving this earth could change how I felt about everything. I was left with a knot in my chest that wouldn't be loosened anytime soon.

Kaitlyn invited me to spend the night at her house. I was in my room packing my duffel bag when I saw the ladybugs. I had seen a couple here and there inside the house, and I had scooped them up and set them free out the window. But now, there had to be at least half a dozen of them climbing up the windowpane. Trapped.

I raised the window and tried to shoo them out. "Go on, get out of here. You don't belong in here."

A few of them flew the wrong way, disappearing into my room. But most of them flew outside, happy to be free.

The doorbell rang. Kaitlyn hadn't been to my grandparents' house before. I shut the window, grabbed my bag, and dashed down the hall, almost colliding with Grandma.

"What's your hurry?" she said. "Kaitlyn's waiting for you."

Kaitlyn stood in the living room, studying Grandma's collection of angels inside the glass curio case. Grandma had a look on her face I couldn't quite read. I expected her to say something about her collectables, but she just stood there with a tight little smile on her face. Her eyes roved all over Kaitlyn, taking in her goth look.

Grandpa walked in from the garage where he'd been working on the Mustang.

"I thought I heard someone pull up," he said. "I'd shake your hand, but . . ." He displayed his greasy palms.

Kaitlyn laughed. "That's okay. It's nice to meet you."

"You are staying in tonight, right?" Grandma asked.

I nodded, and Kaitlyn answered for me. "Yep, we're just hanging out."

"And I've got Kaitlyn's phone number," Grandma said.

We inched toward the door, and they followed us outside.

"Look at that! A Woodie-Wagon!" Grandpa darted past us to check out Kaitlyn's beast of a car.

Kaitlyn laughed and followed him. He walked all around the car, examined the wood panels, and fired off questions. Kaitlyn explained about how her brother found the car and wanted it as a joke, but then it really grew on all of them, and her neighbor was a mechanic, so he helped them keep it running, blah, blah, blah. Grandpa hung on every word. Finally, he stopped asking questions and stepped aside so I could open the passenger door.

Grandma and Grandpa stood on the porch watching as Kaitlyn backed out of the driveway. Despite his greasy palms, Grandpa reached out and held Grandma's hand. They waved with their free hands, and I waved back. They acted like I was a little kid leaving for a week instead of just one night. How was I going to tell them that I needed to go back home to California?

I mumbled sorry to Kaitlyn for my Grandpa's questions and grumbled about my oddball grandma and all her clutter.

"Your grandpa's funny. That was nothing. I was trapped at a gas station for like an hour one time because everyone had to come over and look and tell their story.

"And I think it's sweet, all those angels. I only read the inscriptions on a few of them. There was one for a twenty-fifth wedding anniversary."

"I guess," I said, remembering the five baby angels that I'd always liked as a kid. It wasn't like Grandma had any other grandchildren. What were those babies supposed to be?

I still hadn't met Kaitlyn's parents. They were out again when we got back to her house.

"They're at some shindig for my dad's work, so they probably won't stagger in until two in the morning. They've become quite the socialites."

"What does your dad do?"

"He's in sales. He works for a company that designs parts for Ford."

"What does he sell?"

"Some switch that goes on an engine or something. He was promoted this year, and now he has to travel all the time, but he's usually home on the weekends."

Then she had that awkward look on her face again, like she wanted to ask me questions about my parents.

"You want to order pizza?" I said.

We were flipping through magazines in Kaitlyn's room when someone rapped on her window. She ignored it.

"Uh . . ." I looked at her.

She shook her head. "It's Nick."

"And why . . ."

"Is he not at the front door? Good question." She glanced at her phone. "And I told him to text first, not just show up."

More knocking on her window. Rap dap de do dap. Rap, rap.

Kaitlyn still didn't move. "My parents don't really like him, so he doesn't like to come to the front door. But if he had texted first, I would have told him they're not home." She texted as she talked.

The doorbell rang a minute later, and I followed Kaitlyn to the front door. She peered through the peephole, laughed, and flung open the door.

"Pizza!" she yelled.

"At your service," Nick bowed and held out a large box.

The delivery guy backed out of the driveway. "You owe me twenty bucks," Nick said to Kaitlyn.

She took the box. "Fat chance, it was only fifteen."

"Hello, tip?"

"You just bought yourself one very expensive slice. That's all you get." Kaitlyn opened the lid, and I got a whiff of steamy tomato yumminess.

Nick flopped on the couch. He was wearing shorts even though it couldn't be more than fifty degrees out. He propped his legs up on the coffee table, scratching at them. "Stupid mosquitoes. They were eating me alive out there. Shouldn't they be dead by now?"

"Serves you right, sneaking outside my bedroom window."

"So what do girls do when you sleep over? Sit around in your panties and have pillow fights?"

"You wish." Kaitlyn grabbed a slice of pizza, sat down at the other end of the couch, and nudged Nick with her bare feet. "Foot rub," she said.

I thought Nick would tell her fat chance, but he obliged. I couldn't help but notice that his legs were perfectly smooth, like he had shaved them. Kaitlyn saw my look and explained, "He's a swimmer. He actually thinks he'll swim faster if he shaves off his body hair. If he would shave his head, too, then I might get it, but no . . ."

"Hey, don't knock the locks, man." Nick dropped Kaitlyn's foot and ran his fingers through his hair.

"You haven't cut yourself shaving again have you, no trips to the emergency room?"

"Very funny," Nick said.

I gave them a quizzical look.

"He passes out at the sight of blood," Kaitlyn said.

"It's a physiological quirk, it happens to a lot of people," Nick said.

"Uh-huh. This is the guy who passed out in biology when the teacher pricked his finger. We were supposed to be studying our blood under the microscopes, and there's Nick, slumped on the floor."

"Come on, the guy practically shoved the needle straight through my finger."

Kaitlyn rolled her eyes. "So you'd think he'd know better, right? But no, he decides to do his own piercing. He never even got past his ear. He numbed it with ice and before the needle even touched his delicate earlobe, he was passed out cold."

Nick slumped back on the couch, closed his eyes, and groaned. "You're killing me."

"So I guess you don't have any tattoos, huh?" I asked.

Kaitlyn laughed. "Oh, wait till you hear that story—"

Nick popped up from the couch. "Okay, I'm outta here. I'd stick around for more fun and games, but I've got places to be."

He made a grab for the last slice of pizza, but Kaitlyn slapped his hand. "Don't you dare."

"All right already. Geez. You two are quite the welcoming crew."

"Who invited you?"

Nick thumped his chest with his fist and let out a huge burp.

"Sicko." Kaitlyn shoved him out the door.

"He totally likes you," I said after she shut the door,

"Come on. He's Nick."

"Yeah, and he's got it bad for you."

"No way. We're just friends. Sometimes I even wonder if he's gay."

"Really? Why?"

"Just look at him. I thought for sure he was going to pierce his right ear, but he started with the left."

"Does he wear eyeliner?"

"See! He does sometimes."

"But that doesn't mean he's gay."

"Well he's never had a girlfriend. He never even talks about liking any girls."

"Duh, because he has the hots for you. Don't you see how he looks at you?"

"Please." Kaitlyn held up her deformed hand. "No one wants a girlfriend with this."

Kaitlyn half-laughed, but our joking mood came to an abrupt halt. I fumbled with my words, wanting to say the right thing. "Kaitlyn, that doesn't matter."

"It's okay." She busied herself carrying our dirty dishes to the kitchen.

I followed, still struggling with what to say. *It's what's on the inside that counts*. People had probably been spewing phrases like that her whole life. But it was true.

She opened the refrigerator and took out a jug of milk. "You ever have hot chocolate with Baileys?"

"What's Baileys?"

She held up a squat black bottle. "You know, Irish cream. Alcohol. Liqueur. My parents put it in their coffee all the time. You'll love it."

"I don't know . . ."

I'd tried beer once during a camping trip and hated the bitter taste. I took a tentative sip of the mug Kaitlyn handed me.

"There's alcohol in here?"

She nodded. "Told you."

Before I knew it, I had gulped down two mugs of the spiked hot chocolate, and Kaitlyn poured us thirds. The lights clicked off, startling me, as we returned to the living room couches. I sloshed the drink onto my hand.

Kaitlyn laughed. "Midnight. They're on timers."

The streetlights lit the edges of the windows, and soft yellow light drifted in from the kitchen. She didn't switch the lamps back on, and I sunk into the comfy couch cushions, licking the sticky drink off my fingers.

"What one thing would you take with you if you were stranded on a deserted island?" she asked.

"I would have advance warning that I was going to be stranded?"

"Just answer the question, smarty-pants."

"Okay, so I could bring matches to light a fire and signal for help, or maybe I'd *want* to stay stranded there on a beautiful island, so then I'd probably take a book."

"Which one?"

"Hmm, could I take two?"

"Nope, just one."

"You're harsh." My trusty Thoreau or my new friend Agatha Christie? Thoreau's words would probably make sense again on a deserted island.

"Something by Thoreau. Probably *Walden*."

"Thoreau? Who reads Thoreau!"

" 'Not till we are lost, in other words, not till we have lost the world, do we begin to find ourselves, and realize where we are and the infinite extent of our relations.' "

Kaitlyn chucked a pillow at me. I dodged it, laughing.

"Next question—"

"Hey, you didn't answer the deserted island question," I said.

"Too tired." Kaitlyn yawned and curled deeper into the corner of the couch. "I'd take a blanket. Next question: What do you want to be when you grow up?"

Her yawn was contagious. My eyes watered, and I took another sip of my spiked hot chocolate. "I don't know, I just always assumed I'd be a climber."

"You can't just climb. I mean, you can be really great at it, but what else do you dream about? I want to be a CIA spy."

I giggled and choked on my drink, sputtering.

"No one would suspect me. I'd play up the whole poor-girl-with-a-deformed-hand thing." She waved her hand in the air. "You would not believe how many people think you're a simpleton because of this. As if my hand directly affects my brain."

"People are idiots."

"Come on, I know what kind of an imagination you have," Kaitlyn said. "I see you daydreaming all the time. Fess up. What do you want to be when you grow up?"

I smiled. "Okay, but promise you won't laugh."

"You just laughed at me!"

"Sorry. Okay, I kind of imagine myself as a female Indiana Jones–like person."

Kaitlyn tried to keep a straight face for about two seconds, then burst out laughing. "I would pay to see that movie!"

"Seriously. I probably wouldn't be an archaeologist, but maybe a botanist, because I like plants and trees and stuff. And I'm pretty adventurous; my climbing would come in handy. I could discover medicinal herbs in the rain forest and uncharted mountaintops. You know."

"You are too funny, Cara."

After draining my third mug, I could hardly keep my eyes open. Maybe that hadn't been such a good idea. Kaitlyn had said it was alcohol, even if it didn't taste like it. The beige carpeting swirled like a sandstorm as I shuffled back to her room.

I had brought only a long T-shirt to sleep in, and Kaitlyn's house was freezing. I was used to my grandparents' house, with the heat cranked up to a balmy eighty degrees.

"Sorry, my parents have the heat set to go down at midnight too. You want to borrow a sweatshirt?"

"Yeah," I said, rubbing my arms.

She tossed me a green Michigan State sweatshirt. "My brother, Josh, goes to State."

"What year is he?"

"He's a junior. Here he is." She showed me a picture on her phone of the two of them standing next to each other wearing matching sweatshirts like the one I had on now. Kaitlyn's hair was a deep, glossy red in the photo.

"I used to want to go to State, too, but not anymore."

"How come?"

"Long story." Kaitlyn shrugged. "U of M's a better school anyway. You have any brothers or sisters?"

"Nope, I'm the one and only. My parents didn't even want me; I was an accident. One kid was hard enough to fit into their plans."

"My parents are like that now. When Josh left for school, I think they were ready to be empty nesters. But I'm still here. They moved us into this smaller house, and I had to switch school districts. They didn't even think about what a big deal that was. Mostly they're too busy with their life to notice me." She sank down on her bed and closed her eyes. "Which is fine by me." She opened her eyes. "I don't think I can sleep up here. It feels like I'm on a Tilt-A-Whirl."

We spread blankets on the floor and turned out the light. Kaitlyn pulled the soft purple afghan off the bed and draped it over both of us.

"It's spinning down here too," I whispered.

"Yeah, but at least we can't fall off." She giggled.

"Do you miss your brother?"

"Yeah, kind of, I guess. I mean, I'm used to it now, he's been away almost three years. And he comes home a couple times a year, it's not like he's gone for good . . ."

She stopped talking for a second, then started again, stumbling over her words. "I didn't mean . . . I just meant that . . ."

I changed the subject. "How come you dyed your hair black?"

"Well, it's not like I turned goth overnight or anything. I just started wearing black clothes, it sort of fit my mood. It was hard starting over at a new school. I was the new girl freak with the weird hand, and then last year it got even worse."

"What happened?"

Kaitlyn went on talking about goths in a faraway voice. "I met Nick at work over the summer. We started hanging out, and I could totally relate to his friends." She half-laughed and her voice grew softer, sleepier. "I dyed my hair just for kicks, and then added the dark makeup."

"Did your parents freak?" I asked.

"They thought I was into drugs or something. Came right out and asked me. But I get good grades and stuff. I stay home most of the time. Nick and I go to concerts sometimes, down at the Majestic or the Shelter, but it's not like I'm a groupie following bands every weekend. My parents pretty much dropped it."

Kaitlyn yawned and rolled over, facing away from me. I thought she was going to sleep, but she continued.

"No one understands."

I could barely hear her voice.

"I know," I whispered.

Silence. Steady breathing. Kaitlyn was asleep. The lava lamp oozed and swam in the purple light.

No one understood. I knew my parents would be back; I just didn't know when, and I didn't like the not knowing. I didn't know what our life would look like when they got back. If we'd be moving again, if I'd be going to school somewhere else. What it would be like without Uncle Max, who had lived with us more often than not ever since I was a baby.

It was something that was hard to explain to others. Why he lived with us. I just accepted it; it was the way it had always been. It was like I had two dads.

Mom and Dad and Max had all worked at the same summer camp all those years ago. Mom had even dated Max before my dad. She said that relationships were complicated, and it was hard to be gay in our straight world. Confusing. It had taken Max years to accept that he was gay. I knew it was selfish, but I used to be kind of happy in a way when Max's relationships ended. I'd feel bad that he was sad, but it meant he'd spend more time with me again. I knew he'd be a great dad, but I didn't like to think about him getting married and adopting kids of his own. Now, I'd be his only daughter.

My mind spun with all the unknowns while the room tilted. I wanted to feel the weight of the smooth stone from Chimborazo in my hand, rub my fingers around the curves to calm my mind, but my body was too heavy to get up and find my jacket.

Kaitlyn whimpered and thrashed under the blanket. I peered into the purple murkiness of the room. A sob. I patted her shoulder and whispered, "It's okay. Shh, it's okay."

Kaitlyn sucked in another sob and curled up on her side, returning to quiet, rhythmic sleep. She hadn't answered my question about what had happened last year to make her already tough experience even worse. I pulled the soft afghan up around her shoulders and inched closer, snuggling in beside her. The room was no longer spinning. It was dark and still.

20

In the morning, I wondered if Kaitlyn remembered her middle-of-the night sobbing. She acted like nothing had happened. My eyes looked redder than hers. My head throbbed. Kaitlyn had scrubbed off her makeup, revealing strawberry-blond eyelashes and faint freckles sprinkled over her nose and cheeks. Her red hair just barely peeked out from her side part. I wondered how often she had to touch it up. She looked so fresh faced. She looked like a Katie, not a Kaitlyn. For the first time I had a hint of why she wore her dark layer of protection.

"Here," she said, handing me a big glass of water. "One of Josh's tricks. Alcohol dehydrates you."

"Thanks. Do you have any tea?" I asked.

"Like hot tea? Probably. Let's go look."

Despite their late night, Kaitlyn's parents were up and dressed in matching dark blue velour sweat suits. Neither had red hair, although her mother had so many freckles she looked tan, and she had the same strawberry-blond eyelashes as Kaitlyn. Her dad pulled two tennis rackets out of the coat closet; they even had matching bags.

"Sure you girls don't want to join us?" her father asked. "We could play doubles."

"Or we could have breakfast," offered her mother.

My stomach lurched at the thought of food; it was all I could do to sip my cup of tea. I sneaked a sideways look at Kaitlyn. She met my eyes and shook her head. "No thanks."

"Well, at least let me make you some breakfast here."

"It's okay, Mom, we're not hungry yet. We'll get something later."

The irritation in Kaitlyn's voice was clear.

"Well, if you're sure . . ." Her mother's voice trailed off.

I stood in the middle of their silence, dunking the tea bag in my mug. Kaitlyn wanted her parents to leave; my parents were gone, but I wanted them to come home.

As they gathered their things, Kaitlyn's mom said, "Say, Cara, do you have a dog?"

Totally random. I glanced at Kaitlyn again.

Kaitlyn exchanged a look with her dad and rolled her eyes.

"She's on a dog mission," Kaitlyn's dad explained.

"I still can't believe you're serious about this," Kaitlyn said. "I asked for a dog, *begged*, for like ten years, but no . . ."

"That's because you wanted a chocolate Lab." Kaitlyn's mom turned to me. "Can you imagine a chocolate Lab in this house?"

"I wanted to name it Cocoa," Kaitlyn said in a little girl voice.

I smiled, picturing the puppy named Cocoa. "I used to have a dog, Tahoe. She was a husky. But she died three years ago. She was really old, fourteen."

"Did you have her since you were a kid?" Kaitlyn asked.

"She was my dad's dog before I was even born."

"A husky, now that's a dog," Kaitlyn's dad said.

Kaitlyn's mom was shaking her head.

"Mom has something more like a Chihuahua in mind." Kaitlyn and her dad wrinkled their noses and frowned.

I agreed. Tahoe was no yippy lapdog.

Kaitlyn drove me home later in the morning. My next driver's ed class was at one o'clock.

"I don't think your mom's ready to be an empty nester if she wants a dog," I said.

"Tell me about Tahoe," Kaitlyn said. "I've wanted one forever."

"She was really sweet. My dad named her Tahoe because he always wanted to move out West. And she was great in the mountains. We had a little doggy backpack for her, and she carried her own water and stuff."

"Now that's cool."

"Yeah, but it was really sad when she got old. She limped and shuffled around, and had cataracts so bad, she could hardly see."

"Aw."

"One morning, she couldn't walk at all. My dad carried her to the car, and we drove out to one of our favorite spots, a rocky clearing with a view of the gorge. Tahoe stretched out on a ledge and closed her eyes."

"Oh my God, she died right there?"

"No. The rocks were warm from the sun, but a cool breeze drew up from the depths of the gorge. The wind ruffled her fur, and she looked so peaceful. We carried her back home, and she died in her sleep that night."

"Oh, I'm going to cry," Kaitlyn said. She waved her hand in front her face, her eyes tearing.

"Yeah, she was a good dog."

"That's the way I want to go," Kaitlyn said.

Tahoe's death was the way it should happen. She lived a full life, and we were there with her right up to the end. We buried her in the woods near our cabin, beside a giant fir tree, and marked the grave with a small cairn, carefully balancing the stones.

That pyramid-shaped cairn on Mount Chimborazo, stones piled as tall as me. Uncle's Max's life had been snatched away in a terrifying instant, without a funeral or a body to bury. Did my parents add a rock to the cairn at Chimborazo for him? The thought made me light-headed, and I closed my eyes.

I slipped my hand into my jacket pocket and rubbed the smooth little stone I had taken from near the cairn. At the time, it had felt like some kind of protection, a way to ensure that my parents and Uncle Max were still alive. Now, it felt like the only piece of them that I could hold on to.

The brakes on Kaitlyn's car groaned and screeched as she stopped in front of my grandparents' house.

"I know, Beast, it's so sweet and sad," Kaitlyn said, patting the steering wheel.

I opened my eyes and steadied myself as I scooted out of the car. My legs felt wobbly. If this is what a hangover felt like, I wanted none of it.

"Don't forget, climbing gym tomorrow," Kaitlyn said. "Miss Indiana She-Jones. There's gotta be a sound track. I'm going to look it up when I get to work!"

In the Road Rules driver's ed classroom, I sat in the seat behind Tom. He turned around, raised his eyebrows and smiled. I had a sudden impulse to reach out and touch the faint scar on his lip. I wanted to ask how he had gotten it, but I just smiled back, then moved my gaze to the instructor. Mr. Demetrios was huge, like a pro wrestler, with a booming voice.

"This is it, your first day to hit the road. Car number one: Nathan, Keith, and Elizabeth. Car number two: Cara, Trudy, and Tom."

My heartbeat quickened. I wasn't particularly nervous about driving, just driving with Tom in the same car. The two older women, Trudy and Elizabeth, exchanged rueful smiles; they'd been hoping to be together.

Tom must have noticed their look too. "I can switch to the other car if you want, so you two can be together."

My heart beat even faster. I wanted him to go, but I wanted him to stay too.

Elizabeth nodded and started to speak.

"Oh no, it's okay," Trudy interrupted her. "We better do what the teacher says."

She winked at me so fast I barely caught it. I flushed.

Tom looked at Elizabeth. "You sure?"

Elizabeth interpreted a knowing look from Trudy. "I'll be fine. You go ahead. Those other boys look like they need a mother in their car." She smiled and left to join her group.

I got Tom but also Mr. Demetrios—he sent his assistant off to the other car. I cringed. I could already imagine him yelling at me.

I was chosen to drive first, and Trudy and Tom sat in the back. Mr. Demetrios pointed out the mirror adjustments, turn signal, and how to switch gears. Thick black hair covered his forearms and hands, even his knuckles. A nervous giggle escaped from Trudy in the backseat. I forced myself not to turn around and peek at Tom.

"What are you waiting for, young lady?" Mr. Demetrios said, pointing straight ahead. "Drive."

I pulled out of the parking space, and switched the right blinker on, waiting for a car to pass. I turned onto the street and cruised down the right lane, keeping my speed steady at forty. *Oh yeah, I got this.*

The stoplight ahead turned from green to yellow. My foot hovered between the gas and the brake. Red! I slammed on the brakes.

Mr. Demetrios slapped his palm against the dashboard and barked, "Should have gone through it. Take the next left."

I waited in the left turn lane at the next light, green, but too many oncoming cars. Yellow, still more cars. Red.

"Go!"

I hit the gas and squealed around the corner, oncoming cars taking their left turns out of the corner of my eye.

I glanced in the rearview mirror and met Tom's gaze. His eyes were wide. Could this be any more embarrassing?

"Pull into this parking lot. Blinker on!"

I found a wide, open space and jerked to a stop.

"In the back," he said to me. "You," he pointed to Tom, "up front."

Tom puffed out his cheeks and released a loud breath as we switched places.

He kept glancing at me in the rearview mirror. His eyes crinkled into a smile, and sometimes he'd raise his eyebrows.

"Eyes on the road," Mr. Demetrios grunted.

But I kept my eyes on him, and soon his brow was furrowed, like he was intensely concentrating. And he drove really slowly. Cars zoomed around us at every intersection.

"Give it some gas, Granny."

What a jerk. I glared at the bald spot on the back of Mr. Demetrios's head and exchanged a look with Trudy. She bit her lip.

I tried to be ready to smile reassuringly in case Tom looked at me in the rearview mirror again, but his brow furrowed even deeper. When his turn was up, he slumped in the seat and let out another long breath.

Trudy moved to the driver's seat, and Tom slid into the back next to me.

"Whew." He spread his long legs out to the sides. His knee bumped mine, but neither of us moved.

I peeked sideways. The small scar on his lip almost disappeared when he smiled. I lowered the window halfway to let the breeze cool my burning skin.

"Windows up!" Mr. Demetrios barked.

I grimaced at Tom and we burst out laughing. Mr. Demetrios was going to yell at us again, but it didn't matter, there was no holding it in. We grinned at each other through the rest of the ride.

After the lesson, I walked with Tom to the front of the building where Grandpa would be picking me up.

"Hey, I brought you something." He dug in his pocket and pulled out a beaded bracelet. "This is what I was telling you about. From Brazil. The acai beads."

The beads were speckled shades of cream and brown with spidery lines. "Wow, it does look a lot like mine."

Tom slid the acai bracelet over my wrist. "Now you have two."

I encircled my hand around my wrist. "Oh no, I can't take it. I thought it was your mom's?"

"Don't worry, I asked her if it was okay. My dad gave it to her a long time ago, but they're divorced now."

"I'm sorry."

Tom shrugged and stuffed his fists into his pockets.

"How old were you when they divorced?"

"Ten. Fifth grade. It's okay. My dad has always traveled a ton for GM. It's really not that different now, even holidays aren't hard to share because my mom's Jewish and my dad's Catholic."

"Wow. So which are you?

"I don't know. They've kind of left it up to me. So, I'm a little bit of both, but not really either one. And I always have a mix of Yiddish and Spanish in my head."

He moved his hands like mouths talking to each other. "Meshugna," the right hand said to the left. "Loco," he said, twirling his finger beside his head.

I laughed. The shining sun turned his eyes to the color of honey. "So, Torres is—"

"Mexican, but my dad grew up here. Chicano."

I nodded and fiddled with the bracelets, the tagua beads rubbing against the acai beads. So similar, almost the same size and colors, with their own unique swirls. They looked like they were meant to go together.

"I get to see my dad this week. I have dinner with him every Wednesday if he's in town. It's our pupusa night."

"Pupusa?"

"You've never had pupusas?" He said it with a heavy Spanish accent.

I laughed again, shaking my head. "Is it like a taco?"

"Oh, you are missing out. Salvadoran. Delicioso." He rubbed his stomach. "I'll take you to the pupusaria sometime."

"Pupusaria?"

"Ooh, nice rolling r's. Tú hablas Español?"

"Un poco."

Tom paused at the bike rack and unlocked a mountain bike. "Bicicleta."

"Sí." I couldn't stop laughing. "I know that one."

"Hasta mañana," he said, wheeling his bike away.

"Hasta mañana." I held up my wrist with the bracelets. "Muchas gracias por el . . . beads, bracelet!"

"Pulsera de cuentas! De nada."

He threw his leg over his bike and pedaled off. I watched until he turned the corner, looking back at me with a wave.

"Pulsera de cuentas. Pupusaria," I repeated the words softly, rolling my r's, smiling to myself. "Pupusarrrria."

21

I was so distracted by Tom that I went along with Kaitlyn's plan to go to the climbing gym. When she picked me up, Nick was already in the car, but he moved to the backseat to let me sit up front. He was dressed in his usual getup, all black with a hemp-rope necklace. I couldn't tell if he was wearing eyeliner. Maybe his eyelashes were just super thick and dark. It looked like he had spent a lot of time making his hair look messed up. Kaitlyn was wearing a black T-shirt and leggings but no dark makeup. Her hair was pulled back into two low braids, revealing a few stray red strands at the nape.

"I'm just here for observation purposes. And moral support," Kaitlyn said, glancing at me out of the corner of her eye.

"Come on, you have to climb," Nick said.

"If I'm climbing, you're climbing," I said. Had I decided I was actually climbing? If I did, I was only planning on doing the bare minimum. I wasn't a circus performer. If anyone thought I was putting on a show, they were wrong.

"I'm afraid of heights," Kaitlyn said.

Nick rolled his eyes. "Please."

"What do you know?"

"You're a natural," Nick said. "You just don't know it yet. And if you weren't planning on climbing, how come you didn't put on your face?"

Kaitlyn looked at Nick in the rearview mirror and stuck out her tongue.

"I wasn't saying you looked bad or anything. You've got the whole pale glamour thing going on."

At Planet Granite, Kaitlyn gave Nick a shove and said, "Hope your eyeliner is waterproof."

"Maybe you should dye your hair blonde to match your real eyelashes," Nick said.

They continued their banter all the way inside, but I had stopped listening. A parade was marching in my chest heading down to the pit of my stomach. Get a grip, Cara! It wasn't like I was about to compete or anything. I didn't have to impress anyone. It was just climbing. Just like always. Nothing had changed.

But that wasn't true. Everything had changed.

Nick's brother was working behind the counter, wearing his usual smirk. "Hey bro," he said as Nick approached.

The smirk must be a family trait or something. But Nate, Nick's brother, didn't have Nick's dimples to soften the look. Even when he was being nice, he still looked like a jerk.

Nick had a pass and his own gear. Kaitlyn continued to say she wasn't actually climbing.

"Put on a harness and shoes to get a feel for it," I said. "Then I can teach you how to belay, but you don't have to actually climb if you don't want to."

She wore a size seven shoe, same as me. I should have thought to bring her my extra pair.

"These shoes are so gross," Kaitlyn said. "How can you guys stand wearing them without socks?"

Then again, maybe it was a good thing I hadn't offered my extra pair.

"It's different when it's your own sweat," Nick said. He stuck his nose in his shoe and inhaled.

Kaitlyn wrinkled her nose. "You. Are. Disgusting."

We headed into the climbing area. Instead of stressing me out like the time I came with Grandpa, the sweaty chalk smell felt like home. My body was truly itching to climb. I pulled my fingers backward to stretch my wrists.

"There's a new 5.10 route over there called Bliss," Nick said. "Stupid name, but it looks good. Might be kind of reachy for you two shorties though."

"You're one to talk," Kaitlyn said, popping up on her tiptoes to reach Nick's height. "We're not really here to climb, remember? We're on a mission. What do those numbers mean again anyway?"

"The higher the number, the harder the climb. 5.5s are for wusses, 5.13s are for climbing gods and goddesses like Cara," Nick said.

I rolled my eyes.

Nick smirked at me and continued. "The route is marked with colored tape at the bottom. You just follow the holds with that color tape all the way to the top. We might as well get a few good climbs in while we're here. If you can stop playing Sherlock for five minutes. I don't know what you think you're going to see anyway."

"We need to be on the lookout for anyone who looks suspicious, anyone who's really checking Cara out," Kaitlyn said.

"Yeah, good luck. You really don't have any idea who she is in the climbing world, do you?"

"Will you two stop talking about me," I said. "Let's just climb already."

"Oh my God, Cara." Kaitlyn squeezed my shoulder. "He's right. Look how many people are checking you out."

Nate had entered the climbing area. His head was tilted toward another guy, talking, but he was looking straight at me. Why didn't he just announce my presence with a megaphone? It's not like I was Hollywood famous. Just a good climber. At least I used to be.

"Let's jump on a wall, and I'll flail away and fall off," I said. "Then maybe people will get tired of watching me. See, I really suck. I bombed at the World Championships. I'm all washed up now."

Nick snorted.

Kaitlyn elbowed him. "Okay, where are you going to start? And don't you dare fall off, Cara. If the wimpy-ass note writer is here, he'll show his colors."

"Let's just rainbow this 5.8 to get warmed up," I said.

"Translation please," Kaitlyn said.

"Sorry. Instead of following one of the colored routes, just grab whatever color holds are within your reach. Rainbow it. It's easier that way. Then when we're warmed up, we can try an actual route."

"*You* and *Nick* can try an actual route."

"You want to belay Nick while he climbs this one?" I asked her.

"Whoa, hold up," Nick said. "She's going to learn to belay while I'm climbing? What if I fall?"

"You're not going to fall while rainbowing a 5.8, and besides, she'll catch you."

"I could die."

"That would be tragic," I said.

Kaitlyn crossed her arms. "I'm just watching, remember?"

I wasn't going to pressure her. I explained all the steps as Nick and I took turns climbing the easy route, but Kaitlyn was more focused on looking for suspicious characters.

"I want to keep my eye on that guy over there," Kaitlyn said. "Does he look familiar?"

The nice buzz-cut guy from my first visit was belaying a climber but looking in our direction. He smiled, then looked up to follow his partner.

"That's Blake," Nick said. "He works here, but he goes to Harrison High."

"Darn."

"Come on. Let's hit that 5.10," Nick said.

Nick climbed the route first while I belayed.

"You don't look very *blissful* to me," Kaitlyn called out as Nick grunted, slipped off a hold, and swung on the rope.

"Just wait until you get up here."

"I'll pass, thanks."

"Fuck this! Let me down," Nick called after he missed the same hold two more times.

"Stop trying to frog it," I said. "Try doing a drop-knee instead."

"What do you mean?" Kaitlyn asked. Finally, we were getting her a little interested.

"He's not making the best use of his body. Watch, he looks like a frog splaying his legs out like that. If he dropped one knee instead, then back stepped, he'd be able to twist and reach his arm up much higher."

Nick sailed off the wall again. "I've lost my juice. Let me down."

I lowered him to the ground where he knelt, catching his breath.

"There's no way that's a 5.10a. That crux move has got to make it a c, even a d. It might be a 5.11."

"Let me see," I said. I switched places with Nick, tying into the rope. "On belay?"

"Belay on."

"Climbing."

"Climb on."

I dipped my hands in chalk and started off in a left layback, reached up with my right hand, right foot up, left foot flagged. I twisted and pivoted up to the crux, dropped my right knee, reached far up with my right hand, and motored to the top.

"Take," I called down to Nick.

He lowered me down and said, "That was sickening."

"That was beautiful," Kaitlyn said. "How did you feel?"

"Blissful," I said with a mock sigh. "It might only be a 5.9."

"Fuck you," Nick said.

Kaitlyn swatted him.

"I had the advantage. Next time I'll go first so you can get the beta. You ready to try a route, Kaitlyn?"

"Nope." She scanned the room some more. "What about that guy?"

"Way to go," Nick said. "The only black kid here, and you think he looks guilty."

"I didn't mean it like that! God." She swatted him again. "He's been looking over here, okay?"

"Why does it have to be a guy? It could be a girl, you know," Nick said. "That's Jaquon Reed. Goes by Jake, and he's one of the best climbers here—that's probably why he's checking Cara out. But he's only in eighth grade."

"Eighth grade! He's so tall," Kaitlyn said.

"Let's check out the route he just finished," I said.

"There's no rope on it," Kaitlyn said.

"It's a lead climb, and it's a 5.12b." Nick shook his head. "There's no way."

Before I could talk myself out of it, I grabbed a rope that was coiled on the ground and tied a figure eight onto my harness. "You belaying?" I asked Nick.

"I'll be your belayer," a voice cracked behind me.

I turned around and looked up to Jake, the super-tall eighth grader. His tiny dreads were dusted with chalk. He wiped his hands on his T-shirt, leaving two chalky prints.

I glanced at Kaitlyn. Her eyes bulged.

"I put up this route myself," Jake said. "It's called Nemesis. See if I gave it the right rating."

Great, if Stretch here put up the route, it was probably pretty reachy. Outside on rock, I could find any kind of little nub to make the moves, but the choices here were limited on plastic. Indoor climbing was the only time my height could do me in. I scanned the route. It didn't look that bad. It wasn't like it was a tricky competition route. I didn't have anything to lose.

I climbed on and entered my zone. Calm breaths, feeling every movement, pull, push, reach, grasp, clip the bolts one by one. Slow and steady, inch by inch, like a spider spinning a web. I was almost at the top of the wall, about to go horizontal, upside down. My core muscles tightened. The next hold looked like a big old jug but it was out of my reach. Nothing for my next footstep. I took a deep breath, smeared my foot on the wall, and sprung up to the jug. Yes, bomber! Feet up like on monkey bars, wiggle across, upside down. Clip to the anchor.

"Take!"

Jake lowered me to the ground. "Way to on-site. You climb like a freakin' snail though. I don't know how you can go so slowly without burning yourself out."

"I don't win the speed contests."

"Where'd you pull that dyno move out of? I didn't think you were one for dynamos."

"You didn't give me much choice."

"5.12b?"

"Close, but I'd say 5.11 b/c. It's pretty juggy. A couple of them are major bombers. Maybe swap one for a sloper or get some more tiny pinch grips up there."

"Yeah, maybe." Jake peered up at the route.

"Your turn, Nick," Kaitlyn said.

"It's top-roped for you, unless you'd rather lead it," I said.

"Screw this. I'm going bouldering."

Kaitlyn and I looked at each other and shrugged.

"Thanks, Jake," I said, as we left to follow Nick.

"Later," he said, without looking back.

We left him standing at the base of the climb, arms crossed, studying the route. Nemesis.

22

On the ride home, Kaitlyn said, "Don't even tell me that wasn't suspicious. That Jake kid sounded just like that one letter." She imitated Jake, but with a deep, sinister voice: "I'll be your belayer."

"Dude! He doesn't go to our school." Nick stuck his head in between the front seats. "Change the station, will ya." He reached for the radio.

Kaitlyn elbowed him. "Get out of here." The car swerved. "I'm trying to drive."

I rubbed my left wrist. It throbbed a little, I should have taped it. I felt like the old days, chalk under my nails, toes happy to be released from the cramped climbing shoes. My mind free of clutter. For the first time in two months. Climbing does that to you—frees you up.

"Don't worry, Cara, we'll get to the bottom of this," Kaitlyn said as she pulled up in front of Nick's house.

Nick lived in a mansion. "Care to join me for tea at the castle," he said in his fake English accent.

"Can't. Sorry," Kaitlyn said. "Tonight is pretend-we're-a real-family-that-eats-dinner-together night."

"Oh well. It appears that I shall dine alone again. Adieu, ladies." He bowed as he got out of the car. Then he skipped up the walkway.

"I told you. He's so gay," Kaitlyn said as she zoomed around the long, circular driveway.

"He's something, I don't know what." I counted five garage doors. "What's up with that house?"

"I know, it's monstrous. I told you, his parents are loaded. Nick's dad is some hotshot lawyer and a big time Republican. He's made a couple bids for state representative, but so far no go. He does his best to keep Nick and Nate undercover, but somehow they always end up in some photo, totally punk and goth, messing up their dad's family values image."

I smiled, picturing the campaign poster, and wondered what Nick's mom was like.

"Nick hates that his family is rich. His thinks they're a perfect example of our wasteful society, destroying the planet. His mom shops all the time, it's like her job. But Nick buys half of his clothes at the Salvation Army and wears Nate's hand-me-downs. He's really serious about it."

"So why does Nick have a job? He doesn't need the money."

"He doesn't want to have anything to do with his dad's money. Nick thinks his dad is hypocrite supreme. Besides, he's really into music, like me, so it's fun working at the music store."

"You think music stores will even exist in a couple years?"

"That's why I took the job! Someday I'll be able to tell my kids I worked in one of the very last music stores."

"And they'll say, 'What's a music store?'"

"Exactly!"

The car brakes groaned and squeaked as Kaitlyn slowed for a red light.

Kaitlyn rubbed and patted the steering wheel. "Hang in there, Beast, you know I love you."

We reached my grandparents' house, and I stopped on the porch in front of the ceramic goose. She was dressed like a witch. Doll-size black dress, pointy hat. She even had a pint-size broom. Grandma! She was something too.

In the living room, I curled up into my papasan chair and opened my latest Agatha Christie to where I had folded the page.

Oldies music drifted out of the kitchen along with the clink of dishes. Was Grandma humming?

The muscles in my forearms trembled the slightest bit, exhausted from climbing, as I held the book open. I wished Tahoe could be curled up beside me, her body warm against my legs, her head resting in my lap. She never liked when I climbed. She would bark as soon as I tied into the rope. When my feet left the ground, she would jump up and rest her paws on the rock below me, barking again. She never did this to my parents, only me, from the time I was a little girl. Like she thought it was her job to protect me. She paced and circled the ground beneath me, and didn't rest until I was safely back on the ground.

Nick had asked if Kaitlyn and I would go to the climbing gym with him again. Kaitlyn and I had looked at each other, eyebrows raised, and then we'd shrugged and said, "Sure."

Was it that simple? Just say yes, and figure it out as you go. That had been my dad's answer every time a climbing route had scared me, every time I hesitated and wanted to turn away, climb a different route, a safe one that I knew I could do.

If I kept climbing at the gym, could I get Kaitlyn to actually try it? Friday night, she'd said she'd gone through a rough time the year before. Like what? She had transformed her entire appearance to black; all the brightly colored clothes shoved to the back of her closet, her pretty red hair hidden under dark dye. She had gone from Katie to Kaitlyn. What had happened to her?

I longed for that warm, safe feeling that Tahoe had brought me. The need washed over me with a shudder. I really, really wanted a hug from my mom.

I almost called my parents right then. But as soon as the need washed over me, the anger surged as well. They were the ones who had left me. They should be calling me. And always the worry, nibbling away at my anger, what if they got hurt, or worse? What would I do when all my anger had been eaten away, and I was only left with worry? My stomach ached at the thought.

23

My underwear was shrinking. For that matter, so were all of my clothes. My jeans were tighter around my butt, my shirts tighter around my chest. Maybe it was the way Grandma did laundry. My clothes were definitely getting washed more often these days. Not that I would wear the same pair of underwear two days in a row—okay, maybe if I was camping. But my jeans and sweaters could usually make it through a few days. Not in this house. Grandma went into my room while I was at school and gathered whatever clothes she could find that weren't safely tucked in a drawer. She grabbed the jeans I had tossed over the stool or a shirt that was left hanging from the closet doorknob. When I got home, they were folded, smelling flower fresh, and stacked on top of my dresser. Didn't she have anything better to do?

Who was I kidding? My clothes weren't shrinking, I was gaining weight. I had no idea how much I weighed. It wasn't something I ever worried about. No more organic whole wheat macaroni and cheese with hidden chunks of cauliflower like I'd had at home. Grandma cooked the real deal. And after growing up on natural peanut butter and nine-grain bread, I had been scarfing down Jif and Wonder any chance I could get. With hardly any exercise for the past couple of months, it was no wonder my butt was busting out of my underwear. But now, even my bra was getting tight. Before, most people wouldn't even notice if I went braless. Maybe I was going through some late stage of puberty. That would just figure. Not only had everything else changed completely in my life, now I didn't even recognize my own body. Couldn't just one thing stay the same?

Kaitlyn's car was in the shop getting new brakes, so Nick was forced to drive her to school for the day. He tried convincing Kaitlyn to ride her bike, but no go. We met in the student parking lot after our last class, and I stared at Nick's sleek, black car. I wasn't a car person, but even I had to admire this machine.

"Wow, what is it?" I asked.

"Mazz-err-atti," Kaitlyn stretched out the name.

We climbed in the car, and I sang softly. "Nick's Maserati goes 185. His dad busted him, and now he don't drive."

Nick whipped around and grinned.

"Way to go, classic-rock sister!" Nick raised his hand for a high five. "California Cara grooving on Joe Walsh."

"Who?" Kaitlyn was looking at us like we had lost our minds.

"For shame, do you not work in a music store?" Nick said.

Kaitlyn stuck her tongue out at him.

"My parents listened to him," I said. *And Uncle Max.*

"Actually, I only know it from my older brother," Nick said. "In honor of Cara, it's classic rock hour." He punched the button for 94.7 on the radio.

Eddie Van Halen's electric guitar ripped through the car. Kaitlyn covered her ears and groaned, and Nick peeled out of the parking lot, tires squealing.

At the climbing gym, Blake greeted us from behind the counter. No sign of Nate, and my shoulders relaxed an inch. We stopped in the locker rooms to change out of our school clothes. Kaitlyn pulled her hair into a ponytail and scrubbed her face clean. Rather than ghostly white, her cheeks were rubbed to a rosy, fresh-faced glow. Katie was back.

"You gonna climb with us today?"

"Probably not."

I smiled. She was moving in the right direction; I didn't need to push her.

We found Nick working a route in the bouldering cave, and I automatically got into position to spot him as he attempted to maneuver an overhang. He fell, and I half-caught him with my hands on his back.

He jerked around. "Shit, where'd you come from?"

"Your nightmares," I said with an evil grin, my hands curved into claws.

Nick cracked up and mock shuddered.

Kaitlyn watched while I bouldered to warm up. She ran both of her hands over the various holds, but didn't attempt to climb on.

"I'll spot you," I offered.

She shook her head but continued to gaze at the holds, following them up and down and side to side with her eyes.

Nick had disappeared, and we found him at the base of Nemesis. It was still labeled a 5.12b. No sign of Jake today either.

"Doesn't look like he changed much," I said, scanning the route.

"Give it a go," Nick said.

It was easy to say yes to this one. I'd already done it once, easily. I grabbed a lead rope, tied in, and hopped on the wall. I swiveled all the way up to the crux, lunged for the big bomber hold, grabbed it, and slipped right off.

"Falling!" I yelled, but Nick wasn't expecting it. He dropped me a few feet before locking off the rope. I swooped and swung sideways, tipped upside down, and got tangled in the rope.

"Sorry!" Nick called up.

"Let me down."

"Don't you want to get back on?"

"Let me down!"

He lowered me to the ground. "How come you didn't just stay up there and work on it?"

I didn't answer him. My heart was spastic. Kaitlyn was wide-eyed.

"I'm okay," I told her. I studied the route. "Jake changed out that hold. Serves me right, I told him to do it. It looks just like the bomber jug, but there's nothing behind it to hold on to. It faked me out."

Kaitlyn still looked spooked.

I turned to Nick. "I'm going again. Ready?"

"Climb on."

I climbed the route again, fell off again. And again.

"Too bad Jake's not here to see this," Nick said.

I stood at the base of the climb, fuming. Nick wasn't even trying to hide his amusement. I had attracted a small crowd. Including Nate.

"How's it going?" He smirked.

"How's it *not* going?" Nick smirked back at him, dimples flashing. I glared at both of them.

"Your turn," I told Nick and started to untie from the rope.

"No way. This is your Nemesis."

Kaitlyn didn't look spooked anymore. She looked . . . intrigued. She gave me a nod and a smirk of her own. It said, "Do this."

I blew out a big breath, shook out my hands, and retied my rope. "One more time."

"Belay on," Nick sang.

"Climbing."

"Climb on."

I studied the crux move again and jumped on the wall with an energy I had never had before. I was one of the calm climbers. Light on my feet, slow and steady. But now I felt power and strength, fueled by anger. It had been simmering inside me for months and now it was flowing and oozing like lava boiling up to my shoulders, down my forearms, into my fingers. I was on fire. Grab. That. Hold.

Aaaarrrrgh! A deep grunt erupted from my chest, I lunged and palmed the hold with an iron left grip, hooked my right toes, and swung my right arm up to the next hold. Bomber! I motored through the rest, clipped the last bolt, yelled, "Take," and the rage settled back down to a low simmer in my stomach.

"Way to go! High five!" Kaitlyn and Nick said as soon as my feet touched ground. Then they laughed and slapped each other's hands.

"5.12b?" Nick asked.

"Oh yeah."

Grandpa was sitting in his usual chair when I got home. He lowered the newspaper. "Your mom called while you were gone."

I sighed. "Great timing. What did she say?"

"Not too much, we got cut off again. They climbed a mountain in Patagonia. I meant to look up the name afterwards and find it on the map, but now I've forgotten it. She said to tell you how much they miss you."

I scoffed. "Did she say when they're coming home?"

Grandpa shook his head. "Nope, that's when we got cut off."

"Convenient." I jumped up and hung from the doorframe.

"Monkey. Don't let your Grandma see you."

I hopped down and shook out my wrists. My fingertips stung and my forearms burned from all my attempts on Nemesis.

"That Kaitlyn looked different today," Grandpa said. "No raccoon eyes or black lips."

"Yeah. She took off her goth face to climb. Didn't want to sweat and smear it all over."

"How does she do climbing with her hand?"

"You know about her hand? She usually keeps it hidden in her long sleeves."

"I noticed it that first day when she picked you up. I was about to shake her hand, but all at the same time I realized my hands were greasy from working on the car and that her hand was misshapen."

"She's pretty sensitive about it."

"My father lost some fingertips in his woodshop. I'm sure it was hard at the time, but I never saw it slow him down."

"Kaitlyn's like that too. She does all kinds of stuff with that hand. She hasn't actually tried climbing yet; she just watches. But I think she's getting closer."

He nodded. "You said 'goth?' As in gothic? Hmm. She wants to be left alone, but also to be seen, to be noticed."

"Huh?"

"Oh, every generation has a version. When your mom was that age it was the punk rockers. She even went through a punk stage herself."

"*My* mom?"

Grandpa chuckled. "She came home from a friend's house once with chunks of hair streaked bright pink. Oh, she gave your grandma fits. Still does," he said and went back to his newspaper.

24

The week before Halloween, Grandpa bought tons of candy and hid it so we wouldn't be tempted to eat it before trick-or-treating started. I looked all over the house but never did find it. Grandpa wouldn't reveal the hiding spot, but did say that he moved the candy several times. I noticed that some of the bags were open when they finally came out of hiding. He's a sneaky one, that Grandpa. Grandma was her usual cranky self.

She walked into the living room just as I jumped up to hang from the doorframe.

"Cara, get down! How many times do I have to tell you?"

I hopped down and cracked my knuckles.

Grandma winced. "We're shutting off the porch light at eight o'clock. I'm only giving out candy to the little ones. Those big kids are nothing but trouble coming round here in the middle of the night. Norman, you bought too much candy again."

Nick was going to a college party with his brother, but Kaitlyn said she wasn't into dressing up. (I could see why, she did it everyday.) We decided to hang out at Kaitlyn's house and pass out candy. Her parents had their own party to attend.

"My mom went as Cat Woman in this slinky-dinky outfit. She kept twirling her tail and meowing and rubbing up against my dad who was dressed as a flasher. Trench coat with shorts on underneath, I hope to God. They're so disgusting."

It was a perfect sweater-weather night. Cool and clear. The moon shone through the skeleton tree branches, porch lights lit up the street.

We passed out miniature chocolates to miniature princesses, ghosts, and a string of cartoon characters. Later in the evening, Nick stopped by on his way to the party.

I wouldn't have recognized him if he had just walked by. He was dressed all preppy with a pink oxford over a pastel-yellow polo shirt with the collar flipped up, and a sweater tied around his shoulders. Tan chinos with shiny penny loafers. The only clues to his previous identity were his purple black hair and the ever-present hemp necklace.

"What do you think of me now?" he said, turning around to model his outfit.

We cracked up. "What did you do, raid your dad's closet?" Kaitlyn said.

"Yes! I did. Just call me Chip the Third. Where's my tennis racket?"

Too funny. He continued, "Come with me. I've got extra clothes, you can go as Buffy and Muffy. No wait, you guys should just switch clothes. Cara's already got the prep thing going on."

"Hey," I protested.

"She's not a prep," Kaitlyn said. "She's got more of an REI thing happening. Or Moosejaw."

"True," Nick said. "She could be one of their cover models."

"What's Moosejaw?"

"A local shop," Kaitlyn explained. "They always have funny ads with hot, *au naturel* adventure girls."

"Oh please." I rolled my eyes. I could see Becky on a magazine cover. I was just one of the guys.

"You're no stranger to photo shoots," Nick said. "You're in the climbing magazines."

"I was climbing, not posing."

"Whatever. Are you two having another sleep-over? Another pillow fight in your-"

"Give it a rest," Kaitlyn said and whizzed a miniature Hershey's at his chest. "What do guys do when you sleep over? Sit around in your boxers having burping contests?"

"You ever see someone light a fart on fire?" Nick said.

"You. Are. Disgusting. Go away!" We pelted him with more candy bars, and he jogged away, laughing.

We retreated to the house with a handful of candy each, leaving the rest in the bowl on the porch for the late crowd.

"You sure you don't want to go to the party?" I asked.

"Not me. You?"

"No. I don't really get into stuff like that."

"Me neither. Not anymore anyway. I used to go with Josh sometimes, but…"

"What?"

"Nothing." She shook her head. "You're the sophisticated world traveler. You've probably been to some awesome parties."

Ha! Maybe I had experienced different things than Kaitlyn and Nick and others who never really left their hometown. But sophisticated?

"I've been all over with my parents, but we usually camped. We weren't high-styling luxury travelers. I've learned a lot about other cultures though."

"Like what?"

"Like, there are German words that we don't have at all. A single word that captures an entire idea. Like, waldeinsamkeit."

"Bless you," Kaitlyn said.

I laughed. "It means forest solitude. Thoreau used hundreds of words to describe that, and the Germans just sum it up in one perfect word. And did you know that in Chinese there is no such word as 'coincidence.'"

"Really?"

"Yeah. So think about the meaning of that. That nothing ever happens just by chance. There's a reason or some sort of force or energy behind it."

"God?"

"Maybe. God, spirits, angels, nature, fate. The Chinese call it yuan. Destiny. But I guess it depends on what you believe."

"I don't know what I believe," Kaitlyn said. "But it's interesting. Like with us. The way we met. It seemed like a random event, just a *coincidence* that you sat at our lunch table and we started talking. But maybe there was more to it. We were meant to be friends. Something drew us to each other."

"Exactly," I said.

"Do-do-Do-do." Kaitlyn wiggled her fingers. "Spooky."

25

Kaitlyn gave me a ride to my next Road Rules class, and I couldn't help thinking about yuan, destiny. How maybe it wasn't just a coincidence that I ran smack into Tom my first day in the cafeteria and then he turned up in my driver's ed class. As Kaitlyn pulled up in front of the building, Tom rode up on his *bicicleta*. He hopped off, locked his bike around a lamppost, and loped through the doors without noticing us.

Kaitlyn swatted me with the back of her hand. "That was Tom Torres!"

"Yeah. He's in my class."

"Get out! He's such a cutie."

"Yeah. Too bad he's gay," I said.

"What?"

"Ha-ha. Gotcha."

"Oh funny, ha-ha. But you know, he's never had a girlfriend."

"I was kidding! Don't even go there."

"He's one of the cutest guys at school. Such a baby face. Most of the jocks are getting it on with some chickadee, but not Tom. He flirts and everyone loves him, but he never asks anyone out."

"Maybe he's waiting until he gets his license."

"I never thought about that. I wonder why he didn't take driver's ed earlier. What do the Chinese call it again?"

"Yuan."

"Go *yuan* with Tom." She shoved my shoulder.

I laughed and scooted out of the car.

"Keep your eyes on the road!" Kaitlyn called out.

This time, my group was assigned to the assistant teacher. We gave Elizabeth a "sorry for you" frown as she followed Mr. Demetrios. Tom and I walked to the other car.

"How was the pupusaria?"

"Ooh, listen to your *rrrrr*'s. Bien, bien." He grinned and nodded at me. "Delicioso, as usual. I totally stuffed my face."

The assistant teacher wore jeans tucked into cowboy boots that clomped, clomped on the asphalt. He told us to call him Billy, and he asked me to drive first.

I glanced at Tom in the rearview mirror, and he gave me a thumbs-up. I was so distracted I shifted the car into reverse instead of drive and lurched backward.

"Whoa, whoa, easy does it," Billy said. "Slow down and focus on what you're doing." He said it in a nice, encouraging way. He didn't yell like Mr. Demetrios.

I forced myself to ignore Tom.

"We're going on the freeway now. Take a right."

I headed down the entrance ramp to the freeway, slowing down as cars whizzed by in the next lane.

"No, no, speed it up. You want to go as fast as the other cars. Put on your left turn signal. There you go, a little faster. You're going to merge in a second."

Merge! There were too many cars. They were all in the way. Where was I supposed to go?

"Don't slow down, keep up your speed. The other cars will let you in. You can do it," Billy said, continuing in his calm, soothing voice.

And just like that, I was over in the other lane. It worked! Cars were passing me in the left lane. I pressed down on the gas pedal again.

"Woo-hoo! Way to go!" Tom and Trudy yelled from the backseat.

"Pick up your speed just a bit, keep up with the rest of the traffic. You're doing great."

I was afraid to take my eyes off the road for even a second, but I grinned the whole time.

Parallel parking was our final task to accomplish. We practiced in a parking lot with bright orange cones. Billy let us listen to the radio, and Jason Derulo came on. Tom gyrated in his seat, spun the wheel, and sang, "Wiggle, wiggle, wiggle," before Billy changed the station. Trudy's jaw had dropped at the lyrics, Tom ran over two cones, and we all ended up in hysterics.

We staggered out of our car, still laughing, and caught up with Trudy's sister, Elizabeth.

"Donald Demetrios is despicable," she said with a scowl. "You three were having too much fun out there."

"How come you two are just learning to drive now?" Tom asked the sisters.

"Oh, we just never got around to it," Elizabeth said. "We're old-fashioned ladies."

"And we had old-fashioned husbands," Trudy added. "But now it's just us, and we've got places to go!"

"You go girls!" Tom gave them a double high five.

Trudy and Elizabeth giggled again as they slapped his hands.

When they left, I walked with Tom over to his bike.

"I can give you a ride home if you're game," Tom said and patted the handlebars.

I would have hopped on in a second if Grandpa weren't already on his way.

"My grandpa's picking me up."

"Yeah, that's probably a better idea. But I'll offer it to you again when I get my license."

I felt like jumping into the air and doing a backflip, but I just grinned, holding his gaze for a second. I spun the beaded bracelets around my wrist. "How come you didn't take driver's ed over the summer?" I asked. "I think Kaitlyn took it last summer."

Tom shoved his hands in his pockets. "It's kind of embarrassing," he said, hunching his shoulders up around his ears. "I was in an accident a few years ago. After that, I was afraid to ride in a car. It got better, but it still makes me nervous to be the driver."

He bent over, pretending to walk with a cane, and said in a shaky voice, "I drive like a little old lady."

I laughed.

"I was busy teaching at a basketball camp in the summer, so it was easy to put off."

I was about to ask him about the car accident, but Grandpa pulled up in the rumbling Mustang.

"Chido." Tom let out a soft whistle and walked over to check out the car.

I settled in the front seat, and Tom leaned in the window. I introduced him to Grandpa.

"Wow, this is an incredible ride," Tom said. "It's totally mint."

"Yep, I've tried to take good care of her."

"You gonna let Cara drive it when she gets her license?"

"Sure, before I put it up for the winter. I'm guessing she's going to want her own car down the road though."

"You are so lucky," Tom said to me. "My parents both drive Cadillacs. GM has tried to make it sleek looking, but it's still a boring middle-aged boat of a car."

Grandpa chuckled. "My winter car is a Taurus. Now that's a boring boat of a car, but it drives a lot better in the snow than this machine." He revved the engine. "Cadillacs are good, safe cars, too. You can pick Cara up anytime if you're driving a Cadillac."

Grandpa winked at me. I stared at him, eyes wide. Grandpa!

"It's a deal," Tom said.

I sneaked a peak at Tom, then eyed Grandpa again, warning him not to say anything else.

Tom waved good-bye as Grandpa pulled away from the curb, and I waved back. I watched him in the side mirror. He was still standing there, admiring the Mustang as we roared away.

26

The next day at school, Tom jogged up behind me and Kaitlyn and draped an arm around each of us. He flashed a grin, said, "Morning ladies," and then he was gone, motoring down the hall. Two girls brushed past us. One of them bumped into Kaitlyn, threw a nasty glance her way and said, "Excuuuse meee," then giggled with her friend. They hurried ahead, catching up to Tom, and flanked him on either side.

"What was that all about?" I asked.

"Ann-Marie Fidesco. Wannabe cheerleader. Birdbrain, skank. That's about all you need to know."

"She has a problem with you?"

"She has a problem with everyone outside of her elite group of phonies. She went to my old middle school for a year before she moved to this school district. Swimming was part of our gym class, so we had to change and shower before we got into the pool. She went around and told all the guys that I was a true redhead. You know, meaning that I had red hair *everywhere*. She was responsible for my nickname that year. You don't even want to know what it was."

"What?"

"Not telling."

"Come on."

"Fire bush."

My eyes popped wide, and my lips twitched into a grin.

"Yeah, funny now, not then."

"It's not funny, I'm sorry. Is that why you started dying your hair black?"

"God no. That was ages ago, in seventh grade. Ann-Marie moved the next year. Unfortunately, I had to follow her to this high school, but the nickname did not come with me. I don't know if she even remembers me."

We saw Nick at his locker and stopped to say hi. He was wearing a studded dog collar around his neck.

"What's this?" Kaitlyn asked, reaching out to touch the black, studded band.

Nick stepped back out of her reach. "What's it look like?" he snapped.

"Bite my head off already. What happened to your hemp rope? You never take it off."

Nick glanced at me then back at Kaitlyn. "My brother came back."

"When?"

"Last night. He just got out of jail."

"Wow."

"This morning he was gone. So was the cash from all of our wallets and my dad's credit card."

"Oh, Nick." Kaitlyn stepped closer and touched his shoulder.

Nick slammed his locker shut, shook his head, and stalked off.

Kaitlyn looked like she was trying to decide if she should go after him. "Did you follow that?"

"Not really. He has another brother?"

"Yeah, Mike. He's a few years older than Nate. Nick's the baby. And he's always worshiped Mike. But Mike started getting into drugs and trouble a few years ago. He wasn't crazy bad or anything, he just had a hippie-Grateful-Dead-free-love kind of attitude. His dad bailed him out a couple of times, trying to keep everything quiet, then he turned into a total control freak. Mike had these amazing long dreads, and his dad made him cut them all off. After that, Mike took off with some girl and no one knew where they were for a while. Then they found out he was in jail down in Florida. And his dad wouldn't even help him. He's a lawyer! His dad said it wasn't his job to be Mike's lawyer, it was his job to practice 'tough love.'"

"What about their mom?" I asked.

Kaitlyn shrugged. "She doesn't like things to be messy."

"That's crazy. I don't get it."

"Me neither. That hemp rope that Nick always wears, it's Mike's. I've never seen him without it."

Nick's parents had abandoned his brother when he needed help. It shouldn't have surprised me after these past few months without my parents. But still, it's just not what parents are supposed to do. I was in the way, and they pushed me aside. Mom was devoted to Dad, Dad was devoted to Uncle Max, but where did that leave me? Dumped at my grandparents', that's where.

I went home for lunch that afternoon for the first time in a month. I thought I'd let Nick have a chance to talk to Kaitlyn in private. And I needed to think. My thoughts were clumped in my head like strings of cold spaghetti, and I needed to pull them apart. Where was Miss Marple when you needed her?

Kaitlyn used to have red hair, she wore bright-colored clothes. She said she went through a rough time last year and wrapped herself up in darkness. She covered herself in black, painted her room midnight. Agatha Christie would call it *The Mysterious Case of the Transforming Girl*.

And Nick. Always goofing around, hamming it up, dressed as darkly dramatic as Kaitlyn. Wearing a necklace to hold on to the memory of his brother.

And me. What about me? Hanging out with my new friends, going to school as if everything was normal. Dreaming about me and Tom and destiny. I'd stopped responding to texts from Coach Mel as if that part of my life had never existed. As if the questions about my parents and Uncle Max weren't screaming inside my chest, trying to pound their way out past my rib cage. Nothing was as it seemed.

27

I hopped on my mom's old bike and sped down the street. The wind whipped my hair back off my face, cold air rushing into my ears. Kaitlyn had missed two days of school. I had tried texting and calling her, but she wasn't responding. Nick said he tried calling her too, but she hadn't called him back either.

I had found the bike in the garage, an old ten-speed with two flat tires. Grandpa pumped up the tires and gave them a kick. "Good as new," he said.

A car drove by, and the sound of Fleetwood Mac drifted out of the open window. The beat settled in my chest. I remembered the time I came home to find Dad blaring the stereo, singing along with Stevie Nicks. "Come dance with me," he had yelled over the music. And we had danced, swaying and twirling around the living room.

My mother's hands had gripped these same handlebars. The warm sensation traveled right up my arms to my neck, my skin tingling at the base of my skull. Like I was about to experience another earth-tilting moment, like the day I fell off the competition wall, the day Uncle Max was swept in an avalanche. Where were my parents now?

Or maybe the sensation had to do with Kaitlyn. Something was wrong with Kaitlyn. I gripped the handlebars tighter, my hands stiff from the cold.

I leaned the bike against Kaitlyn's garage and rang the doorbell. No answer. I knocked on the door. No answer. I pounded on the door. No answer. I peeked in the kitchen window; the house looked deserted.

I walked around the back to Kaitlyn's bedroom window. The shade was drawn. I rapped on the window. Nothing.

What was going on? A bubble of panic was spreading through my lungs. Kaitlyn wouldn't have gone anywhere without telling me or Nick. She would have called us back unless something was really wrong with her.

Then I heard it as much as felt it; a faint thumping, rumbling behind Kaitlyn's window. The rhythmic beat of music. I rapped on the glass again and shouted her name. Kaitlyn's pale face peeked around a corner of the window shade. I jumped back as if she were a ghost.

She opened the window and squinted in the afternoon sunshine.

And I don't want the world to see me,

'cause I don't think that they'd understand.

The music pulsed around her like an aura.

"Are you okay?" I asked.

She just looked at me.

When everything's made to be broken,

I just want you to know who I am.

"I was worried about you."

Her eyes filled with tears.

"Kaitlyn, what's wrong? Go open the front door, okay?"

She nodded and disappeared from the window.

The door was open when I got back to the front of the house, and I followed Kaitlyn to her room. She wore baggy gray sweatpants and her hair was fuzzed up and tangled. She climbed into bed and pulled the purple afghan up to her chin.

The music had stopped, but a Goo Goo Dolls CD had been tossed on the carpet. I sat down on the floor next to her bed and looked up at her. "Are you sick?"

"Kind of."

"Did you go to the doctor?"

"No."

"What did your parents say?"

"They don't care."

"I tried to call you. Nick too."

"I broke my phone."

I saw her phone then, on the floor by the bookcase. The screen was cracked, nearly shattered. I sat with her in silence for a couple of minutes, unsure what to say. Then Kaitlyn said, "How do you do it?"

"Do what?"

"You had to move all of the sudden. Your parents sent you away. Does it make you feel like they don't care about you? You don't even talk about it. How do you do it?"

It was like she had plucked the thoughts right out of my head. How did she know? I picked up her busted phone and fingered the cracked screen.

"I don't know," I said. "I don't even know what I'm doing half the time. You should see my grades. It's like I'm just starting to feel again. I miss them. But I'm mad too. I'm mad at them for going off and leaving me, and . . . and for not staying home where we would all be safe together, especially after losing Uncle Max. He lived with us for almost my whole life. It was like I had two dads."

"I'm sorry," Kaitlyn whispered. Her eyes were wet again.

I looked away as tears sprung to my eyes too. Kaitlyn sat up and wiped her eyes with her fingers. A faint smudge of black shadow encircled her eyes as if she had been rubbing them with her fists. She reached for a box of tissues on the nightstand, pulled out two and handed one to me.

I dabbed my eyes and tried to laugh. "If you had a dog, she'd be licking our tears right now."

Kaitlyn gave me a sad smile, then took a deep breath and let it out slowly.

"Something happened last year. Around this time, after Halloween." She took another slow breath. "I thought I was dealing with it. I keep trying to let it go, to put it behind me, but . . ."

She pressed her hands against her stomach.

"My first couple of years in elementary school, my teachers would talk to the class about my hand. They let me show the kids how I could still use it, and this other boy would show everyone his glasses and how things looked different through them. It was the same kids for years and years, and they just accepted me. It was like, 'Yeah Katie has a funny hand, so what, who cares?'

"Freshman year was so awful, switching school districts. We had this seminar where the teacher had the awesome idea to teach us all how to properly shake hands to prepare for job interviews and stuff. No limp, dead fish handshakes to turn people off. She actually wanted us to walk around the room shaking hands with everyone."

Oh no. My eyes fell to Kaitlyn's deformed right hand, the smooth pink skin where fingers should be.

"All these kids are coming up to me, holding out their hand to shake, and so I do it too, thinking maybe . . . maybe—" Her voice wavered. "They couldn't get away from me fast enough."

"For weeks afterwards, this stupid group of guys . . . they'd come up to me in the halls and hold out their hands to shake, pretending to introduce themselves."

My face flushed with heat. "Assholes."

Kaitlyn nodded and pressed a tissue against her wet eyes. She released a big huffing breath. "Everyone always says high school is better than middle school, that everyone is maturing and more accepting. Right—not if you're the new girl with a freak hand.

"But then sophomore year, I met a guy, and I thought he really liked me. I thought we had something special."

I breathed a little easier. Kaitlyn wasn't sick. She wasn't dying. This was about more than her hand; she had a broken heart. I was used to hearing broken heart stories from climbers like Becky.

Kaitlyn continued. "Eric. He was in my brother's fraternity at State. It just started so randomly. I had called to talk to Josh, but Eric grabbed Josh's phone, goofing around. And we just started talking. He was so funny. We texted and followed each other. He looked so incredibly hot in the pictures. Not like the guys at school. A *college* guy. He was really interested in me, what I had to say. He called me Kaitlyn, not Katie. He made me feel so grown-up."

Kaitlyn looked up at the ceiling and sighed. "A few weeks later, it was Siblings Weekend at State."

I adjusted my position on the floor to get more comfortable, settling in for Kaitlyn's story. It was going to be okay. Broken hearts can be made whole again.

"I didn't even care about seeing my brother, I was so excited to see Eric in person. I never told him about my hand. I just thought that Josh had probably told him, you know? I wanted to believe that he could look past it. That he knew the real me."

She looked down at the tissue crumpled in her fist. "As soon as I saw him, he ran over and gave me a huge hug. It felt so good to be in his arms. But then we pulled apart, and he grabbed my hands, and . . . and . . ." Kaitlyn's voice broke.

Oh no. I inched closer to her and touched the purple afghan, poking my fingers through the loops of soft yarn.

"The look on his face . . . I'll never forget it. It makes me feel sick . . . my stomach . . ." She sucked in a sob.

"Oh, Kaitlyn," I said.

She sniffed and started tearing the tissue into shreds.

"He couldn't even look at me after that. He just ignored me and made an excuse to leave. I was supposed to be up there the whole weekend, but Josh drove me home that night.

"I actually thought I was in love. Just from talking to him for a few weeks—I can't believe I was so dumb."

"You weren't dumb," I said. "He was a jerk."

Kaitlyn was quiet a minute, looking down at the pile of shredded tissues.

"He texted me the other day, out of the blue. To say sorry for how he acted. My brother probably put him up to it."

"Maybe it's been eating him up," I said. "He felt guilty. As he should."

"Well he wasn't calling to try to start something again. Nothing has changed. And he has a girlfriend."

"He told you that?"

She shook her head. "I had blocked him before, but like an idiot I looked him up again. I should have known better."

"That's how you broke your phone?"

"Against the wall."

I followed her gaze to the wall where the midnight paint had been chipped, revealing a streak of lavender beneath.

Her voice turned hard. "It's always going to be like that. The revulsion and pity in people's eyes. God, it has to be my right hand, the one that everyone automatically tries to shake. You have no idea what's it like to see them recoil in disgust."

She thrust her hand in front of my face and I jumped. Smooth skin wrapped over the stubs of her missing fingers. I grabbed the hand with both of mine and squeezed. "No, Kaitlyn. It's not always going to be that way."

My voice was thick and quivery. Tears dripped to my lips. Tears for Kaitlyn. Tears that I'd kept tucked away for all these months. I released her hand to swipe the wetness from my cheeks and moved to the bed next to her.

We hugged each other and cried.

28

I pumped the pedals on the bike as fast as I could, wind stinging my face. To have to dread something as simple as a handshake. She fell hard for a guy who turned out to be a total creep. I had crushes on guys, other climbers, and now Tom, but nothing like what Kaitlyn had experienced. I didn't even talk to Tom outside of school and driver's ed. Kaitlyn thought she was in love. She trusted Eric, and he broke her heart. It was so unfair.

What a different person she must have been before then. Katie with red hair and a sprinkle of freckles, happy and in love. Anger squeezed out all of my other feelings, and I pumped the pedals even faster, gasping for breath.

Back home, I stowed the bike in the garage. I wasn't ready to face my grandparents. My eyes were probably red from crying, and tears threatened to spill again, remembering the pain in Kaitlyn's voice. I tried to push away the panic that was creeping around my throat. Was this how Grandma's anxiety attacks started? I swallowed a rush of saliva, feeling like I could puke.

I sat down next to the goose on the front porch, focused on my breath, and waited for my heart to stop hammering.

I knew how Kaitlyn felt to some degree. Both of our lives had changed course in the past year; we couldn't go back to the way things were. Kaitlyn had confided in me, trusted me to share those painful feelings with her. I still hadn't told her much about my parents and Uncle Max. Why was I having so much trouble opening up to her?

I looked at the goose, and she looked back with her knowing glass eyes.

Because, if I talked about it, it would make it real. And I didn't want it to be real. I didn't want to open up to anyone. I didn't want to feel settled here. I wanted to go home. And some part of me truly expected my parents to show up tomorrow, the next day, two weeks from now. And we'd all go home together.

I thought about the woods surrounding our cabin and the walks I used to take with Dad. When I was little, we'd walk hand in hand. I'd feel the pressure of his fingers squeezing mine and knew that meant to pause.

One time, he whispered, "Shh. Can you hear it? The trees. They're talking."

I stood perfectly still, head tilted, listening. Then I said, "I can hear them breathing!"

And my dad laughed and laughed. It became our private joke. "Wait, I hear someone *breathing* out here," Dad would say in a scary voice. "Oh, silly me, it's just the trees."

Since they were homeschooling me, Mom and Dad would often recite poetry when we were hiking and climbing. One of my dad's favorite lines was, "Give me my scallop shell of quiet."

"That's our cabin, Cara, and these woods. Our own scallop shell of quiet."

That was what I needed right now, and I wasn't going to find it inside my grandparents' house.

I was careful not to meet Grandpa's eyes when I finally went inside. Somehow he always seemed to read my mind. He was watching the news on TV from his usual spot. Grandma's phone voice drifted out of the kitchen. Then she came into the living room, phone to her ear with one hand, smooshing ladybugs with a tissue in her other hand.

"Damn things all over the house," she muttered. "They're not ladybugs. They're Japanese beetles. They bite."

I curled up in my papasan chair and watched the news with Grandpa. A West Coast correspondent came on the air with an update about the wildfires raging in Southern California. As they had feared, the Santa Ana winds had fueled the fires. Thousands of acres were burning out of control, and neighborhoods were threatened near the Angeles Forest. Evacuations were underway.

I could feel Grandpa glancing at me. I was already feeling overwhelmed by Kaitlyn's story, her pain poured on top of my own. I was like a cup filled to the brim, and now the liquid was foaming and spilling over the edge.

The fire had to be near the cabin. My skin crawled with the heat. Heat from the flames, heat from the parching, gusting Santa Ana winds. The urge to run away flared inside me like a struck match. Run away from all the bad news, run away from the panic clutching my throat, run away to the shelter of the mountains, hide from the crackling winds, hide in my scallop shell of quiet. I didn't know where my new life in Michigan was leading me. I only knew I wanted to turn around and run through the flames.

29

Kaitlyn was at school the next day, wearing her goth face, looking the same as always except for a slight redness in her eyes. It was the end of the trimester and grades were posted.

Kaitlyn and Nick received their usual good grades, mostly As, a couple B+s.

"You saved my butt in physics, thank you very much." Kaitlyn high-fived me.

Physics was easy to understand in the climbing world. You could see the theories in motion; weight, gravitational pull, velocity. You name it, it's there. The other subjects were a different story.

"How'd you do?" Kaitlyn asked.

"No comment."

"Come on, it can't be that bad," Nick said.

"Oh yes it can."

And it was. One B, two Cs, and three Ds. I shouldn't have been surprised. It wasn't like I had been doing my homework. I would have aced an exam about Agatha Christie. My teachers were probably feeling sorry for me, otherwise I would have gotten Fs instead of Ds.

Grandma and Grandpa didn't say anything when I got home from school. I guessed they were waiting for me to tell them. Grandpa finally brought it up at dinner.

"We got a call from your school counselor today about your grades, and we saw them on the computer. Not like it used to be in my day when you brought home a piece of paper."

His voice was light, but Grandma was tight-lipped. My jaw tensed.

"Well, I guess we should have been asking you about your homework every week," Grandpa said.

Grandma's lips pinched even tighter.

I stabbed my fork into the rubbery chicken on my plate. "I'm not used to school like this."

"No, I guess you're not," Grandpa said. "This has been new for you. You've been through a lot. I can see how it would be difficult to concentrate on your schoolwork."

Blood pounded against my skull. *That's right, Grandpa. This is all new to me. Uncle Max disappearing off the face of the earth. Being dragged clear across the country. My parents traipsing around the Southern Hemisphere with barely a thought about me. And you expect me to even care about idiotic schoolwork?*

Grandpa continued. "But now it's time to buckle down. You'll have to put your mystery novels away for a while and limit your time at the climbing gym. I want to see you doing your homework every night. And I'll look it over. I know they do things differently nowadays, but I should be able to help you with some of it. Or we'll find a tutor for you if necessary."

My hands trembled. It was an effort to keep my voice steady. "Homeschooling works better for me. I can't concentrate at school."

Grandma slapped her palm on the table. "You can't drop out of school to climb!"

I flinched.

"Margaret," Grandpa said.

I shoved my chair back from the table. "Who cares! Who cares about stupid school anyway! It doesn't matter. Nothing matters anymore!"

Grandma stared at the light fixture hanging over the table; one of the four bulbs was burned out. She wasn't even looking at me. I had become my mother. I glared with all the fury raging inside me, then stood and stomped to my room. I slammed the door.

I pulled the cardboard box out of the closet and pushed my hair out of my face. It had grown longer than I'd ever had it. I couldn't stand the thought of cutting it. I couldn't lose anything else. My life was out of my control. At least I had control over my hair.

I twisted it on top of my head into a messy bun and sat cross-legged, looking at my old climbing magazines. I had to get back home. I had to find a way to get back to the cabin. It was all that was left of Uncle Max. Maybe that's what it would take to bring Mom and Dad home. If I ran away, back to the cabin, back to the mountains.

The phone rang, and a minute later there was a knock at my door. I shoved the box back into the closet.

Grandma opened the door and held out the phone. "It's your dad."

I didn't move from my spot on the floor. Grandma held out the phone, her other hand on her hip, chin jutting out in irritation. I grabbed the phone and shut the door back in her face.

Dad's deep-throated voice calmed the storm inside me. "Cara, I'm glad I caught you. I wanted to tell you not to worry. The cabin's still there. They were able to keep the wildfire back and the winds have shifted. It should be safe now."

"Dad—"

"We've heard there's some smoke damage. Quite a bit actually. But it's still standing."

My dad knew. He'd been gone for months with barely a word, but he knew that I still needed the cabin. He understood that it was still my home.

"I want to go home." My voice broke over the words. My face crumpled and a sob escaped into the phone.

"It's okay Cara, shh. It's okay. Shh, it's okay."

I sniffled and swiped my fingers beneath my eyes. "I can't stay here."

"The cabin will be there waiting for us, when the time is right."

"I want to go now!"

"Going back isn't going to change anything. You need to be in school now."

"It's not fair! You can't just send me away, throw my life away."

The words were out of my mouth before I realized how they might sound. Dad was quiet. I didn't mean to bring up Uncle Max, to suggest that Dad had thrown his life away too. Or did I?

"I can go to school back at home," I said, my voice quieter.

Dad's voice was even and soft. "Cara, we're trying to give you a life, to give you a home. Because I just can't do that right now."

The finality of his words settled inside me, smothering my anger.

"Cara?"

"*Dad.*"

"I want you to think about something." Other voices spoke in the background, shuffling, like people coming and going. I concentrated on Dad's voice. "We want you to join us down here for Christmas, back in Ecuador. I think it will help you understand."

"Why can't we just go home for Christmas?"

"I don't know where my home is right now, where it should be. I can't go back to California yet."

"What happened to your 'scallop shell of quiet?' That's what we need now."

Dad was silent for a minute, and the voices behind him grew louder. Spanish. *Hasta luego.* A door slammed. I gripped the phone tighter to my ear, afraid to lose him.

"Right now, I need vast space, like a fire that needs to rage and burn. The cabin can't contain what's going on inside me now."

The phone connection crackled in my ear, as if it was responding to my dad's words. I waited for it to clear.

"But you have all the woods around the cabin to roam in. Remember, you used to talk about the difference between raging rivers and calm mountains?"

"You mean when I stopped kayaking?"

"Yeah, you said the white water stirred you up until your blood was frothing, but in the mountains you felt calm, they shared their peace with you."

"You don't forget anything, do you?" he said.

"Not the important stuff."

"I don't know how else to explain it to you, Carabou. This is new territory for me. I just need to go into the gaps. You know, deep into the mountains to suck out its marrow."

"And then you'll find some peace, enough to bring it back home with you?"

"You'll understand better when you come here. I need you to have faith in me. Okay?"

"I don't know what I have faith in anymore."

The line crackled again. "Let's just get you down here with us for Christmas. I need to talk to your grandparents about it."

"Okay," I said, even though it wasn't.

I opened my door and found Grandma hovering. I brushed past her, handed the phone to Grandpa, and returned to my room without a word.

Going into the gaps. I had read those words before. Wild words about wilderness. I dug past the magazines in the box to my books underneath. Annie Dillard's *Pilgrim at Tinker Creek.* I flipped through the pages with folded corners and found the phrase, the passage underlined.

The gaps are the spirit's one home, the altitudes and latitudes so dazzlingly spare and clean that the spirit can discover itself for the first time like a once-blind man unbound. The gaps are the clefts in the rock where you cower to see the back parts of God; they are the fissures between mountains and cells the wind lances through, the icy narrowing fiords splitting the cliffs of mystery. Go up into the gaps. . . . Squeak into a gap in the soil, turn, and unlock—more than a maple—a universe.

Dad was clutching and grasping, searching for meaning in the only way he knew how. The books in my box, that's what they were about too. Annie Dillard, John Muir, Thoreau, and me too—we needed wild places, wilderness.

Annie Dillard wandered and observed the wilderness and its creatures. I had read some of her work before, part of my homeschooling with Mom and Dad. Her words were entrancing, honest, yet often puzzling to me. There was an essay about an animal, what was it? Something in water, a beaver? He had surprised her one day, his fierce face; they locked eyes. She was in his brain for that moment, and he was simply living. Living in necessity, while we live in choice.

I dug through my box again, trying to find those words. I found the essay tucked in a notebook. A weasel, that was the animal she'd stared down. Now I remembered. She wrote about how the weasel bites its prey out of instinct and doesn't let go. And we could live that way too, if we wanted. *I could very calmly go wild. . . . We can live any way we want. . . . The thing is to stalk your calling in a certain skilled and supple way, to locate the most tender and live spot and plug into that pulse.*

In California these words had puzzled me, but I was beginning to understand.

I think it would be well, and proper, and obedient, and pure, to grasp your one necessity and not let it go, to dangle from it limp wherever it takes you. Then even death, where you're going no matter how you live, cannot you part.

I read the last paragraph three times, thinking of Mom and Dad and Uncle Max. Grasping their one necessity. It nearly took my breath away. It didn't matter if I didn't completely understand the words, I *felt* their meaning. My body reacted with goose bumps. Okay, Dad.

I closed the notebook and stood at the window. A few clumps of brown, droopy leaves clung to their branches, but the trees were mostly bare now, exposed to the chill that saturated the air. Heavy clouds had veiled the sun all day and made the night even darker. I couldn't see a single star in the sky. The moon was nothing more than a fuzzy halo, a promise in the distance.

And what was up with these ladybugs? Japanese beetles, according to Grandma. They looked like ladybugs to me. I counted four. Two on the windowsill, another on the glass, and another climbing up the curtains. I scooped the ladybugs into my palm and raised the window. Their tiny legs tentatively tapped my skin, but they didn't attempt to explore.

"What's the matter with you?" I asked. "You don't belong in here." I held my hand out the window. "Now go, before Grandma finds you.

"Go on," I said, but still they remained on my palm.

"This is not your home. Go." I blew them off into the darkness and they flew away.

If only I could do the same.

30

There's a concept in sports training called maximizing your weakness. The gist of it is that you focus on your weakest areas in order to improve your overall performance. My weakness was dynamic power moves, requiring a burst of speed and strength. Now I had an emotional power ball inside me that surged and exploded while I climbed. I attempted moves I never would have tried before. I'd leap right off the wall, suspended in the air. The old Cara would have slowly maneuvered around, finding rinky-dink tiny holds to delicately grasp and balance on. Now I looked for the straightest line and lunged and leaped.

Sometimes Nick and Kaitlyn would come to the gym with me, but they had their jobs to keep them busy. Jake became my main climbing partner. Nick was having fun teasing me about Jake. His favorite line was, "Jake's on the make." Jake's googly eyes were a little annoying, but he was really the only climber near my level at the gym. The only one as obsessed as I was.

On school days, I couldn't climb until I had finished my homework; my grandparents' rules were in effect, but I spent the Friday after Thanksgiving break at the gym. Jake belayed me on a 5.12 route he had put up a few days before. I let out a huge grunt as I lunged for a hold shaped like a unicorn's horn.

"You're climbing like a freaking nutjob!" Jake called out. "You were supposed to do a locking twist up to that tiny crimper, then grab the horn with your other hand."

"What are you? My personal route setter?"

"Yes!"

I finished the route, and he lowered me to the ground.

"That was awesome," he said. "You gotta start competing again. Your style has totally changed. You're gonna blow everyone away."

Maybe, but my old life of traveling with my parents and competing seemed so far away. And without the cabin to ground me, it was difficult to even think about real climbing outside on the rocks.

Coach Mel had left me a message about an exhibition event in Tennessee. If only it was in California.

I untied my figure-eight knot and gazed around the gym at the colored holds, the funky shapes, neon tape marking the routes. Buzz-cut Blake was watching me with a group of little kids sitting at his feet.

I had talked to him about getting a job here, thinking that I could earn money to buy a plane ticket back to California. But they only needed an occasional hour or two for little kids' birthday parties. They didn't need more help until their summer camp. I couldn't wait that long. My best chance was to talk Mom and Dad into coming home when I met them in Ecuador for Christmas.

Jake unclipped the rope from his belay device and shook out his wrists.

"You can't let that Becky girl dominate the scene."

"Becky?" I scoffed. "How do you even know about Becky? She doesn't have what it takes to dominate."

"Oh yeah, then how come she's burning up routes all over the country?"

"What are you talking about?"

"Hello? She's everywhere."

The last climbing magazine I had read was the one sitting in my closet, left over from August. I hadn't done more than glance at the covers at the gym. I hadn't even bothered to text anyone to keep in touch.

"I'm tellin' you, she's trying to take your place," Jake said.

Hearing about Becky stirred up something in me, a competitive edge maybe, but I didn't know what to say or quite how to feel. Competition climbing was behind me, at least for now.

"How come you've never competed?" I asked Jake. "You're way good enough."

He shrugged.

"Seriously, you should try it."

He looped the rope through his harness and tied a figure eight. "I don't got the money to travel to comps. Besides, my family and everyone I hang with thinks it's a stupid sport. Not even a real sport, you know, like basketball. I'm so tall that everybody thinks I should play basketball and get a college scholarship. Climbing's fun, but it don't get you nowhere."

Jake lived in Pontiac. You can tell the difference as soon as you cross over the city limits from Bloomfield. What I had seen didn't look like the slums or anything, although people said parts of it were really rough, like a smaller version of Detroit.

"Which do you like better, climbing or basketball?" I asked.

"Both. But if I play basketball in high school next year, I won't have as much time to climb. You know Tom Torres?"

I pinched my finger in the carabiner on my harness. "Ow!"

"You okay?"

"I'm fine," I said, sucking on my finger. "How do you know Tom?"

"He's my big brother. I mean not for real, just at the Y. We shoot hoops all the time. He was my coach at basketball camp last summer."

I tried my best to sound casual. "Yeah, I hear he's really good."

"He's the best," Jake said as he climbed on the wall, his long arms reaching a foot higher than my longest twisting stretch. He was made to climb.

I dug my feet into the rubber chips and braced myself as Jake launched over an overhang. A flash of silver as he clicked the carabiner into the bolt. He was wrong about climbing not getting you anywhere. It can take you places most people only dream about. It can take you all around the world. It can take you up so high, you get a completely new view of the world around you. It can take you to places deep inside your own mind that you never knew existed. It can take you places where maybe you shouldn't go.

31

In Spanish class, I opened my notebook and found a new note, but it was folded like a paper airplane. This time, the handwriting was completely different than the others.

THE 7PM SHOW

Small, neat printing, all in capitals, written in black pen. The person with the messy scrawl could not possibly be capable of this level of penmanship. I didn't think *I* was capable of this writing, so perfect were these letters. At lunch I flattened the note on the cafeteria table for Kaitlyn and Nick.

"What the hell?" Kaitlyn said. "That's all it says?"

"That's it."

"Is someone asking you out, like to a movie?" Kaitlyn said. "What show? Where?"

"Maybe they're not talking about a movie. *The 7pm Show* is the name of a climbing route. Rifle, Colorado. My first 5.14a."

Nick whistled. His brother Mike's hemp necklace hung around his neck again, replacing the dog collar he had been wearing.

"I am so confused," Kaitlyn said. "What's it supposed to mean?"

"And how did it get in my notebook?"

"Creepy, creepy," Kaitlyn said.

Nick recreased the paper airplane lines, propped it into shape, and sent it soaring across the row of tables. It plummeted to the ground a couple feet before Tom's table, but no one paid any attention. A girl almost always squeezed in next to Tom, and today it was Ann-Marie

Fidesco, Kaitlyn's middle school nemesis. I fiddled with my beaded bracelets and gazed at Tom's back.

I'd finished driver's ed and was happy to have my learner's permit but bummed that I wouldn't get to see Tom anymore. I wondered how he was doing with his practice driving. The car accident he mentioned must have been pretty bad if it had made him so afraid. Maybe that was how he got that scar on his lip.

"Check this out," Nick said and tilted his phone toward me and Kaitlyn. A snowcapped peak filled the screen. "Mike's in Colorado."

His brother who had taken off with his family's cash had sent them all a text, saying thanks for giving him a fresh start, and he would repay them as soon as he earned enough money. Apparently, Mike had bought a snowboard from a local ski shop with his dad's stolen credit card. But that was all, no other charges showed up.

"Colorado, huh?" Kaitlyn said.

"They just legalized pot."

"Right."

Nick shrugged. "Maybe he's teaching snowboarding. He was really good."

"Do you think your dad will try to track him down?"

"I don't think so. He didn't report his credit card as stolen, or even cancel it. My mom convinced him to wait and see what happened. Dad said he'd give Mike until the end of ski season to pay him back, then he's cutting him off."

Kaitlyn was going skiing in Colorado with her parents for most of the school break. She'd tried convincing her parents to let me and Nick tag along, but no go. It was a family trip. And that was final. Nick especially wanted to go, hoping to find his brother.

"There are probably a hundred ski resorts in Colorado," Kaitlyn told him. "What are the chances he's at the exact same one as my family?"

"Just keep your eyes out for him, will ya?"

Nick clicked his phone off and looked at me. "We gonna climb every day over break?"

"Well—"

"What? I'm not good enough for you?"

"I'm visiting my parents in Ecuador."

"That's great!" Kaitlyn clutched my hands. "Why didn't you tell me?"

I shrugged. "I don't know. I just have a bad feeling, like something isn't going to work out."

I couldn't explain it, but in my heart, I didn't believe the trip was going to happen. Or maybe I was afraid it wouldn't turn out as I hoped. That I wouldn't be able to convince them to come home. Even when the airline confirmation was e-mailed to me, and I had printed out the details on paper, I wasn't convinced. I touched the paper and examined the flight numbers and times. Maybe it was Uncle Max. Going back to Ecuador without him felt wrong, like picking the scab off a wound that doesn't want to heal.

The basketball group stood and piled up their trash, draining the last of their drinks. Tom picked up his tray and left with his friends, Ann-Marie Fidesco trailing behind him, the paper airplane trampled under their shoes.

32

I pulled on wool socks, laced up my hiking boots, and grabbed my coat, hat, scarf, and gloves. My boots thunk, thunked as I walked into the kitchen. Grandma and Grandpa were waiting for me, ready to head out for a Christmas tree. I was looking forward to tromping around a Christmas tree farm; it was the closest I was going to get to being back home in the mountains.

"Ready?" Grandpa asked.

"Yep. You got the hot chocolate?"

"You want to take hot chocolate?"

"Yeah, in a thermos. Isn't that what you do too?"

"Well, I don't see anything wrong with that. I'm always up for a warm drink. Hot chocolate it is."

Grandma pulled the milk out of the fridge while Grandpa went in search of a thermos.

We all piled into the Taurus, Grandpa's winter car, and I was surprised that Grandma didn't object to going. It must be a long drive to get all the way out in the woods where there was room for a Christmas tree farm. Imagine that, the Christmas spirit was even giving Grandma a boost.

Grandpa found a radio station playing Christmas carols. We sang and hummed as Grandpa weaved his way through subdivisions and out onto the main drag of Woodward Avenue. He slowed down and pulled into a parking lot on the right. A huge blow-up Santa and a snowman flanked a banner that said Tim's Trees. Behind the banner were rows and rows of evergreens.

My jolly mood evaporated. This wasn't a Christmas tree farm. This was a parking lot! No wonder it wasn't a big deal for Grandma to come with us. We weren't even on the road for ten minutes.

And she didn't even get out of the car. She waited inside with the heat running while I followed Grandpa.

"What do you think? Is one of them calling out to you?" Grandpa asked.

I shrugged. My cabin and parents were as far away from this place as possible.

"You're going to make me choose?" Grandpa said.

"I don't care." The faint tune of "Frosty the Snowman" piped from a speaker, almost drowned out by the roar of traffic. Grandpa was eyeing me, but I stared off into the rows of nearly identical trees. At home, we would have hiked into the woods and cut down our own tree, leaving gifts of pinecones smeared with peanut butter and bird seed.

A guy carried the Fraser fir to our car and helped Grandpa tie it to the top. "Now how about some of that hot chocolate. Glad you thought to bring it, Cara."

"I don't want any. Let's just go."

"Well, I'm going to have some."

I could feel Grandpa studying me while he shared a cup of hot chocolate with Grandma. I turned away, hugging myself against the chilly air. I slipped off my glove and reached for the stone in my coat pocket, turning it around and around in my fingers.

Another guy hoisted a tree onto the minivan next to us. He stopped to debate with Grandpa about his choice of a blue spruce.

Blah, blah, blah. Who cared? The trees had been trucked from a forest a hundred miles away.

I dropped the stone back into my pocket and yanked on my glove. I kicked one of the car tires with the toe of my hiking boot.

Back at home, I helped Grandpa carry the tree into the house. I shuffled backward, carrying the heavier trunk end, then I went straight to my room. I knew I was acting rude, but I couldn't seem to make myself care.

Later that evening, Grandpa stopped in my room.

"You okay, Cara?"

"Sure."

"Sorry about this afternoon. I wasn't thinking. I should have known that might have made you miss your parents even more. The holidays can be a tough time of year."

"Is that where you always get your tree?"

Grandpa looked surprised at the question.

"For a while now, but not in the old days. We used to head out to the real Christmas tree farm. It was a whole day's adventure." He stopped, then slapped his forehead. "What a knucklehead am I! The hot chocolate, those hiking boots. You thought we were going to a real Christmas tree farm!"

I couldn't help smiling as he face-palmed again.

"Nope, your grandma never would have made it all the way up there. But that's what we used to do when your mom was little."

"That's what we did at home."

"I'm sorry you were disappointed."

"It wouldn't have been the same anyway."

"No, I guess you're right. It probably wouldn't."

33

The next morning, Christmas music drifted into my room. In the kitchen, Grandma had changed the radio station from oldies to Christmas carols. I peeked from the doorway and grinned. She hummed and swayed as she measured and stirred at the counter. She was even cracking eggs to the beat of music!

In the living room, Grandpa was surrounded by large cardboard boxes. He opened one and pulled out strings of Christmas lights. One by one, he plugged them in to see if they worked. They lit up the room, tiny red lights, just like we had at home. Mom won that argument years ago. Dad grew up with big multicolored flashing lights. Mom grew up with tiny red lights. Our tree and my grandparents' tree, the only ones I had ever seen with red lights. That warm feeling perked up inside me again, that little bit of holiday spirit.

When we'd finished decorating the tree, Grandpa asked if I wanted to get some practice driving in.

"Sure, I guess I should."

"Let's take the Mustang out before we get snow. What do you say, Margaret? It'll be a pretty drive with all the Christmas lights."

"You want me to go for a ride with Cara driving?" Her voice was incredulous.

"Thanks a lot," I said.

"You just keep practicing with Grandpa, and I'll go with you when you officially have your license."

"I'm going to hold you to that, you know."

Grandma shook her head. "Oh go on, already. Shoo, you two."

She waved the feather duster at us, then turned to the curio cabinet of porcelain angels.

Grandma would be appalled at our cabin in California. We definitely didn't have a regular dusting routine. I cringed thinking about the smoke damage. What would our cabin look like when I finally made it back home? Charred and blackened, covered in soot? Neglected. Abandoned. And the forest? How many trees had we lost in the fire?

Driving took all my concentration. I was nervous driving the Mustang, but it gave me a spark of energy too. There was so much power in that engine.

Grandpa directed me toward the freeway ramp, and I held my breath at the sight of the speeding cars. I remembered Billy's words and merged onto the highway.

"Nice job," Grandpa said.

I smiled and stomped on the gas.

"Ah, you've inherited the family lead foot, I see."

I eased up a bit and glanced at Grandpa, but he was grinning.

"Just stay on 75, I'll give you a little tour of Detroit. This highway will take you all the way to Florida. Sometimes I get the urge to hit the road, just go and see where it takes me."

"Road warrior," I said, smiling. I cruised along with the steady pattern of traffic.

"What's so special about Grandma's collection of angels? Like all those babies?"

"Your mom never told you about the babies?"

"No, I don't think so."

"Well, maybe she was waiting until you were older. When it was time for you to have your own family." Grandpa cleared his throat.

I had a moment of panic thinking he was about to talk to me about sex.

"When I told you about your grandma's problems with anxiety attacks, I guess I wasn't starting at the beginning. It goes way back to before your mom was even born. It even goes back to before me."

Now he had really lost me.

"Your grandma married her high school sweetheart right before he got drafted to Vietnam. She got pregnant, but miscarried, and then her husband was killed in the war."

Whoa. My eyes widened and I gripped the steering wheel tighter. I wanted to look at Grandpa, but I was afraid to take my eyes off the road.

"I know. Terrible. Maybe I should wait and tell this story when you're not driving."

I shot him a quick glance. "I'm okay, keep going. I never knew she was married before you."

"We met a few years later. She was the pretty teller with long blond hair at my bank." He grinned. "I always tried to time my spot in line so I'd end up at her window. When we got married, we wanted to start a family right away, but it didn't turn out like we hoped."

"She had two more miscarriages before we finally had Lori. And it was a rough delivery. Truthfully, we almost lost her. Your grandma, not your mom. Lori came out healthy and bursting with life, but Margaret was rushed off to surgery. Needed an emergency hysterectomy. No more babies for us."

I didn't know what to say. *Who knew?* I guess there had never been a reason for my mom to bring it up. But now a light flickered in my mind trying to reveal something to me, like the glowing circle of a campfire. I knew this was important somehow, that there was meaning there, but it remained hidden in the shadowy trees beyond the campfire's reach.

"There's the Ambassador Bridge to Canada," Grandpa said. "It's pretty when it's lit up at night."

He was right. It was pretty. "Just go a little farther, then we better head home before Grandma gets worried."

Ahead, the highway rose up. Down below, off to the sides, were row upon row of factories. Yellow-gray smoke billowed against the purple-rose sky and flames burst out of pipes. A rotten-egg sulfur smell filled the car and stuck in my nose and throat.

"The Rouge plant," Grandpa said.

"It's disgusting," I said.

Grandpa closed the car vents to block the smell. "I saw a photo documentary once. This man had taken pictures of the Rouge at interesting angles. Some of the shots were at this time of day with the sunset as the backdrop. He was able to make it beautiful in a way. To turn it around into something positive."

He directed me to get off the highway, drive over the overpass and back on, heading north. Heading home.

We were quiet for a while, the sky darkening, red brake lights glowing in front of us, headlights zipping by on the other side of the highway. My ears filled with the lulling, steady sound of the tires on pavement. I felt so tired, drained. Grandpa must have been feeling the same way because all of a sudden he sat up straighter, rolled his window down halfway, leaned his head out, and sucked in the sharp cold air.

He rolled the window back up, shook his head and said, "Brrrrr. Thought I was going to nod off a minute there. It's time for some tunes."

He switched on the radio and punched the preset buttons, passing up talk and jazz, stopping at classic rock. "This is what we need," he said, and turned up the volume.

Bob Seger's scratchy voice filled the car. *Sunspot baby, we sure had a real good time.*

Grandpa joined in, *I looked in Miami. I looked in Brazil. The closest I came was a month old bill . . .*

My Brazilian acai bracelet from Tom was on my wrist, and I couldn't help grinning. Grandma was bebopping in the kitchen, now Grandpa was rocking! Bob Seger was one of my mom's favorites too. The bass thumped in my chest, and we sang along. Grandpa swayed in his seat. I got off the freeway at our exit and followed the suburban roads home, the stores and houses decorated with wreaths and garland and a rainbow of lights. More lights twinkled in the trees.

If only there was snow. And mountains.

34

The day before I left for Ecuador I awoke with a jittery stomach. It wasn't right to feel nervous about seeing my parents, but I couldn't help it. I felt like something important had changed, the thousands of miles of distance between us were like an actual physical barrier to be broken down.

I opened my window shade to gray skies and brown earth, no sign of a white Christmas yet, but on the nightstand next to my bed was a Christmas cactus, bursting with coral-colored blooms. A flat, rectangular-shaped object wrapped in shiny red paper was in the middle of my floor. I picked it up and turned it over in my hands; it felt like a book. I opened my bedroom door and found another wrapped book at my feet. A trail of shiny, red papered gifts led down the hallway, into the living room.

"Santa came early," Grandpa said with a wink. "Come see what else he left for you."

I followed him into the basement. Hanging on the wall was a campus-board, wooden rungs lined up vertically for climbing training.

"Wow! How'd you know how to do this?"

"I remembered seeing one at your house in Tennessee. Amazing what you can find on the Internet. Give it a try," he said.

I jumped on, maneuvering from bottom to top then back down again. I hopped down and shook my stinging hands.

"No more hanging from the door frames, okay?"

"Okay," I said with a grin.

Grandpa and I sneaked a couple Christmas cookies out of the

tins while Grandma cooked a French toast brunch, cinnamon scenting the house. I cleared the dishes afterward, while Grandpa retreated to his chair with a book. Grandma picked up the phone to call friends and relatives out of town. I kept looking at her, trying to picture her with a soldier husband and then as a pretty bank teller with long hair instead of her short curly mop of gray.

I stood at the kitchen sink, enjoying the warmth of the sudsy water on my hands, looking out the window at the heavy gray sky.

If only I knew what awaited me tomorrow. Christmas in Ecuador just felt wrong. But it was my best chance for convincing my parents to come home.

It finally snowed later that afternoon, and I perked up at the first sight of those fat, swirling flakes. I pulled on my coat and mittens and stood on the front porch. Grandma's goose was dressed in her red coat and Santa hat. After all the gloomy gray days, the world was white and magical. A silent, fluttering storm of down feathers. The sky lilac. So quiet, a hush settling in all around.

The snowflakes dusted my mittens long enough for me to study their star shapes before melting. They brushed my nose and cheeks, clung to my eyelashes, mixed with my tears. I had been closing my mind and heart trying not to think about what had happened to Uncle Max. Tall and strong, lean, ropy muscles, his face etched from sun and laughter. I couldn't help imagining him dragged under the snow, buried, suffocating, freezing. His face frozen in horror. Frozen in time.

35

The next morning, snow covered the rooftops, cars, and trees like frosting. My flight to Ecuador wasn't until later in the afternoon, so I helped Grandpa shovel the sidewalk. We turned in opposite directions, working our way to the neighbors on either side.

Splat! A snowball nailed me in the back of the head.

"Hey!" I whirled around, the snow dripped down my neck.

Grandpa laughed. "Sorry, I was aiming for your back!"

I scooped up a handful, packed it into a ball, and chucked it at him.

He ducked just in time, but I was quicker with the next one.

Splat! It smacked him on the chest, exploding, right where he had unzipped his coat.

"Oh, no fair!" Grandpa shouted.

"Gotcha!"

"Got you!" he said, whizzing another one at me, catching my leg.

I wound up to throw another, but he held up his hand. "Mercy. I need some hot cocoa."

Now that we had stopped, my fingers and toes were stinging with cold. My jeans were stiff and wet.

We picked up our shovels and returned to the house.

I lingered in a hot, steamy shower, the water pounding my shoulders, but I still felt chilled. I cringed against the cold blast of air as I stepped onto the bath mat and dried my goose-bumpy skin. I shivered and grabbed a second towel. A headache lurked behind my eyes. My throat felt parched and scratchy. I was about to leave for an exotic trip, to finally see my parents after four months apart. I should have been happy, but my feelings were all tangled up. I just felt tired, drained.

I curled up in my bird's nest chair and realized for the first time that it was like a scallop shell—my own shell of quiet here in Michigan. I tried to read, but couldn't focus. A snowplow rumbled down the street. Snow was clumped on the twiggy bushes like big, white blooms. Unless we went high into the mountains, I wouldn't see snow in Ecuador.

Grandma's music drifted out of the kitchen. *Have yourself a merry little Christmas.* It didn't feel right to be leaving Grandma and Grandpa alone for Christmas. I didn't even know what they usually did; we hadn't seen them in so many years. They hadn't said anything about going to church. I never went with my parents either. Dad used to say he felt closer to God when he was on top of a mountain than he possibly could in any church.

It was almost time to leave for the airport. My lunch churned in my stomach. I curled up tighter. I couldn't get warm. I wrapped a fleece blanket around myself, but still, I shuddered, my skin crackling with goose bumps. I longed for the toasty warmth of the fireplace in our cabin. I crawled out of my chair, heading to my room for a heavier sweater. My legs wobbled, and the floor tilted.

"Cara?" Grandma said. "Are you okay?"

She was by my side in an instant. I wrapped my arms around my body, squeezing. My teeth chattered. Why was it so cold in here? A chisel chopped at my skull. I closed my eyes against the pain.

"Your cheeks are flushed." Grandma's hand on my forehead was like an icicle. "Oh dear, you're burning up." She called to Grandpa, "She's burning up, Norman."

The weight of blankets on my bed kept me still, but I trembled inside. Every muscle ached, every inch of skin felt bruised. My eyes scalded behind my closed lids. Yet I felt like I was on an icy mountaintop, snowy wind whipping all around me.

I woke to the sound of Grandpa's voice. "Good morning, Carabou."

I squinted against the hazy daylight filling my room. Grandpa was sitting in a chair near my bed. My head was full of grating rocks. I tried to talk, but was overcome with coughing. A razor blade was lodged in the back of my throat.

"You slept all night. How are you feeling?"

I groaned. "I missed my flight?"

He nodded.

I groaned again. "What am I going to do? I need to get to the airport." I tried to sit up, but the pain behind my eyes knocked me flat.

"Sorry, Cara, you're not going anywhere for a while. We called your mom."

"I shouldn't have stayed out in the cold yesterday."

"Nah, that's a myth. Can't catch the flu just from being cold. Grandma and I got our flu shot, so we should be safe. But you, you're going to be under the weather for a few days."

Grandma appeared in my doorway, carrying a steaming mug. "Sorry you're sick, Cara." Her voice was gentler than I'd ever heard it.

I pushed myself up in bed, slowly this time, and Grandpa propped my pillow behind my back.

"I wasn't feeling good yesterday, but I thought I was just nervous about my trip."

"That's the way the flu hits you, all of a sudden." Grandma handed me the warm mug. "Old family recipe, sip it slowly, and it'll make you feel better."

I sipped the golden liquid. Sweet and citrusy, spicy and more, it lit a path down my throat.

"What is this stuff?" I rasped.

"Dandelion wine," Grandpa answered.

He chuckled at the confusion on my face. "You never read that book? Ray Bradbury. I'll have to dig it up for you."

"It's tea, lemon juice, honey, and a secret ingredient," Grandma said. "Now that you're awake, I'll make you some toast." She felt my forehead again. "And get you some ibuprofen for that fever."

"I never get sick," I grumbled. Another round of coughing racked my ribs. I took another sip of the soothing liquid, and asked Grandpa, "What's the secret ingredient?"

"Whiskey," he whispered with a grin.

I slept on and off throughout the day. Coughing left me gasping for breath with tears in my eyes. Shivering, I let myself feel pitiful.

I shuffled into the living room when my fever moderated, then retreated to my bed when my temperature soared, burrowing under the mound of blankets. My parents had called, but I slept without even hearing the phone ring.

Grandpa found his copy of *Dandelion Wine* and left it on my nightstand next to the blooming Christmas cactus. For the next two days, I read and slept, hardly leaving my bed.

Kaitlyn stopped by when she returned from Colorado.

"Enter at your own risk," I croaked.

She brought my Christmas present, a pint-size stuffed Husky dog, white and silver gray, just like Tahoe.

"Ooh, she's wonderful," I said, cuddling the plush dog.

I gave Kaitlyn a book of poems and hot chocolate mixes that I had found for her.

"Thanks! Perfect to curl up with before we go back to school. I'll save the Baileys for another night when you're recovered, so you can reveal more of your deep, dark, Indiana She-Jones secrets."

She backed away from my hacking coughs and retreated home as my fever spiked again. I tucked my new, plush Tahoe dog under the covers beside me. Even my dreams were feverish that night.

I struggle through the freezing, blinding, white wind. I reach out and pat Tahoe's damp fur. Up ahead, a wall of darkness. I trudge closer, closer. Clutched in my hand, a tiny bottle of golden nectar. The air turns warm, heavy. I want to stop, rest, let the warmth seep into my bones. But the darkness beckons. It hums. Alive. My heart pounds, or is the sound coming from the murky dark? We're at the edge now, peering down. Tahoe's pink tongue curls out, panting. Moisture seeps from the swampy ravine, sweat trickles down the back of my neck. Uncle Max's voice. Tahoe barks once. She leaps. No! The darkness reaches out, and I slip, falling . . .

I woke up on fire. I tossed aside the layers of blankets and swiped damp strands of hair away from my sweaty face. The fever had broken, and I drifted back to sleep, floating on the cool night air.

The next morning, Mom was sitting in a chair beside my bed.

36

"Mom!" I sat up in bed and kicked myself free of the tangled sheets.

She laughed. "Don't get up, you're sick."

"I feel a lot better," I said. My words came out in a rush. "I didn't know you were coming. When did you get here? Where's Dad?"

A fit of coughing stopped my stream of questions.

"You still *sound* sick," she said. "I wanted to surprise you. Your dad's not here, just me. You know how he is about coming here."

Grandma had made it clear plenty of times how she felt about my dad. But still, he would be coming to see me—who cares if Grandma made him feel welcome or not.

"To be honest, we only had money for one plane ticket, and I didn't want to ask Grandma and Grandpa to borrow any." She reached out and tucked a strand of hair behind my ear. "I tried to come sooner, but a lot of flights were canceled because of the snow. It didn't feel like Christmas without you there with us."

Tell me about it.

"How long are you staying?" I asked.

"A few days. Grandma and Grandpa said you were really sick. We were worried about you."

I sighed and flopped back on my pillows. Even though I felt better, I was still shaky and weak. A layer of frost had crept onto my bedroom windowsill. The wind howled outside.

Mom's beaded bracelet from Ecuador, the twin of mine, was on her wrist. *Buena suerte para una madre y su hija.* She straightened and smoothed my covers, just like how she used to tuck me in as a little kid. My body melted to her touch.

"Grandma's making chicken noodle soup. I'll bring you some a little later," she said. "Then we can call Dad. He can't wait to talk to you."

I smiled and closed my heavy eyes.

The sun shone in patches of blue sky the next morning, the snowy yard sparkling and smooth except for a trail of squirrel prints.

"You feeling up for a walk?" Mom asked.

I nodded. Fresh air sounded great.

We bundled up and strolled down the block. Snow dusted off the tree branches, shining like glitter in the sunlight.

"I haven't heard from Coach Mel in a couple months," I told Mom.

"Do you know why Coach spends more time teaching rather than climbing?" she asked.

I shrugged. "She's older."

"Not much older than me," Mom said. "A very long time ago, your coach lost her fiancé on a climb. They had just become engaged."

Oh my god. What was with all these people dying? I knew Coach Mel had been one of the top sport climbers before she began coaching, but I had never heard about an accident.

"When we were missing on Chimborazo, it was really hard on her. And for you too, I know that, and I'm still very sorry. For Mellie, it stirred up her grief from years ago, especially when she heard about Max."

"Why didn't she tell me?"

"She was just doing the best she knew."

Coach Mel had tried to stay in touch, but I'd basically ignored her. I guess she understood more than I realized.

Clouds had moved in, covering the sun, and the cold air made my nose drip. I sniffed and tugged my hat further down over my ears.

"Let's turn around," Mom said, linking her arm through mine. "You're not completely over this bug yet."

Back inside, Mom watched as I tugged off my boots and shrugged out of my coat.

"What?" I said.

She shook her head, her lips curving into a soft smile. "It's only been a few months, but you've grown. You look so mature." She ran her fingers through my hair. "Your hair is so long. You've grown out your bangs. It's darker too."

"Not enough sun here."

"You're beautiful." She pulled me into a hug. "I love you so much."

"I love you too, Mom," I said, softening into her embrace. She smelled like the crisp fresh air.

She pulled back and cupped my face. "Do you have a boyfriend?"

I rolled my eyes.

"Uh-huh." She turned to my Grandpa, sitting in his reading chair. "Spill the beans. Cara has a boyfriend, doesn't she?"

"Mom."

Grandpa lowered the newspaper. "Boys are calling here every night, knocking on the door at all hours. We can't keep 'em away."

"Grandpa!" I laughed. "Don't listen to him," I told Mom.

"It won't be long," she said. "Your dad's really not going to know what to do then."

On New Year's Eve, I talked to Dad again. He yelled into the phone, his words slurred. "Cara! I wish you could see this. Do you hear it?"

Loud fizzes and pops, crackling and explosions. The noise nearly drowned out his voice. But he was still there, on the line, and I thought I heard him whimper, a sob breaking free.

I handed the phone to Mom. She looked at me questioningly. I swallowed, but couldn't speak. Dad crying. So brief, but horrible; a sob of pain escaping from deep within. I had never heard my dad cry before.

She listened for a minute, then said, "I love you," and ended the call.

"He's had a little too much to drink," she said.

"Is he okay? What was all that noise?"

"New Year's Day is a major celebration in Ecuador. Sort of how we talk about cleaning out the old to bring in the new. Their celebration is like a huge party in the streets. People dress up in costumes and make effigies out of old clothes, stuffing them with sawdust or newspapers and firecrackers. The effigies are called años viejos."

Mom's Spanish had improved during the time she was away, and she pronounced the words without hesitation. Firecrackers, that was the noise I had heard. It sounded more exciting than the night Grandma and Grandpa had planned: *The Sound of Music* and popcorn.

"They build small huts out of eucalyptus, and the años viejos are put inside. At midnight, they're set on fire. It's quite dramatic. All of the hardships and troubles of the past year are burned away."

In bed that night, fireworks and flames exploded behind my eyes. Instead of a eucalyptus hut, I saw our cabin bursting into flame, swept by the forest fire. And inside stood Uncle Max, looking out the window, not in fear, but in awe of the spectacle surrounding him.

The night before Mom left, she told me their plans. I had heard her correctly on the phone, they were training for K2. Uncle Max's dream, to summit the deadliest mountain on Earth.

I stared at her. Hard.

"I know what you're thinking," she began.

"Really?" I snapped. "If you did, we'd be back home in California now. One out of every four people die trying to summit that mountain. That's what I'm thinking."

Mom was quiet for a minute. I knew my stuff. K2 was called the Savage Mountain. The second highest after Everest, but even more dangerous. More climbers had died on K2 than on any other mountain due to its treacherous terrain and unpredictable, relentless storms. Not to mention that it was in Pakistan. Their journey would begin in Islamabad, right in the heart of a terrorist insurgency.

"Did Mr. S. ever tell you why he stayed in Ecuador?" she asked.

"No. What, he fell in love with the country?"

She shook her head. "He lost a partner on Mount Chimborazo."

Mr. S. had definitely not shared this information with me. How could he? My own parents had been heading to Chimborazo and then were nearly killed.

"He's never been able to move on, to put it behind him. He's been stuck in the same place ever since," Mom said. "If your dad can live out Max's biggest dream for him, I think he'll be able to truly move forward from there."

So many arguments exploded in my mind. She'd just given me two more stories of climbers dying. The practical question jumped out.

"How are you going to pay for that kind of expedition?"

"That's the crazy thing. Like this was meant to be. Max's death brought more attention to us, our story. We didn't even have to seek out sponsors; they came to us. We'll never have this kind of opportunity again."

What more was there to say? They couldn't even afford an extra plane ticket, but someone else was offering to fund their next summit attempt. Mom and Dad knew the risks. They'd been seeking and living these risks my whole life. It wasn't just fear that rippled inside my stomach, it was thrill. K2 was hard-core mountaineering land. Ascending this mountain of mystery was considered a far greater accomplishment than Everest. How many women had summited K2, ever? Ten? Fifteen? My mom could join their ranks.

The day after Mom left, another Ecuador postcard arrived from Dad. On the back, he'd scrawled:

> Doesn't everything die at last,
> and too soon? Tell me, what
> is it you plan to do with
> your one wild and precious life?

Mary Oliver. I sighed. What was he trying to tell me now? I wished the postcard had arrived when Mom was still here, so I could ask her. Was Dad trying to explain what he was doing, or was he asking me what I planned to do?

Mom was returning to Dad to train for their most perilous climbing expedition yet, and I was expected to stay here and finish school. Stuck in the "hills" of Detroit. I was going to have to find my own way back home. To my own wild and precious life.

37

I was healthy again, the snow melted, and school grew interesting after winter break. It was time for all juniors to take a three-week Health Seminar on Human Sexuality. Sex Ed. Letters were sent home giving parents the opportunity to excuse their child from the course if the content was objectionable. Grandpa chuckled when he saw the letter, but Grandma screwed up her mouth and said, "Well, I hope this is an abstinence-based program."

"Don't think so, Margaret. Says here the class will discuss all methods of birth control in the context of healthy relationships."

"Fat lot of good that did Lori," Grandma muttered.

"But she gave us Cara."

"Cara could have come after Lori finished college if it wasn't for Mark and that hippie-dippie commune in the woods."

My grandparents were actually talking about sex. In front of me. I fled for my room. Mom got pregnant with me when she was only twenty. She had taken a year off from college and was living and working with my dad in the mountains. Instead of returning to school, she had me. From what I'd been able to patch together, this was the start of the conflict between my parents and grandparents. Then when Mom and Dad proceeded to travel around the world, climbing, with me in tow, things really got ugly.

But maybe there was even more to it. I was an accident. My mom had had me without even trying. It hadn't been so easy for Grandma.

Back at school, everyone was talking about sex ed and the upcoming Sadie Hawkins dance where the girls were supposed to ask the guys. Hormones swirled through the hallways like gusts of wind before a storm. I couldn't stop thinking about Tom. I was on the lookout for him in between every class. I made sure I walked by his locker first thing in the morning and at the end of the day. In Algebra II, I oh-so-casually strolled over to the pencil sharpener whenever he was there.

"Hola, muchacha. Regular or the super special?"

I smiled and handed over my pencil, wishing I could think of a smart comeback.

"Super special it is." And he hunched down and grinned that amazingly cute grin.

Grandpa had bought me a mechanical pencil with refillable lead. No way was I using it.

At lunchtime, I met Kaitlyn as usual at the fringe of the goth table.

"Nick won't be here," she said. "He got sent to the office."

"How come?"

"His T-shirt. Did you see it?"

"Uh-uh, he still had his coat on when I saw him this morning."

"It said 'son of a b——' on the front."

"Who sent him to the office?"

"Mrs. Cooper, AP English. Nick calls her Mrs. Plaster, you know, the one who wears so much foundation it looks like you could smack her on the back of her head and her face would crack."

"So what'll happen?"

"Nothing. They'll make him turn it inside out. But it's good he's gone 'cause we gotta talk. I think we should go to Sadie Hawkins."

"I thought you didn't like that kind of stuff," I said.

"I don't. I mean I don't know. I used to, before, you know. I've just been thinking, and I think it would be good for us. To get out, you know, and try to move, like forward or something."

I burst out laughing, I couldn't help it. "Smooth, Kaitlyn."

"You know what I mean."

"Who would you ask?"

"I was thinking about asking Tom Torres," she said.

My eyes popped.

"Psych! Just kidding! He's all yours."

"No way am I asking him."

"You have to! This is the perfect chance."

"I thought we were talking about you?"

"There's not really anyone I like. So I was thinking about asking Nick, you know, to go as friends."

"You do like him, don't you?"

"Please, I told you, he's totally gay."

"Uh-uh, he's so in love with you."

Kaitlyn stuck her tongue out at me. "Is not. At this very moment, Virgin Goth Girl is waiting outside the office for him. She's probably going to ask him to Sadie Hawkins, and then we'll have to come up with a Plan B."

"Virgin Goth Girl?"

"You know, Ashley, the one who usually sits over there, always wears white, ruffly peasant shirts and dresses, and those lace-up boots."

"I thought goths always wore black."

"You have so much to learn. Being goth is about expressing yourself as a unique person—we don't follow a mold."

Except for Virgin Goth Girl, they all looked pretty much the same to me. But I didn't say that to Kaitlyn. It wasn't like I had any style of my own. I didn't buy my jeans with artfully ripped holes; they were thin and torn at my knee from wearing them so much.

"So when are you going to ask Tom?"

"Shh," I said, looking around to see who was in earshot. "I'm not asking him." I picked at the frayed cuff of my flannel shirt, the beaded bracelets peeking out.

"Now you're messing with a . . . son of a bitch," Nick appeared next to Kaitlyn and pounded out the drumbeat on the table. His shirt was inside out and backward with the tag in front.

"You'll never guess who just asked me to Sadie Hawkins," he said.

"Virgin Goth Girl," Kaitlyn and I said at the same time.

"Ooh, her fatal attraction to *moi* has been that obvious?"

"Please . . ." Kaitlyn rolled her eyes. "What'd you say?"

"Actually, I didn't let her finish. She started fishing around, and I bolted. Save me?" he whimpered.

"Of course. Would you like to go to Sadie Hawkins with me?"

"That would be lovely," Nick said and bowed and kissed her hand. *The* hand.

For a second, I think we all held our breath.

Kaitlyn recovered first and waved Nick off, her hand disappearing under the table. "Okay, enough already. Now we have to find a date for Cara."

"Go Tom, go Tom, go Tom," Nick rolled his arms and chanted.

"Shut up!" I hissed. Two rows over, Tom sauntered toward his table, carrying a loaded tray.

"I heard all about you and Tom in your Road Rage class," Nick said. "Way to go." His dimples flashed and he raised his eyebrows up and down.

And they both had the nerve to sit there looking innocently at me.

"I'm not asking him," I said, crossing my arms.

Tom slid onto the bench with his basketball buddies. No Ann-Marie Fidesco. No other girls. Just a group of guys, sharing food, gesturing, acting goofy.

38

I had missed Tom at his locker in the morning. I chickened out when he was sharpening my pencil before class. I twisted my beaded bracelets together while our teacher droned on. I couldn't believe I was actually doing it. If my blood pumped any harder, it would spurt out of my ears. I hadn't even been this nervous at the World Championships.

In the hallway we were swept along with the tide of students, pausing at a jam up in front of the library. Katniss Everdeen peered out from a poster, her bow and arrow aimed straight at me. I forced the words out of my throat. "Do you want to go to Sadie Hawkins with me?"

He stood dead in his tracks while the crowd surged and swarmed past us. "Oh Cara, that'd be fun, but I'm already going with someone else."

"Sure, okay, no biggie," I stammered. We were still standing in the middle of the hallway, and someone knocked into my shoulder, shoving me closer to Tom.

He reached out a hand to steady me, but I kept my eyes down. I twisted out of his grasp and bolted. At least that's what I tried to do, weaving and dodging my way through the crowd.

"Cara!"

I kept going, blood roaring through my ears.

In English, the teacher gave us the prompt, "How does one define love?" and told us to write for fifteen minutes. *Are you kidding me?* I stared down at my paper, replaying the scene with Tom. Mrs. Smith walked up and down the aisles offering help. She paused at my desk and touched my shoulder.

"Cara, are you feeling okay? Your cheeks looked flushed."

"I'm okay," I muttered and ducked my head while my cheeks flamed even more.

What was I thinking, asking him in person? I should have let Kaitlyn ask him for me. Or I should have just texted him first and asked if he was going to the dance. Idiot. It was going to be awkward every time I saw him now.

At the end of the day, I headed straight outside into the freezing air. Tears filled my eyes, blurring the path. Who did I think I was? How did I get caught up in this superficial high school life? What was I doing here?

Spring was around the corner in California. It was nowhere in sight in Michigan. Piles of polluted sludge lined the streets. More snow was forecasted overnight. I stepped over the slick patches of ice on the sidewalk. My nose dripped, and I sniffed—a familiar smell from home—a campfire? Wood burning from someone's fireplace.

I fingered the smooth stone in my pocket.

Kaitlyn pulled up at my house just as I rushed up the sidewalk. I glanced over at her but kept walking. She hopped out of her car.

"Cara!"

I paused but didn't turn to look at her. I just couldn't.

She caught up to me. "Hey, how come you didn't wait at school?"

I shook my head, and she followed me into the house, past my grandparents' questioning looks, to my room.

"What's wrong?" she asked.

I flopped on my bed face first, grabbing my Tahoe dog and squeezing her tight. "I'm such a loser." My eyes filled with tears again.

Kaitlyn sat on the edge of my bed and rubbed my back. "You're not a loser. What happened? It's Tom, isn't it? That asshole! What did he say?" She got up and came back with a tissue. "It'll be okay."

I sat up and blew my nose.

"He's already going with someone else."

"Did he say who?" She scratched my back.

I shook my head.

"Was he a jerk about it?"

I shook my head again.

"Well, what did he say?"

"He said he was already going with someone else. End of story."

"I mean, did he seemed bummed or anything, like he really wanted to go with you, but . . ."

"It doesn't matter. It's not just Tom. I shouldn't even be here. This isn't my life." My lips trembled.

Kaitlyn was quiet for a minute. Then she said, "It might not be the life you had before, but it's good to try new things and have fun. You don't always have to be a serious climber girl."

I tugged at Tom's bracelet to take it off, but it was twisted and tangled with my other one. I slid them both off and tossed them on my nightstand.

"I know bad stuff happened when you were in Ecuador. And when something bad happens, it's okay to feel bad for a while, for a long time even, but you have to keep going. Good things will happen again. You need to let them."

"I need to go home. I need to go back to California."

"Why?"

"I don't know." I pressed my fingers over my eyelids, trying to halt the tears inside. "I just need to."

"You mean to go back and live there or like right now, soon, to visit?"

"Yes. Both. I don't know. I just can't stay here. I don't belong here."

We sat in silence, my blunt words hanging in the air.

"Okay," Kaitlyn said. "Well, I will miss you terribly, but if you need to go back, I guess that's just what you need to do. Will your grandparents take you?"

"Yeah right," I said with a snort. "My grandma can barely ride in a car for more than ten minutes. They wouldn't understand."

"I have money saved up from my job," Kaitlyn said. "We could hit Nick up too."

"Oh Kaitlyn." My tears flowed. "I would never—"

"Come here." Kaitlyn opened her arms, and I leaned into her.

She gave me a squeeze then released me. "You need to eat some ice cream, read some Agatha Christie, and we will figure out a plan tomorrow. 'Kay?"

I nodded. "Okay."

I stayed in my room for the rest of the evening, telling Grandma and Grandpa I didn't feel good. It was true. My skin burned. I felt feverish. I didn't cry. I just turned out the lights and crawled into bed.

I woke up with a gasp at three a.m. My skin sweaty and clothes twisted around my body. I took off my jeans and sweater and tried to drift back to sleep, but my mind had been revved to racing speed. I peered into the darkness, feeling more lost than ever.

Four a.m. Still couldn't sleep. Tahoe rested in the crook of my arm. The darkness of my room was actually full of color, like glitter, hovering in the air above me. When I closed my eyes, I could still see the tiny pinpricks of color on my eyelids.

What an awful friend I had been. Such a baby to fall apart over one rejection from a boy compared to what Kaitlyn's been through. She wanted good things to happen. For both of us. She must have thought that she didn't matter enough for me to stay here. That I could just leave her behind. I hadn't said anything about missing her if I left, or even if I would come back.

39

I got to school early and waited for Kaitlyn by her locker.

She took one look at me and said, "Were you up all night packing?"

I shook my head. "I'm not going. Not anytime soon anyway. It's okay. Thank you for being such a good friend. I would miss you so much if I left."

We hugged each other tight.

"Girly hug! Girly hug!" Nick wrapped his arms around both of us and jumped up and down.

We laughed and shrugged him off.

"Okay, I heard that you are still dateless for Sadie Hawkins, and I have the solution," Nick said. "You should go with my brother Nate."

Kaitlyn and I both opened our mouths in shocked disgust.

"Ew," Kaitlyn said.

"No way," I said.

Nick looked hurt. "What's wrong with my brother?"

"You know very well what's wrong with your arrogant ass of a brother. No offense," Kaitlyn said.

"No way," I said again.

"Fine, who's it going to be then?"

Kaitlyn and I looked at each other. I shrugged and said, "I'm just not going."

"You have to go," Kaitlyn said.

"You could ask Jake," Nick said, snickering. "You'd make his day. No, you would make his life. He'd be the talk of his school. The first middle schooler asked to a high school dance. And you only come up to like his belly button. It'd be like—"

I held up my hand. "Not funny."

"So not funny," Kaitlyn said.

And we linked arms and marched down the hall.

My stomach convulsed all the way to Algebra II. I spotted Tom as soon as I walked in, but I quickly looked away. When I took my seat, he got up to sharpen his pencil. I followed his back with my eyes, but looked down when he reached the pencil sharpener. I don't know if he looked my way. I was busy digging out the mechanical pencil from Grandpa. I dashed out of class the second the bell rang.

Kaitlyn rushed by my locker at the end of the day. "I've got to go to work, you okay to walk home?"

"Oh yeah, go ahead."

She waved, then called out from down the hall, "I have an idea! I'll call you later."

An idea about what? She was gone before I could ask. I turned back to my locker, and Tom appeared out of nowhere.

"Hey Cara, how's it going?"

I opened my mouth but my chest was caving in.

"You get to drive your grandpa's Mustang much? You're so lucky. I've got an old beater now. My parents surprised me with it. Not that I'm not grateful, but it's a hand-me-down ancient Escort wagon from my neighbor."

I managed a smile. I think. Maybe it came across as a wince.

"Well, I just wanted to say hi. I'll catch you later."

And he was gone.

God, I needed to go climbing.

Jake was already at Planet Granite when I arrived.

"Cara, come look!"

He hung about twenty feet in the air, just below an overhang, and dipped his hands in the chalk bag tied at his waist.

"I think this is it. A 5.14. Nate and I put it up yesterday. I can't get past the darn crux!"

A cute, middle school girl was belaying him. Jake always had girls checking him out, but he was too into his climbing to pay attention. Or too into me, as Nick would tease.

"Climbing," he called down to the girl.

"Okay," she called back.

He hooked his right ankle on a pretzel shaped lump, smeared his left foot on the wall, stretched with his left arm, grabbed a moonrock hold, reached his right arm up and—

"Falling!" he yelled.

His belayer girl popped about two feet off the ground from the force of his fall, and I grabbed her harness to pull her back down.

"Let him down," I said.

"I don't know if he wants to. He's almost got it."

"Let him down."

She let out the rope and Jake sunk to the ground, trying to catch his breath.

"Your turn, Cara."

I tied in to the rope, and Jake took over belaying.

"Climbing," I said.

"Climb on."

I motored up the first stretch until I got to the spot where Jake had fallen. I hooked my right heel on the pretzel like he did, but I couldn't stretch far enough to reach the left handhold. I backed down and used the pretzel simultaneously as a handhold and foothold, pushing up with my triceps, balancing my weight. I stood on my tiptoe on the tip of the hold and inched my way up, smearing my other foot, my right hand finding a tiny pincher hold that Jake had later used as a foothold.

Now I was within reach of the moonrock that Jake had used. My fingers pressed into its divots. I matched both hands on it, pushed my feet off from below, let out a huge grunt, and dynoed to the next hold. I danced to the finish and clipped the last bolt.

"Take!" I called.

Jake lowered me down.

"5.13," I said with a grin. "Maybe even 5.12."

"You make me sick," he said, tying into the rope to give it another go.

Kaitlyn texted me later, but I told her I couldn't talk. I didn't want to think about plans for California or Sadie Hawkins. I just wanted to keep the feeling from climbing. Contented and weightless, like floating on a cushion of clouds. It was the closest I ever came to the feeling of being home. I went to bed and slept until my alarm woke me up.

40

It was a good thing I entered school well rested the next morning. I had forgotten that it was sex ed day. I had no idea what to expect. For some reason I expected the girls and guys to be separated, but we were all together, herded into the auditorium. Girls huddled together on one side, jittery and giggling. The boys sat on the other side, yelling down the aisles and shoving each other. Only Nick straddled the imaginary line that divided the sexes. He sat in the middle of the back row, Kaitlyn beside him. I filed in next to her, spotting Tom down toward the front in the middle of a guy row. He was slumped in his seat, long legs sprawled out to the sides. As if he could feel my eyes on him, he turned around and scanned the room. I sat down before he could catch me.

A hush fell over the room as our assistant principal, Mr. Halloway, and Nick's favorite, Mrs. Plaster, took the stage. A few twitters and elbow jabs went around the room. Nick had a name for Mr. Halloway, too. It was Hal, short for halitosis. Which was kind of mean, but his dragon breath was enough to make you gag. Hal was an ex–football star, looked big and beefy in his suit and tie, and walked like he knew he was a stud. It turned out that our two teachers had minored in Human Sexuality in college. For real. Who does that?

They began with a brief introduction of the class, saying that we had already been taught the mechanics of our bodies in previous health classes, so they would be focusing on relationships.

"We want to hear directly from you. What concerns you, what are you struggling with?" Mrs. Plaster said. "You are growing up a rapidly changing time with technology, social media, like we've never seen before. You spend much of your time in an online world, and we're going to talk about how that is altering relationships for better and for worse."

"I want everyone to pull out a piece of paper and write down at least one question," Hal instructed. "Anything that's on your mind. Friendships, dating, sexuality. Don't put your name on it. We'll collect them and try to answer as many as we can."

I glanced at Kaitlyn, and she crossed her eyes. Nick scribbled away. I had no idea what to write. *What do you do when you get up the nerve to ask a guy to Sadie Hawkins, and he turns you down?* Yeah right.

I twirled my ponytail. In Spanish, the word for "questions" is "preguntas." I wrote, "No preguntas," and folded up my paper, smiling to myself.

Hal and Mrs. Plaster circled the room, collecting all the folded up notes. Then they began, which I thought was pretty brave of them. I assumed they'd take a few minutes to review them first. I mean who knows what kind of perv questions some kids were going to write down.

Hal read the first question. "What do you do if someone you know has bad breath?"

Half of the room burst out laughing. Kaitlyn and I looked at Nick, but he was sitting with a perfectly straight face, as if he was eagerly anticipating the answer.

"Now, now, this is a good question. It's a touchy subject. You've got to find a way to tell the person without hurting their feelings, but sometimes honesty is the best policy. Do you have any thoughts, Mrs. Cooper?"

Mrs. Plaster looked at Hal with a sly smile, and said, "You could offer them a breath mint." She reached into her pocket, pulled out a roll of mints, and held it out to him.

Laughter exploded around the room. Nick was physically shaking in his seat, doubled over.

Hal laughed with us, clueless. I felt a little bad for the guy.

Mrs. Plaster read the next question. "What do you do when you're friends with a girl but you like her more than that?"

Whispers spread around the room. The basketball guys craned in their seats, trying to guess who had written the question. I couldn't see Tom's face.

Kaitlyn stretched her legs out in front of her, tapping her clunky boots together. Nick looked bored, doodling on his notebook.

Mrs. Plaster continued, "It sounds like this is a popular question. I'm sure many of you will find yourself in this situation at one time or another, both boys and girls. And in fact, some of the best, loving relationships start off as friendships."

I sneaked a look at Kaitlyn. Her face was blank.

"So what do you guys think you should do? You like someone more than a friend, how do you let them know?" Hal threw the question out to the crowd.

"Have a friend tell her for you," a boy shouted.

"Yeah, saves you the embarrassment if they don't like you back."

"Text her."

"Ask him to Sadie Hawkins!" A group of cheerleaders cheered.

I couldn't help it, my cheeks flamed. I tugged my hair out of its ponytail and let it fall in front of my face. I hung my head and doodled in my notebook like Nick. I wanted to see what Tom was doing, but no way was I looking anywhere near his direction. I drew a tiny snowcapped mountain peak. By the time the bell finally rang, I had an entire mountain range stretching across the top of my page.

I stopped at my locker before lunch and out fell another note. Seriously, I was so done with this place. I shoved the note into my back pocket unopened.

Kaitlyn and I were the first to arrive at our lunch table. The sun shone through the windows and glistened off a row of icicles dripping off the roof.

"I've been thinking," Kaitlyn said.

"Uh-oh."

"Come on. Listen. This is serious stuff. You want to go back to California, right?"

"It's not going to work. Don't worry about it, Kaitlyn."

Ashley the Virgin Goth Girl and Brett the pierced face guy actually smiled at me as they came to the table. I nodded hey, then leaned closer to hear Kaitlyn over the increasing clamor.

"No, listen," she said. "I was thinking about what you should do. Even though your parents sent you here, they wouldn't want you to lose touch with the rest of your life that was important to you. Wouldn't they want you to go back to California at least for a visit?"

"What are you trying to say?"

"I'm saying that you should go back, but you don't have to do it on your own. We could plan it as a trip, together. I mean, if you wanted me to come too."

I looked at her, digesting this new idea. I smiled. "I'd love for you to go with me."

Kaitlyn clapped her hands. "Yay! We could go for spring break."

"What about spring break?" Nick plunked down his lunch tray. "You in bikinis, running wild?"

"Shut up. *We* are going to California," Kaitlyn said.

"Oh man, I want to go to California."

"*You* are not invited."

"How come? I'd behave. Please."

Kaitlyn rolled her eyes. "We haven't even made any plans yet. So hold your horses. First things first. We need to find Cara a date for Sadie Hawkins."

"Did you hear who asked Tom?" Nick asked.

"I don't even want to know," I said.

"Ann-Marie Fidesco."

"No!" Kaitlyn scrunched up her nose.

Big surprise. "Forget it. I don't even like him anymore."

"Maybe he's such a nice guy, he just didn't know how to say no to her," Kaitlyn said.

"He's Mr. Basketball Star. She's Miss Wannabe Popular Cheerleader Skank. I don't see anything wrong with this picture," Nick said.

"If she were, like, a nice cheerleader, a sweet person, then it could be understandable," Kaitlyn said. "Or if she was irresistibly gorgeous, or smart, or anything, just not Ann-Marie Fidesco."

"Maybe he just wants to get laid." Nick said.

Kaitlyn crossed her arms and glared at him. I had already been crossing my arms and glaring for most of the conversation.

"This is Cara's crush we're talking about. We are not going to give up on him that easily."

"Says who?" I said.

"Maybe he'll need rescuing at the dance. There's no way he can actually like her. So, all the more important for you to be there."

"I still think you should ask my brother," Nick said.

"No, she should ask *my* brother!" Kaitlyn said.

"I'm not going," I said, crossing my arms even tighter.

One of the dripping icicles broke from the roof and shattered on the sidewalk below. The shards sparkled like cut glass.

"Just as friends, you know, no pressure, just fun." Kaitlyn reached over and touched my arm with her missing-fingers hand. "And this is the other thing I was thinking. Your parents sent you here, to go to school because they wanted you to have these experiences, right? And your uncle, he would want you to go to the dance and have fun too. Don't you think?"

She gently squeezed my wrist. "Maybe it's time to move forward. For both of us."

And that's how I ended up going to Sadie Hawkins with a totally hot college guy.

41

The high school powers that be decided this year's Sadie Hawkins dance was not going to be a casual affair. Last year's theme was a country barnyard dance, and there was more activity in the haystacks than on the dance floor. So I've heard. This year's dance was supposed to be classy, to encourage students to be on their best behavior. Not quite semiformal like homecoming, but classy chic. Whatever that means.

I told my grandparents the Thursday before the dance, half hoping it was too late to get a dress. Grandma didn't even twist her mouth in irritation, but told me to follow her down into the basement. She went over to the area where I had seen the goose's little clothes hanging up and rifled through a few garments draped in cellophane bags. She took them down one hanger at a time and handed them to me. We carried them upstairs and draped them over the couch. Dresses. Dresses my mom had worn to dances during high school and college. Each one beautiful in a simple, nonfussy way. Just like my mom. I touched the silky fabrics: black, turquoise, red, lilac.

Grandma sniffled, and I glanced over at her. Her eyes were shiny. Grandpa came up behind her and put his hands on her shoulders.

"I remember her wearing these dresses just like it was yesterday," Grandma said, her voice wavering. "You're welcome to wear them, she would want you too. I don't guess they're in style now though. We can buy you something new."

Seeing Grandma on the verge of tears, I swallowed hard. I hadn't thought about Grandma feeling hurt before, just angry. Then I remembered what Grandpa had said about everyone grieving in their own way.

The lilac dress looked the most outdated, with a ruffle around the scooped neckline. But the others were so elegant and simple, they looked timeless. Taylor Swift could have worn them to the Grammys.

"I'll try them on," I said.

I gathered up the dresses and took them to my room. I sat on my bed and stared at them for a long time before I took them off the hangers. I was almost the same size as my mom. The sleeves were a little too tight on the black dress; my biceps were strong from climbing. Mom wasn't a climber back then. Even though I knew I wouldn't wear the lilac dress, I tried it on. Just to see what she had looked like. I stood in front of the full-length mirror that hung from the back of the bedroom door and looked at the nineties version of my mother.

Was she the woman I wanted to be?

I took off the lilac dress and replaced it on the hanger. Red or turquoise? Mom must have looked stunning in the turquoise one, with her electric-blue eyes. But I had my dad's chocolaty brown eyes. I stepped into the red dress, pulled it up over my hips and slipped the spaghetti straps over my shoulders. Once again, I faced my mother in the mirror. The dress was perfect.

I held out my arms and turned a slow circle, following my reflection. My sunshine highlights had faded, but somehow in these past few months, my muscular pecs had morphed into actual boobs. I was no Becky, but I had curves. I turned and looked over my shoulder. My arms looked strong, my triceps cut, my back sleek and ripply when I flexed. I was a climber girl, a climber's daughter. *But I am not you, Mom.*

I opened the door and strutted down the dim hallway. The living room was ablaze with the setting sun through the front window.

Grandma sucked in her breath when I swept into the coppery glow. I smiled and twirled a pirouette, piano notes of smooth jazz drifting in from Grandma's kitchen radio.

"Woo-wee!" Grandpa whistled. "You look beautiful."

"Just like Lori." Grandma looked at Grandpa, nodding. "Doesn't she?" She touched the flowing skirt of my dress, the red satin shimmering in her fingers.

Grandpa tilted his head, studying me. Then he placed his hands on Grandma's shoulders and pecked her cheek. "You know who Cara looks even more like?"

Grandma turned her gaze to Grandpa.

"You," he said.

Grandma shook her head, but smiled, her cheeks flushing.

Me? Look like Grandma? I raised my eyebrows, but Grandma and Grandpa locked eyes and drifted back in time.

The song on the radio shifted to the sultry sound of saxophone. Grandpa grasped Grandma's hand and slowly spun her around, then they waltzed like I imagined they did on their wedding day. He pressed his cheek to hers, and he winked at me. So fast, I almost missed it. They glided across the living room carpet, embraced by the yellow glow of the lamps, the evening sky deepening to violet.

42

Kaitlyn, Nick, and Josh picked me up for the dance. Josh had driven down from Michigan State that afternoon. He was tallish and thin, probably Tom's height, but without the crooked grin and wavy hair. Josh's red hair was cut short and spiky, and a sprinkling of freckles dotted his nose. I saw a flash of Kaitlyn-Katie without her charcoal smudged makeup. Grandpa said he looked like quite the gentleman in his dark-gray suit with a red tie. (Kaitlyn had told him to match me.)

Even with her heavy makeup, Kaitlyn looked beautiful. She wore a black halter dress, and the contrast with her pale, milky skin was stunning. She kept her hand hidden in a loosely draped black cashmere wrap.

No suit for Nick. He wore black jeans and boots, and a T-shirt printed to look like a tuxedo. He kept his arm around Kaitlyn as we walked into the school. There was a look on his face, I had seen it before, but now I knew for sure what it meant. That question from our health seminar popped into my head. *What do you do when you're friends with a girl but you like her more than that?*

The cafeteria had been transformed into a dim and pulsing nightclub. The lunch tables had been cleared away, silver streamers floated from the ceiling, and a disco ball sent sparks spinning around the room. The DJ yelled, "Whoa-oh oh!" over the thumping music. Ann-Marie Fidesco squealed as she flashed past us, boobs bobbing in her strapless dress. She pulled Tom behind her.

I jerked my gaze away before he spotted me and followed Kaitlyn and Nick over to their group of goth friends. They stood in a corner, clustered together, looking bored. Virgin Goth Girl was a southern belle vampire in a white corseted dress. She eyed Nick and swiveled her hips to the music. Nick was oblivious. Josh had a faint smile on his face, bemused. Kaitlyn grabbed my hand and said, "What are we standing around for? Let's dance!"

And we did. The four of us together, crazy on the dance floor. I made myself bob to the mindless beat of Justin Bieber, and I truly let myself go when the music shifted to the classic song from *Footloose*. I wasn't going to think about Tom. We formed a small circle and took turns swinging each other around. Josh and Nick were wild dancers, with their long arms flapping out to the sides, jumping and spinning. Then the music shifted from fast to slow in a second, and Josh was there with his arms around me, and Kaitlyn and Nick were right next to us.

Josh held me at a comfortable distance. He tried talking to me, but I could hardly hear him, so after a couple *what?*s we stopped talking. Kaitlyn and Nick talked and laughed while they danced, moving closer and closer to each other, then Kaitlyn rested her head on Nick's shoulder. He bowed his head against hers.

Would Tom hold me like that? I wouldn't be able to rest my head on his shoulder. I'd rest against his chest, and he could rest his chin on the top of my head. And his arms would wind around my waist, igniting my skin with electric sparks the length of my spine. And if I looked up, and he looked down, our lips might . . . was he dancing right now, holding Ann-Marie close, her big boobs squashed up against his chest? I scanned the room and found Tom on the sidelines. Alone. Well not *alone* alone, but with a couple of guys. Most importantly, he was not dancing with Ann-Marie; she was MIA.

The slow song ended, and our group headed for the jugs of lemonade to refuel.

I was examining a tray of cookies when Tom appeared next to me, bumping his shoulder against mine.

"Hey," he said. "Who's the mystery guy?"

"Oh, he came down from MSU," I said.

"Ooh," he said, raising his eyebrows.

I giggled and rolled my eyes. "He's Kaitlyn's brother."

"Hey, a college guy is a college guy. You look amazing." He swept his arm from my head to my toes. "And you seem to have grown a couple inches taller."

I straightened my spine and lifted my chin. I'd forgotten how tall the heels made me. Not quite cheek to cheek with Tom, but close.

"Where's your date?" I asked.

Tom winced. "I think she's puking in the bathroom, but I'm not really sure. She was trashed before we even got here."

"Too bad."

"Uh-huh, serves me right. I never would have asked her out. She asked me in front of a bunch of her friends, and I just didn't know what to do."

He looked right at me, open and honest, and I held his gaze.

"Would your college guy mind if I stole a dance?" he asked.

I glanced over at Josh. He was standing next to Nick, joking around, pantomiming something. Kaitlyn watched me with a huge grin and wiggled her fingers in a wave. I smiled back at her. Tom took my hand and led me out to the dance floor. He held me closer than Josh, his hands sliding from my hips to the small of my back. Our thighs brushed together, and he peered down into my face, a wavy lock flopping over his forehead. Every molecule in my body roared.

"Tom, I'm back!" Ann-Marie clamped her paws around his bicep. She reeked. One of her dopey friends slurred, "We got to get her out of here. Mr. Halloway's already giving us the stare down."

Tom looked back and forth from me to Ann-Marie and her friend. He stepped away, but grasped both of my hands and squeezed. "Sorry, Cara." And then he was gone. He stalked ahead of Ann-Marie, leading the way, letting her friend half-stumble with her.

Kaitlyn came up beside me. "Well, that sucks."

"Yeah." I sighed. "But it was a nice sixty seconds."

Grandpa was reclining in his chair reading a book when I got home. He wore his usual bedtime outfit, flannel pants and a sweatshirt, which was exactly what I wanted to be wearing at that moment. I kicked off my shoes and flopped on the couch.

"How was it?" he asked.

"It was fun. I like dancing, but my feet are killing me."

Grandpa chuckled. "You'd think your feet would be as tough as stone after cramming them into those tiny climbing shoes of yours."

"I know, but wearing heels is a whole other thing."

"Grandma tried to wait up but she got too sleepy. She said she hoped you had a good time."

"Thanks," I said, yawning. "I'm beat. See you in the morning."

I limped to my room and struggled out of my dress. I hung it back on the hanger, and whispered, "Thanks, Mom."

Freshly laundered and folded clothes from Grandma were stacked on my desk with a note resting on top. Blue-lined notebook paper, folded into a small square.

The note I had shoved into my jeans pocket last week, unread. I unfolded the paper, square after square. Slanted, messy writing, in pencil.

He should have said yes.
Turn him into your belay slave.

43

In the morning, I reread the note. What the hell? Should I be reporting these to someone? But the notes weren't actually threatening; they were just weird.

He should have said yes. Was the note writer talking about Tom? Only Nick and Kaitlyn knew about it, unless someone else at school had heard. I thought I had ruled Nick out, but . . . Who was doing this!

I tossed the note onto my desk and checked my phone for the first time in days. Dead. I plugged it into the charger. Tom had never called me before, but he could get my number. I remembered the warm weight of his hands on my hips, on my lower back. I watched my phone, but the screen stayed black. My rumbling stomach sent me to the kitchen.

"Wait until you go outside, Carabou. It's like spring," Grandpa said with a smile.

He was right! Spring was here. After gray skies and subzero temperatures for months, forty-five degrees and sunny felt downright balmy. I would have bundled up in heavy fleece in California if it was below fifty, but today I only needed a sweatshirt. I knew right where I wanted to go. I stuffed my climbing shoes and chalk bag into my backpack and headed out for a walk. After half a mile, I found the spot. I stopped under the railroad viaduct and ran my hand along the stones that made up the wall. I had ridden my bike past this spot on the way home from Kaitlyn's, but it turned too cold before I had a chance to return and check it out. It was perfect for bouldering.

It was dim and cooler out of the sun, and my breath puffed into the air. I rubbed my palms together for warmth. I was the only one around. Not like back home in the Angeles Forest where there was almost always someone else hanging out in the most popular climbing areas. I had to tell Jake about this place.

"Echo!" My voice reverberated off the stone walls.

I pulled on my climbing shoes and tied the chalk bag around my waist. *Climb on*, I said to myself. No jug holds here, no brute strength needed, no dynos. Just a graceful, deliberate dance across the stones. The rock climbing puzzle. Finding the perfect matching pieces. Crack to crevice to nub to flake. When every piece falls into place, it's like a dance, a delicate but powerful balancing act. The art of holding on and letting go at the same time.

I traversed the wall until my fingertips were raw, my toes numb. I walked home with my forearms burning. I found Grandma standing in the yard, staring down at the soggy, dead flower beds. The plastic flowers from the window boxes lay in a heap on the straw-like grass. They had been covered in snow for so long, I had forgotten about them. She just stood there, surveying the yard, looking lost.

"Are you going to plant some new flowers?" I asked. "I could help."

"Nah." She shook her head. "It'll probably snow tomorrow."

"Whatever." I wasn't going to let her get me down.

I tossed my climbing shoes and chalk bag in the corner of my room and checked my phone. Fully charged with one text. Coach Mel. *Miss you.*

I squinted at the picture. The team was at the exhibition event in Tennessee. There was Becky in a star-spangled skimpy outfit, Zach's arm around her shoulders, one hand raised in the peace sign.

I clicked off my phone. Whatever. I didn't want to think about competition climbing; I just wanted to enjoy the feeling from my dance across the stones.

But I couldn't stop checking my phone. I looked at the picture from Coach again, zoomed in and studied the climbing wall in the background.

Still no word from Tom.

44

Stupid Michigan. Winter was back by Monday. Grandma wasn't being negative, she was being realistic. The last dried-up bloom on my Christmas cactus crumbled in my fingers. The plant arched and stretched toward the stingy daylight. The cold seeped through my jacket as I trudged to school. A mist of frozen rain and tiny snowflakes spat into my face. I couldn't believe it. What kind of place was this? Why would anyone want to live here? Weather that plays tricks on you, never-ending winter.

I shoved my hands into my coat pockets, my fingers automatically searching for the smooth stone from Mount Chimborazo. It wasn't there.

I stopped in the middle of the sidewalk and carefully felt the lining in my pockets. I pulled one pocket inside out, then the other. No holes. No stone.

I nudged the slushy snowy ground around my feet and bent down to peer closer.

I started walking again. Maybe it fell out at home. I'd look for it later. It was just a stone. But my heart thumped and my stomach turned twisty. It wasn't just a stone.

I turned around and half-ran, splashing through slushy puddles. I slipped on a slick patch right in front of the house, landing on my hip, my hands thrust into the snowy bank trying to catch myself. The cold shock made me gasp.

I shoved myself up, my hands stinging, my pants soaked. I blinked back tears and choked on a rising sob.

Grandpa opened the front door and eyed my wet pants. "Oh no, did you fall?"

I threw my backpack to the floor and yanked off my boots. "My stone is gone!"

"What stone?"

"My stone from Chimborazo. Uncle Max's stone. It's always in my pocket."

"It fell out when you fell down?"

"No. It was already gone." I ran down the hall to my room, my eyes scanning the floor along the way. I dropped to my hands and knees in my room, searching the carpet.

"What does it look like?" Grandpa asked.

"It's about the size of my thumb, oval shaped and smooth. Shiny black with a coppery line running through it."

He backed out into the hallway. "I'll check in the living room and kitchen."

I felt my way all around my room without any luck. I sat back on my heels. Think, think, when did I last notice it in my pocket?

Grandma appeared in my doorway. "Grandpa said you lost something from your coat pocket? A precious stone?"

I nodded. "It must have fallen out somehow. I know, don't say it. If I would just hang up my coat like I'm supposed to and not toss it on the floor . . ."

"I washed it yesterday."

"My coat?"

"It was so warm outside and you left the house without it, so I thought it'd be a good time to wash it."

I closed my eyes, trying to contain the explosion of anger rising up from my gut. Why couldn't she leave my stuff alone?

"You didn't empty the pockets first? You pulled that note out of my jeans the other day."

"Let's check the washer and dryer," she said.

I popped up and dashed past her to the laundry room. *Please, please, please.*

Nothing on the floor, nothing in the washer, nothing in the dryer.

"What about the lint trap?" Grandpa asked behind us. "Sometimes I find coins in there."

"I already emptied it and didn't notice anything," Grandma said.

"The trash." I went straight to the bin in the corner.

"Uh-oh," Grandpa said. "I emptied it last night. It's garbage day."

We all froze. The unmistakable sound of the garbage truck was right outside. I ran to the front door. Our silver metal garbage can was upside down at the curb. The truck rumbling on to the next house.

My shoulders sagged.

"I'm sorry, Cara," Grandma said.

I shook my head and retreated to my room. I stripped off my wet clothes and climbed into bed. I curled up and hugged little Tahoe. I wanted to have a miserable-sorry-for-myself cry, but the tears didn't come.

45

I told myself the stone didn't matter. It was just something I'd become attached to, and I needed to let it go. When I got back to California, my real rock collection—the ones that Uncle Max had found for me— would be waiting. If they hadn't been damaged by the fire.

But my fingers still automatically probed the inside of my coat pocket, and I kept my eyes on the ground, always searching.

Back at school, Kaitlyn and Nick acted the same as always. Friends. Tom acted pretty much the same as usual too, but maybe like a closer friend. Was I imagining it? He greeted me with his crooked smile and pink splotched cheeks in the hallways, and he stopped by my locker to chat more often. In Algebra II, he sharpened my pencil like always. But now our fingers brushed each time, and once, he put his hand on my shoulder as we walked back to our seats. My shoulder tingled through the rest of class. But that was it. He didn't ask me out, and we never talked outside of school. Did I dream the dance, the way he had held me close? It was like it never happened. And I told myself it didn't matter. There was no point in me taking the initiative with him; I wasn't staying here.

"That's just like Tom," Kaitlyn said at lunch. "I'm telling you, he's never had a girlfriend, ever."

I had a Spanish quiz next, so I flipped open my notebook for one last scan of the words. Another paper airplane popped out from its hiding spot. I plucked it up by the edge of a wing like it was toxic and tossed it to Kaitlyn.

"Are you kidding me?" she said, unfolding and flattening the note. "I don't even know how to pronounce this."

Nick showed up as Kaitlyn slid the paper back across the table for me to see.

HUECO   TANKS, I read aloud. Perfect block printing, black pen. Such completely differently handwriting from the messy scrawl of the other note.

"Texas," Nick said.

"Yep, there's a big bouldering comp every year. Last time I was there, my wrist was injured, and I totally blew it." I clasped my hands and cracked my knuckles.

"So the first note was about one of your successes, a 5.14 climb, and this note is about one of your failures," Nick said.

"Nick!" Kaitlyn swatted him.

"It's okay," I said. "Maybe it's a challenge. And there was another note in my locker last week right before the dance."

"Fork it over," Kaitlyn held out her hand.

"I left it at home. It was like the other notes with the messy handwriting, but the message was the weirdest one yet." I recited the words in a deep, mysterious voice. "He should have said yes. Turn him into your belay slave."

"You are so busted, Nick!" Kaitlyn said with a shove.

"What? Why am I always getting blamed for these things?"

"We are the only two who knew about Cara asking Tom to the dance."

"Correction, there is at least one other person who knew."

"Who?" I asked.

"Duh. Maybe Tom's the one sending the notes."

"Oh c'mon," Kaitlyn said. "Why would he do that? Why would he pretend to be someone else?"

"Yeah," I said. "He already told me in person at the dance. If he was going to send a note, he could at least be himself."

"Well, maybe he told someone else. I mean, if he liked you, one of his friends would know about it, right?"

"That'll be easy to narrow down. He hangs out with the whole freakin' basketball team," Kaitlyn said.

She turned to look at Tom's table. Just Tom and his basketball buddies wolfing down piles of food. No girls. Ann-Marie had relocated back to the cheerleader table.

"So now we have two mysteries," I said. "Two different sets of handwriting, two different kinds of messages. Different people are sending these notes."

Sleet pelted the window next to our table.

"And what's up with this weather," I grumbled. "This sucks."

Kaitlyn shrugged and said, "You just have to enjoy the surprise warm days, but you can't expect them to stick around for sure until April or even May."

"May!" I groaned. "I'm never going to make it."

"That's why there's spring break. It's less than a month away. We've got some major planning to do."

"California, here we come!" Nick beat his hands on the table in a drum roll.

"*We* does not include *you!*" Kaitlyn said.

Grandma was inching her way around the living room with her feather duster when I got home from school, but she paused in front of the TV.

"Those hotels should turn them all away. Serves them right for letting those kids in without their parents."

Grandpa's face was mostly hidden behind the newspaper. If Grandma was expecting a response, it wasn't coming from him.

I kept moving toward the sanctuary of my room but caught a glimpse of wild Florida spring breakers on TV as I passed through.

Oh great, now how was I supposed to ask Grandma and Grandpa if I could go to California? Grandma was going to think I was trying to go on a party spring break trip.

I opened my closet doors, sank down on my knees, and pulled out the cardboard box filled with my books and magazines. Grandpa had offered to build me a bookcase, but I had told him no. Setting up my books would feel too permanent. I couldn't do it. I was losing myself. I didn't know who I was anymore.

I skimmed my books looking for answers. John Muir wrote, *Here is calm so deep, grasses cease waving . . . Wonderful how completely everything in wild nature fits into us, as if truly part and parent of us.*

Going to the mountains is going home.

I would approach Grandpa first. He was the most understanding, the most reasonable. I didn't want to make Grandma any more anxious. I would tell Grandpa about my plan to go to California for spring break with Kaitlyn. And if he said no, well, I would just have to go without his permission, without his help. I would find a way. I had to.

46

I kept trying to catch Grandpa alone, but Grandma always seemed to be within earshot. Kaitlyn and I needed to make our plans; I couldn't wait any longer. I'd ask Grandpa to take me practice driving after dinner. When it was just the two of us in the car, I'd make my spring break case.

But before I could bring it up, he surprised the crap out of me. We were sitting down to dinner when he dropped the bombshell.

"Cara, we've noticed that you've been making a real effort to study and complete your homework. Your grades have improved remarkably. We're really proud of you."

Grandma nodded in agreement, but her lips pressed together into a firm line. The wrinkles in her forehead furrowed deeper.

I nodded back. We were all sitting around the table like bobbleheads. No one had started eating.

"We have a proposal for you," Grandpa continued. "And if you're not comfortable with this, you speak right up. Because your feelings are the most important here."

What was going on?

Grandma's eyes were fixed on Grandpa's and her fingers gripped the edge of the table. She looked like she was going for a car ride.

"We'd like to take you on a spring break trip. You haven't said anything, so we weren't sure. But we thought maybe you'd like to go back to California for a visit."

My heart rose into my throat.

"I thought it might help you to be back home again, in the mountains."

I met his gaze. Words went unspoken, but they were there: fire, cabin, Uncle Max.

"But if you're not ready for this, we—"

"No, no, I'm ready," I squeaked.

Grandpa beamed. Grandma still had a death grip on the table.

"But how will we get there? I mean, Grandma can't fly, or ride in the car."

"Right, Grandma and I have been talking about that. And we decided to rent an RV."

Oh my God. I was going to be RVing across country like a retiree. Freaking hilarious.

"It'll be just like being in a house," Grandpa said.

Grandma didn't look convinced.

"Can I take a friend? We'd have room, right? In a big RV. Kaitlyn could come with us?"

"If you'd like."

"And our friend Nick? Can we bring him too?"

Grandma and Grandpa raised their eyebrows at each other.

"We'd need to talk to their parents first," Grandpa said.

"This is perfect!" I jumped out of my seat and kissed Grandpa on the forehead. "I have to call Kaitlyn."

Grandma found her voice again. "You can call her after dinner," she said, nodding at my plate.

I sat back down to gulp my meal, my knee bouncing up and down, spastic like Elvis leg on a climb.

47

I squeezed through the hallway crush of students to get to my locker, popped it open, and out tumbled another note. I swiped at it, missed, and my books and folders slid out of my arms, dumping to the floor. The crowd hopped around my mess, and the note disappeared under a trampling of sneakers and boots. It slid down the hall. I snatched it off the ground, brushed off the grit, and unfolded the squares. Slanty messy writing in pencil.

I must confess. Meet me at Planet Granite tonight.

A confession! Really? My insides squirmed. A climber? Jake was a regular at the gym but didn't have access to my school. Tom was at school but didn't go to the climbing gym. Nick had access to school and the gym, but he's sworn up and down that he wasn't my stalker.

I couldn't sit still all day. Mom would have said I had ants in my pants. It felt like ants were running up and down the entire length of my body. I was jumpy and twitchy. In Algebra II, I was so distracted I almost forgot to meet Tom at the pencil sharpener. I scurried over just as the bell rang, stumbled, and dropped my pencil. Tom and I bent over to grab it at the same time, cracking our heads together.

"Oh," we groaned, holding our heads and laughing at the same time. "Not again."

"Oy vey," Tom said, grasping my hand to pull me up. "Call us King and Queen Klutz."

"Muy torpe," I said.

His lips curved into his cute crooked grin. "Ooh, you're getting good."

The algebra problems on the whiteboard made me dizzy, so I focused on the back of Tom's neck as he hunched over his notebook, his cute ears peeking through his wavy hair.

He twisted to look over his shoulder at me. I held his gaze and smiled; he winked.

I must confess. Who?

I told Kaitlyn and Nick about the latest note at lunchtime. They both had to work after school. So that definitely ruled out Nick. Kaitlyn said she'd race to the gym as soon as she got off work.

I found Jake in the bouldering cave at Planet Granite. He traversed the wall, eyes on his next handhold, and didn't notice me coming in. I stood behind him in spotting position as he prepared to pull himself over the roof. He twisted his arm up to reach the next hold and caught sight of me.

"Argh!" he yelled and fell, taking me down with him. He landed smack on his chalk bag, sending up a puff of powder.

"What're you doing sneakin' up like that?" A streak of white chalk smeared with sweat across his brown cheek.

I laughed. "Get off me, you weigh a ton," I said with a shove.

He jumped up and swatted the air to clear the haze of chalk dust. "You're here early," he said.

"I didn't know I had a set time to be here."

"I mean you're earlier than you usually get here."

I shrugged. Was it just me, or did Jake look nervous?

"Over here." He motioned to the corner. "Me and Nate finished puttin' up a new route."

I read aloud the word written on lime-green tape at the start of the climb: "Metamorphosis."

"Yeah, I named it after you."

I raised my eyebrows. "As in Kafka?"

"Huh?"

I shook my head. "Never mind."

"I was trying to think of a song title, you know, 'cause you're a rock star. Get it? 'Rock' star?"

I raised my eyebrows higher.

"Yeah, I figured you wouldn't get it. Metamorphosis. Because you used to climb like a caterpillar, and now you soar like a butterfly." He acted out the transformation, slowly flapping his hands, creeping forward on tiptoe, then floating his arms up and down.

Too funny. I couldn't lower my eyebrows. I couldn't help it, he was just so darn cute. "Are you turning poetic on me?"

Jake hung his head and shrugged.

"Metamorphosis, huh?" I scanned the new route, lime-green tape marking the holds all the way up and onto the ceiling.

"There are metamorphic rocks, too," I said. "It's when a rock goes through a transformation, changing its form, like when it's been exposed to heat and pressure. Chemical reactions, minerals form, different textures emerge."

"Cool." Jake handed me the rope. "Climb on."

I shook my head. "You first." The gym was nearly empty, the ropes hanging in neat, still lines all along the walls. Someone else had directed me to come here today. The ants ran up and down my body again.

"No fair. I put up the route. If you watch me do it, it won't count as an on-site for you."

"Don't care. You go first." I kept an eye on the entrance, waiting for something, anything, I wished I knew what.

Jake looked around too while he tied in to the rope. Who was he looking for?

"Climbing."

"Climb on."

Jake climbed like he had started off on the wrong foot. He made awkward lunges, and almost slipped twice before he even got to the overhang. He tried to maneuver over the crux, came up short, and dynoed toward the next hold. He missed. The force of his fall popped me off my feet, and I dangled in the air.

"Híjole!"

Two hands grasped the back of my harness.

Tom? What was he doing here?

He pulled me down beside him.

"You know you probably shouldn't be climbing with a concussion." He gently touched the spot on my forehead where our skulls collided earlier. "Good, no goose egg this time."

My hands slackened on the rope, dropping Jake.

"Hey! Stop distracting my belay babe! Hold the line, will ya!"

"Sorry!"

"Just bring me down."

I lowered him to the ground and removed the rope from my belay device, waiting for Tom to say something else.

Loud voices erupted from the entrance. Kaitlyn marched toward us, dragging a protesting Nick by the hand.

"I thought you had to work?" I asked.

"We're on our way. Nick has something to tell you." She jabbed him in the ribs.

He looked helplessly at Tom and Jake. More climbers had entered the gym by now. Sensing something going down, they drifted closer to us.

"No, Jake has something to tell you," Tom said.

"I'm confused." I said.

Jake's mouth twisted like he couldn't get his words out, and Tom put him in a headlock. Which was pretty funny-looking with Jake almost a head taller than him.

"I did it," Jake blurted. "I'm the one who wrote the notes."

My eyebrows were glued to my hairline. "What's going on?"

Tom gave Jake a noogie and released him from the headlock.

"It . . . It started off as a way to get you to climb again," Jake said. "We heard you were in town, but you hadn't shown up yet. Then Nick met you at school and said you didn't sound like you were gonna climb anymore. I was like, Whaaaat? I knew you had to climb. I'd read every article ever written about you. I watched the X-games. You couldn't quit. I had to help you."

"Help me?"

"Well yeah, okay . . . it, it was for me too. I wasn't here that first day you showed up. Blake and Nate said you didn't even climb that day. My climbing idol—living in the D! I had to getcha to climb with me."

Jake looked so young and earnest. His tall, skinny body was drooped down, pleading with me, *his idol,* to understand.

"You are such a nut," I said, with a slug to his arm.

"Your turn." Kaitlyn poked Nick again. "Fess up."

"I only said I didn't *write* the notes. I didn't say I hadn't *delivered* them." Nick held his hands, palms up, in his innocent gesture. He leaned toward me and whispered, "Oh hey, thanks for letting me come to California with you guys." His dimples flashed, and he hugged Kaitlyn around the neck.

"You're going back to California?" Tom asked. "When? For how long?"

"We leave on Friday, for spring break," I said.

"But you're coming back, right?"

I glanced at Kaitlyn. "I . . . I'm not sure. I don't know yet." My words faded as I met his eyes. I held his gaze for a moment, but looked away as heat rose into my face.

Kaitlyn spoke up. "There is still a missing piece to this mystery. How come Tom is here?"

"I wanted to make sure Jake fessed up." Tom spoke directly to me. "I made the mistake of telling him about the dance, and how stupid I was, and how I wished I would have gone with you. The next week, he told me about the note he had written trying to get us together."

Jake confessed even more. Now he seemed proud of what he had pulled off. "I gave the notes to Nate, who gave them to Nick, who put them in your locker."

No wonder I hadn't figured it out, there was no single person to blame. Nick was always at school early for swim practice. It would have been easy for him to sneak the notes into my locker when no one else was around.

Kaitlyn shook her head. "You guys are unbelievable. All this time we've been trying to figure this out. You really pissed us off, you know."

"And creeped me out," I said.

Jake looked a little sheepish, but still proud, like the murderer confessing at the end of one of my Agatha Christie mysteries. Nick looked gleeful and way too smug.

"Wait a minute," I said. "So, you've read the climbing magazines and blogs, and you could have Googled me and found out about my first 5.14a and my bomb at Hueco Tanks, but what about the different handwriting? How'd you learn to write like that?"

Jake squinted at me. "Huh?"

"Oh yeah," Nick said, "I didn't deliver those paper airplanes."

"Hang on," I said. "They're in my coat."

I showed them the difference in notes, the slanting scrawl vs. the perfect block printing.

"That's my writing," Jake said, pointing to the messy one. "I've never seen anyone write that other way."

So I was right; two different people had been writing these notes. And I had an idea about stalker number two. I just didn't understand why or how.

"That's engineer writing," Tom said. "My dad writes just like that."

"Why'd your dad send her notes?" Jake said.

"Doofus," Tom faked a punch at Jake. Jake raised his fists and fake jabbed back. "Somebody like him must have done it. And no, it wasn't me," Tom said.

"Not just engineers," Nick said. "My aunt's an architect. She writes like that too."

I kept quiet about my suspicion. I needed to solve this mystery on my own.

Kaitlyn glanced at her phone. "Oh my God! We're going to be so late to work. You okay?" She squeezed my shoulder. "We'll talk more later?"

I smiled and nodded.

"Let's go." She grabbed Nick's hand and pulled him away. I could hear him protesting as they left. "But we were just getting to the good part . . ."

The crowd around us melted away, pointing at other routes, tying in to ropes. Someone turned up the music, "Welcome to the Jungle," and a guitar riff blared from the speaker overhead.

"Darn, I can't believe I fell off my own route," Jake muttered, hands on his hips, head tilting back to follow the handholds and footholds up to the ceiling.

"You going to show us how it's done?" Tom asked.

A calm heat settled deep into my muscles, replacing my jittery, electric-spark nerves. I lifted my sweatshirt over my head, revealing the T-back tank top underneath. I knew I looked as strong as I felt, and thanks to my recent growth spurt, I even had curves. The look on Tom's face added fuel to my confidence, and I tossed my sweatshirt to him. For the first time, I understood how Becky must feel when she climbed. Climbing brings you attention, makes you interesting—to boys.

I tied in to the rope, took a slow deep breath, and climbed. My breath remained steady; my body knew the route before my mind figured it out. I twisted and stretched, reached and pulled, pushed and danced and floated to the top. I slithered upside down across the ceiling and clipped the final bolt. Tom whistled.

"Right on!" Jake pumped his fist, then lowered me down.

"That's why I named it after you." He released himself from the belay and floated his arms up and down. "Butterfly," he called out over his shoulder as he pranced away.

Tom and I cracked up as Jake joined a group of climbers at another route. I lifted my ponytail, cooling the sweat at the nape of my neck.

Tom rested his hands on my bare shoulders, leaned his mouth close to my ear, and whispered, "That was so hot."

The tiny hairs at the back of my neck prickled. Electricity shot straight to the depths of my belly and radiated beyond.

"I could watch you all day," he said and kissed my cheek.

It wasn't ants dancing up and down my spine; I was sprouting wings.

48

Back at home, I found Grandpa sitting in his usual chair. Instead of the newspaper, a photo album rested in his lap. He looked up at me, sniffled, and gave me a soft smile. Had he been crying? I couldn't see his eyes well enough behind his glasses.

"Are you okay?" I asked.

"Oh sure."

"Grandma in bed already?"

"Yup." He motioned me over. "Come see."

I rested on the arm of his chair and peered at the photo album.

"Do you know who this is?"

It was a picture of a girl about my age, sitting on the concrete steps of a front porch. She wore a denim skirt, and her legs were stretched out and crossed at the ankle. The photo was in color, but it looked fuzzy and faded. The girl's hair was dark blond, long and layered.

"My mom?"

"Yep. When she was your age. You look so much like her. Her hair lightened up to a golden shine just like yours when she started spending so much time outdoors with your father."

He turned a few more pages in the album. There was Mom on her high school graduation day. One picture with Grandpa with his arm around her waist, the next one of Grandma with her arm around Mom's waist. Everyone grinning, saying cheese and smiling for the camera. Then a shot of the Mustang loaded up with her belongings to take to her dorm room at Eastern Michigan.

Each page held a year's worth of birthdays, Christmases, and then, there I was. A teeny, tiny baby in Mom's arms. Dad with a scraggly ponytail and beard, standing stooped behind her, his arms encircling her waist. Page after page, photos of me. Riding in a baby backpack peeking over my dad's shoulder. Standing on top of the giant boulders in our yard in Colorado, stretching arms up to the sky; I'm the king of the world! My hair the same color as the Aspen leaves in autumn. And there was Tahoe, her white and gray fur shimmery silver in the sunshine. Bouldering along the beach in Mexico, Dad spotting me from below, arms up, ready to catch me. A monastery in Tibet, red-robed monks kneeling, Mom and I wearing long skirts with our hiking boots, climbing shorts underneath. California, our little cabin in the Angeles Forest, a dusting of snow, Christmas tree tied on top of our Subaru. And Uncle Max. Sitting next to me in the backseat of the car, our faces smashed against the window, smearing our features, grinning like idiots.

The photos swam in front of me. Grandpa patted my back.

"I just miss them . . . And, and everything . . ." I caught a tear at the corner of my eye with my fingertip.

"I do too, Carabou. I do too."

"All these pictures. We hardly ever saw you and Grandma, all those years. Just the couple summers I came and stayed with you."

"I know. We didn't get to see you as much as we would have liked. We didn't do too badly when you were younger, but as you grew up and your mom and dad moved all over the country . . . It was hard on your grandma. She suffered through the drive down South, but when your parents moved to Colorado then California, well that was it. Margaret took it personally and refused to talk to Lori for a while. There was no way she was getting on a plane, and driving cross-country was out of the question for her too. Your mom, she was always good about sending pictures though."

He lifted his glasses off his nose and wiped the lenses with his sweater, his eyes shiny.

"I don't know, Cara. In many ways, Lori has been lost to us. But I think sending you to live here was a sort of peace offering. A way to reconnect our family."

I took a gulp of air and let myself melt into his shoulder.

49

That night I had the dream again. The world was awash in white. Freezing, wet, choking whiteness all around. Uncle Max's voice. But this time I wasn't tumbling, spinning, falling out of control. I swam steadily forward. I knew I was getting closer. To what, I didn't know. But I knew I'd feel better when I got there.

I awoke thinking about the poem "Diving into the Wreck." Dad had scrawled the words on his latest postcard. It's a poem about facing disaster, diving deeper and deeper into it, and I think Dad was trying to explain what he and Mom were doing. They'd be trekking deeper into the face of tragedy in order to understand and accept and move beyond.

I had looked up the author, Adrienne Rich, and tried to understand. In the poem, you can feel her loneliness. She delves deeper under the sea and finds part treasure, part corpse. Was she trying to understand the death of someone close to her, or was she facing death herself? In my parents' case, it was both.

I also found some feminist interpretations of the poem. They talked about the explorer's quest, diving into the wreck of obsolete myths, especially myths about the roles of men and women. Like my mom, breaking tradition and separating herself from me to pursue her passion. My feelings had moved beyond anger to a new place. I wanted her to summit K2 more than I wanted her home. I could wait for her. But *I* still wanted to go home.

After breakfast, I caught Grandpa alone for a minute.

"You really think Grandma's up for this trip?" I asked, remembering what he had said about Grandma not being able to drive across country to visit us.

"She's going to try her best."

I knew it was selfish, and I should be supportive of Grandma, but I couldn't help thinking about what would happen if she backed out. What if she couldn't do it, what if she refused to go?

"Don't worry," Grandpa said, reading my thoughts again. "Everything's different now. Grandma is full of regrets for not visiting you before. Me too. I wish I would have known how to help her better. We're not going to miss this chance. Plus, we've been practicing."

"Practicing?"

"Yep. We've been taking little drives while you've been at school. We go a little farther each day."

Huh. I twirled my ponytail. That was definitely progress, but I was still worried.

"She can do it. But we'll need to be patient with her, and warn your friends."

"Thanks again for letting Nick come too."

"It'll be a good distraction for Grandma; she'll be watching to make sure you're all behaving." Grandpa winked.

The week flew by as I caught up on homework, packed, and got ready for the trip. Two more paper airplanes appeared with their perfect printing, one in my Spanish notebook, and the other in my physics textbook.

WALL OF VOODOO

WONDER WOMAN

I passed the notes to Kaitlyn. She flattened out the creases. "What do they mean?"

"Wall of Voodoo is at this place called the bunker in Berlin. It's an old Nazi fortress that's been taken over by climbers. I was there with my parents a couple years ago. The concrete walls were old and cracked, full of chipped out chunks, even bullet holes. And climbers have glued on rocks and plastic holds. It's a crazy fun place, but it has an ominous feeling too."

"And this one, *Wonder Woman*, your secret Indiana She-Jones identity?"

I smiled. "It's a climb at Diablo Wall, on an island in Spain. The cliffs jut out over the water. So you don't need a rope, it's all free climbing, you fall and splash into the sea."

"How does someone know all this about you? Maybe we need to tell someone. What if he's a psycho stalker?"

"You know, it's not creeping me out anymore. There's something familiar about it, like the person is reading my mind. He knows my special memories, but not in a hurtful way. I don't know, maybe I'll think of something over the break."

After school on Friday, I went over to Kaitlyn's house to help her pack.

"Just because it's California doesn't mean it's warm all the time," I said. "It'll be warm during the day, but we'll be in the mountains, and it cools off in the evening. You'll need sweatshirts and jeans."

I could hardly tell what she had packed, the entire suitcase was full of black clothes. She opened a dresser drawer and dug down to the bottom, pulling out a pair of faded blue jeans.

"I only have one sweatshirt that I can wear. I'm still not wearing the MSU one that my brother gave me."

I nodded. "Just bring a sweater, and you can borrow one of my tops."

Kaitlyn was on the path to healing, but I didn't know how she'd take the final leap and trust a guy again. Or trust herself to be in a relationship again. I'd thought the Sadie Hawkins dance would be the bridge for her and Nick, but they sure were taking their time crossing it.

She tossed the blue jeans into her suitcase. One spot of color on top of the pile of black.

"What about you?" she said. "You finally get to go home. But you're not staying there, are you? Not yet, I mean."

I sighed. "I haven't let myself think that far ahead. It's what I've been wanting—needing—this whole time. I . . . I don't even know if the cabin is livable after the fire. But I can't imagine how it will feel to have to let it all go. Again."

Kaitlyn's lava lamp oozed and mesmerized. A purple blob broke free and swam to the surface.

"You'll know what's right when you get there," she said, squeezing my hand.

Back at home, I set my packed suitcase by my bedroom door and tugged my box of books and magazines out of the closet. I carefully taped the cover back onto my worn, neglected copy of *Walden*. Maybe Thoreau's words would make sense again out in the wilderness, back at home. I slid the book into my backpack and zipped it closed.

The Christmas cactus on my nightstand was loaded with tightly closed coral-colored buds. Grandpa had noticed it that morning.

"How about that. It bloomed at Christmas, and now it's ready to bloom again at Easter. Watch now, it'll probably happen while we're gone, and we'll miss the whole show."

I gave the plant a drink of water and hoped it would be enough to sustain it while we were gone. Outside of my bedroom window, the RV loomed in front of the garage, taking up the entire driveway. The cabinets in the tiny kitchen were already packed with food and dishes and games and Grandma's arsenal of cleaning supplies. I really hoped she hadn't stashed some mothballs in there too.

I looked back at my box of books on the floor, judging its size.

We still had to load our suitcases, and Kaitlyn's and Nick's. But those outside compartments were pretty deep.

I hoisted the box off the floor, grunting with the weight, and poked my head into the hallway. Blue TV light flickered beneath my grandparents' bedroom door. I crept down the hallway, through the kitchen, and out the side door, my arm muscles complaining. I set the box down on the driveway with another grunt and opened the side compartment.

I rearranged the camping and climbing gear, and hid the box at the back of the compartment. Climbing rope coiled on top, rolled-up sleeping bag shoved in front. I closed the door, then hustled back to the house, shivering in the frigid night air. I had one thing left to do.

Back in my room, my clock glowed green, 11:26 p.m. I rested against my headboard, pillows propped at my back, knees pulled into my chest, phone in my palm. I had spent half of the evening rehearsing what I'd say.

Tom answered on the first ring.

"I was afraid you weren't going to call," he said.

The sound of his voice, husky soft, tangled my rehearsed conversation into a knot.

"You okay?" he asked.

"I'm okay."

"So this is it, huh? Your last night."

"I can't believe it's here already."

"I could kick myself for waiting so long to talk to you."

"Me too."

"What? Kick me or yourself?"

We laughed together for a second.

"There's something I've been wanting to tell you," he said.

"O-kay?"

"Remember that day at driver's ed, when I told you I was nervous about driving?"

I rotated my wrist, the beaded bracelets tangled together.

"Well, I didn't tell you the whole story, about the car accident I was in."

He paused, and I felt the chill in the air. I burrowed my feet under the covers, scrunching my toes into the soft flannel sheets.

"I was twelve, and I had spent the weekend with my cousin, Adam. He was just a few months older than me. We grew up together and hung out all the time. By the end of that weekend, at his house, we were fighting like we were brothers or something. When it was time to drive me home on Sunday, he raced to the car and called shotgun. I complained and whined no fair, and we were horsing around. And my aunt said, 'Tom can ride up front, he's our guest this weekend.'"

Tom paused again. "You still there?"

"I'm here, I'm listening." I twirled my ponytail, worried about what was coming next.

"It seems so stupid now. I mean, who cares if you ride up front or not. And why did I even want to ride up front next to my aunt? Why didn't I want to sit in back next to Adam?"

"We were driving home, and my aunt turned left at a yellow light, and a huge SUV plowed right into us."

I sucked in my breath. My fingers knotted in my ponytail.

"The rest of the accident is a blur. Glass shattered, the airbags went off and pummeled me, but I was fine. My aunt was fine. But the SUV had rammed the door where Adam was sitting. And he wasn't wearing his seatbelt."

"Oh, no." I hugged my knees tighter and closed my eyes, wanting to shut out the picture of the accident forming in my mind. Shattering glass, the scar on Tom's lip.

"I remember my aunt telling us to buckle up, but I guess she didn't check to make sure Adam did. I mean, he was twelve. But he was sulking in the backseat since we were fighting and I got to ride up front . . . And he was poking me and kicking my seat, and I half-turned around and yelled at him to cut it out . . . Who knows, maybe he had his seatbelt on at first, then took it off to switch spots . . . and it might have been just as bad even if he was wearing his seatbelt. I can make myself crazy with all the 'what if' questions, you know?"

"I know." I had been shoving those same questions down, stuffing them away, for months. What if I had asked my parents to stay with me at the competition? What if they were there just one day earlier or later? What if the rope connecting to Uncle Max hadn't been severed?

I knew what Tom was going to say next. His cousin Adam sprawled on the ground, motionless. His body battered and broken. Uncle Max swept in the avalanche, pummeled and buried by a freight train of snow.

"He almost died."

My eyes snapped open, and I sat forward. "He survived?"

"Yeah, he made it, but it's been a really long recovery, like years. I wanted to tell you, because . . . I know it's not the same as what you're going through, but I wanted you to know I understand, at least a little, how you've been feeling."

"Thank you. That means a lot. I'm so sorry about Adam."

"Yeah, I was really close to him, you know, like a brother. And it's been really tough for my aunt, too. There were a lot of witnesses, and the police said it wasn't her fault. Her car was almost through the intersection, and the other guy came speeding through as the light turned red. But still. She felt responsible. Like she should have seen him coming or something."

"That's so hard."

"Yeah, they moved away so Adam could go to this special treatment program. It's weird because it feels like he's gone, but really he's still here. I kind of said good-bye to him, but not really. It doesn't even make sense."

"No, it does." I was thinking of Uncle Max. He had just disappeared. There was no chance to say good-bye.

"You really miss him," I said.

"I do, yeah. But more than that, it's like one minute you feel so alive, like playing basketball outside on a hot summer day, you feel the sun, and you're sweating, you're sinking shots right and left, you're invincible. I'm Kobe! And the next minute you realize you could die. You're gone, just like that."

He let out a slow, long breath. In a deep, slow-motion voice, he said, "And that's why driving freaks me out."

I smiled into the phone. "So, how did you decide to take driver's ed? How did you get past your fear?"

"I just decided I had to do it. Suck it up. Get some cojones. The summer program with everyone from school would have been too much. But I thought maybe I could handle a smaller, private class. That way, if I freaked and dropped out, then at least no one from school would know."

"And then I showed up. Sorry."

"No, that was good. Just by being there, you helped me push through it. I had to pull myself together so I didn't make a fool of myself in front of you. That first day we were driving and Mr. Asshat made you take all those left turns?"

"Oh no, just like the accident."

"No cojones. I almost pissed my pants."

He was being funny, but I felt the fear behind his joking.

"I saw you going to school every day, making this new life for yourself, and I knew that I could get through a stupid driving class. I'd just figure it out as I went."

Making a new life for myself. I hadn't thought of it that way. It didn't feel that way. It felt like I was clinging to a rock face with no end in sight. I sank back down onto my pillows and snuggled deeper under the covers. "How's your practice driving going, now that class is over?" I asked.

"Okay. It still makes me nervous. It's embarrassing. I'm just destined to drive like my bubbie."

"Bubbie?"

"Grandma. What do you call yours?"

"Uh, Grandma."

He snort-laughed. "Wait 'til you hear this, it's hilarious. My mom is a psychologist, so she's always trying out her head shrink stuff on me. She gets an idea during the last snowstorm. She drives us to an empty parking lot at night, and says we're going to do doughnuts."

"Doughnuts?"

"Yeah, you know, where you crank the steering wheel and stomp on the gas, and your car spins around in 360s. You need a rear-wheel-drive car for it to work though."

"This was your *mom's* idea?"

"She's nuts, totally meshugna. The idea was to force me to lose control, but in a safe way. Wide open, empty parking lot, no other cars around."

"Did it work?"

"In a crazy way, it did. It was like being on a rollercoaster, and you're going up, up, up, and you get to the top and you're dreading going over the edge, and then you go flying down, your teeth are rattling and your stomach is in your throat, and aaaaaahhhhh! Then you get off, and you stumble around, and you're like, yeah, let's do it again!"

I was laughing now. "You crack me up."

"Good times."

"It's good that you pushed yourself to get through it," I said. "My grandma started off being afraid of driving and flying, and now she's afraid of everything, to go anywhere."

"I guess it sneaks up on you, when you cut yourself off from everything, huh?"

"I guess. It's just easier for her to stay home, where she feels safe. I understand it a little."

"I had been thinking about you, and how you're so far away from home. After the car crash, Adam was in a coma, and we set up sort of a memorial at the scene of the accident, you know, flowers and stuffed animals, pictures. There's a tree at the corner of that intersection, and people kept coming and leaving stuff there. It's been almost four years now, so nothing is left anymore, but there's still a part of me that's drawn there. I just go sit under that tree sometimes."

"Yeah, I know that feeling."

I curled up on my side, tugging the covers up over the phone pressed to my ear, Tom's voice captured in the warm, quiet space.

"Do you think you'll ever go back to Ecuador?"

"That's what my dad wants me to do. But I'm not feeling like I need to go there. I just feel like I need to go home. Sitting under that tree probably helps you remember Adam and feel connected to him. All of my connections are in California, back in the mountains at our cabin."

"Please tell me you're coming back," he said.

I wanted to get lost in his dreamy voice, swept up in this romance, but I couldn't, not yet. My longing for Tom was all mixed up and twisted together with my longing for home. I was tied to California, like a bungee cord that was stretched to its limit.

"I don't know where I'll end up. I just know I need to go back to California right now." I paused. Tom inhaled but didn't say anything. "I'm sorry."

"Don't be sorry. Just don't forget about me. I'll be thinking about you every day."

His words made my heart skip and spark. "Me too," I said.

"I don't want to say good-bye."

"Me neither."

"Sweet dreams, Cara. My dad used to say, 'Que sueñes con los angelitos.'"

"Sleep with the angels? Much nicer than my dad saying, 'Don't let the bed bugs bite.'"

"Yeah, that's what my mom says."

"My Uncle Max would chime in: 'Don't let the mosquitoes bite. Don't let the mice nibble. Don't let the ticks burrow.'"

Tom chuckled. "And then you were wide awake itching for hours."

"Exactly."

Don't let the scorpions sting. Uncle Max's last words to me, the night before he left with my parents to climb Mount Chimborazo, his laugh echoing down the hall.

Tom yawned, and I yawned back, my eyes watering.

"Que sueñes con los angelitos, Cara."

I smiled and sighed. "You too. G'night, Tom."

I slid my phone onto my nightstand, switched off the lamp, and snuggled back under my covers. The heat from Tom's voice slipped away into the darkness. He'd wait a week for me. Would he wait a year? What exactly was I searching for? I wanted to go home, but was it still my home?

The green numbers on my clock glowed 12:01 a.m. My phone chimed with a mini burst of light. Tom. I smiled. He knew my old crappy phone didn't have emojis, so he'd typed out the words instead. Smiley face with angel halo. Sleepy face with zzz's. Kissy face. Heart. Heart. Heart.

PART III: CALIFORNIA

Tell me, what is it you plan to do
with your one wild and precious life?
  —Mary Oliver, "The Summer Day"

50

All aboard! Kaitlyn, Nick, and I were giddy with the hilarity of traveling in the RV. Little stuffed Tahoe took turns sitting next to everyone. Grandpa concentrated on maneuvering the monstrosity through the local streets and onto I-94 toward Chicago. I thought Grandma would sit tucked away in the back somewhere, pretending she was in a house rather than on the road. But she was sitting up front as copilot. I wouldn't say that she looked relaxed, but she looked better than on any other car trip we'd taken before. Maybe sitting up so high, looking down on all the other cars, made her feel a little more in control, a little safer.

Kaitlyn and Nick looked a little less goth than usual, but it was still enough to make Grandma *tut, tut* under her breath. I was pretty sure Nick wasn't wearing any eyeliner; Kaitlyn still wore her thick line of black curved up at the corners of her eyelids, but no purple black lipstick. Her hair was pulled back into a ponytail. She looked cute, and you could tell Nick thought so too. He twirled his fingers through Kaitlyn's ponytail until she finally swatted his hand away.

We sat on the benches around the table, catching our bags of chips and popcorn as they slid with the bumps and swaying of the RV.

Nick and Grandpa debated the environmental impact of the gas-guzzling RV versus cross-country jet fuel if we had flown instead.

"It's just one trip. Let it go already!" Kaitlyn said.

Grandma had packed a ton of food, filling the fridge and freezer, so we didn't need to stop to eat. Grandpa pulled over a few times to stretch, and we offered to share the driving duty.

"Yeah, right," he said.

Indiana, Illinois, and Iowa, were a blur of sleep, music, reading, and card games. We crossed into Nebraska and camped overnight in an RV park, one of those family places with hot showers, an indoor pool, and miniature golf with windmills.

Kaitlyn, Nick, and I roved around the park, the path lit by campfires and party lights strung up outside the RVs. We passed by a neon six-foot-tall palm tree on one site. How did people even call this camping? The sky was clear, but the stars were drowned out in the wash of electricity.

We strolled through humming generators, country music, and crying kids. At the miniature golf place, Nick shook the closed gate, rattling the fence.

"Closed! Aw, come on, it's only ten o'clock.

"Maybe we'll have time in the morning." Kaitlyn pulled him away.

No time for golf the next morning. No sleeping in, either, with all of us crammed into the RV. We'd brought two tents but decided they weren't worth setting up for the quick stopover. We'd wait until California. Kaitlyn and I had slept on the bunk above the cab, Nick on the fold-down benches, and Grandma and Grandpa got the real bed in the back.

Grandma was up early frying bacon, and the smoky grease hung in the air through Nebraska. When I saw the first car with a Colorado license plate—forest green stamped with a snowy mountain range—I pulled out *Walden* and flipped through the pages. The cover held on tight with the tape, but the spine was broken, threads visible, and a yellowed page slipped out, a passage highlighted and underlined.

I left the woods for as good a reason as I went there. Perhaps it seemed to me that I had several more lives to live.

Mom and Dad were living their life, the one they felt passionately about. They weren't afraid. Maybe they were still trying to learn what the mountains had to teach. They had separated me from that life. Like Thoreau, I left the woods, but he went deliberately while I was forced to leave. Because I had several more lives to live?

Nick and Kaitlyn leaned against each other on one of the benches, shoulder to shoulder, sharing Nick's earbuds, heads nodding to the beat. Nick noticed my book. "Hello? This is spring break. Aren't you supposed to be reading some sappy romance novel?"

"Shut up." Kaitlyn swatted him.

"Yeah, you should read Thoreau," I said. "You'd relate to his 'simplify, simplify, simplify' motto. He's a big environmentalist. Individualism, autonomy . . ."

Nick raised one eyebrow, his dimples flashing. "Fork it over."

I handed him the book. He carefully weighed it in his palms. "What did you do to this thing, kick it around in the dirt?"

I smiled. "It's been through a lot."

Nick's cell phone rang, startling Kaitlyn. She tugged the earbud out and passed the phone to Nick.

"RV express," he answered.

A man's deep voice barked through the phone loud enough for the rest of us to hear, but the words were an angry jumble.

"I'm on the retirement train heading through prairie-ville, where do you think I am?"

Nick held the phone away from his ear. The barking continued.

"We've barely crossed the Colorado line," Nick responded.

He listened for a moment, then stood up and huffed to the front of the RV. "For fuck's sake," he muttered.

He handed the phone to my grandpa. "My dad wants to talk to you."

Grandpa took the phone and assured Nick's dad that Nick was indeed still with us and would remain in our sight the entire time.

"Another charge showed up on my dad's credit card," Nick explained. "Looks like Mike just bought a mountain bike."

"Guess he's getting ready for ski season to end," Kaitlyn said. "You think your dad's gonna go after him this time?"

Nick shrugged. "He canceled the credit card, anyway."

We were all quiet, gazing out the windows, the clouds darkening. The windshield wipers squeaked, clearing the first mist of rain. Water droplets ran along the side windows, the scenery a passing blur of rock-strewn fields.

Soon we reached the forested mountains of the Colorado Rockies. We pulled over for scenic views, and I wanted to take off hiking, get lost in the mountains. Nick stood at the edge of an overlook, gazing out at the snow-covered peaks in the distance.

"See those dead trees?" he said.

The mountainside was covered with evergreens, but large swaths of brown stood among the green.

"I wonder what happened?" I said. "It doesn't look like a fire."

"Pine beetle," Nick answered. "Global warming. It only takes the tiniest rise in temperature for them to survive the winter instead of dying off like they used to. They're feasting on the trees and killing them. This entire landscape is going to be completely transformed."

I stood next to him, quiet, gazing out at the destroyed pine trees. Soon these evergreen slopes would be bare and eroded, like the mudslide-prone cliffs on California's coast.

"Maybe a different kind of tree can grow here instead? Aspens?"

Nick shrugged and continued to stare out at the mountain slopes.

We had aspen trees in our yard when we lived in Colorado years ago. Mom and Dad taught me to rub my hand along the tree bark. White powder coated my palm. A natural sunscreen, we rubbed it on our nose and cheeks.

Nick didn't say any more about the trees, and he didn't suggest a detour near any ski resorts, but I'm sure his brother was on his mind.

I slept through most of Utah, but awoke to the rust-orange, wide-open vistas in Nevada. We pulled over for another scenic view in the dwindling daylight. I breathed in the fresh, dry air, and felt my lungs and heart expand. I had forgotten how good it tasted. I could smell California, we were so close!

51

"Grandma's not doing so good." Grandpa stood next to me at the overlook.

I peered over at Grandma, slumped on a wooden bench with her eyes closed.

"Is she carsick?"

"Not exactly."

"Maybe it's just the mountains, you know, fear of heights, a little vertigo."

Grandpa didn't look so sure. "I'm going to ask her to lie down in the back for a bit, see if that helps."

I couldn't believe it. She had seemed fine. I really thought she was going to get through this. We were so close!

Grandpa helped Grandma lie down on their bed in the back of the RV. She clutched his arm and trembled, looking much worse than that day at the cider mill. The color had drained from her face, leaving her skin as gray as her hair.

"She looks really sick," Kaitlyn whispered.

"We need to let her rest for a few minutes," Grandpa said. "Come on, back outside."

We piled off the RV and stood around, shuffling our feet.

"What can we do?" Kaitlyn asked.

"I've been trying to figure that out for years," Grandpa answered.

"Doesn't she have any pills? You know, Valium, or something?" Nick suggested.

Kaitlyn gave him a warning look.

"What? People take medicine for this kind of thing," Nick said.

"You're right," Grandpa said. "But she's proud of being healthy as a horse. She's never taken any medications; she's one of those people who never get sick. Every spring, I'm sneezing my head off, but she's never even had hay fever. To have to take a drug for her mental health . . . she just hasn't been able to accept that."

I knew it was mean, but I didn't care if Valium knocked her out cold for the rest of the trip. I just had to get to California.

"We have to do something," I said. "She seemed fine before, what happened? When did she start feeling sick?"

"She did seem fine, a little nervous, but not too bad. We were listening to the radio, and she even hummed along. Then we hit the mountains, and I shut off the radio when it turned to static. I was enjoying the views and the quiet, and next thing I knew, she wasn't looking so good."

Grandpa boarded the RV while the rest of us stood around, waiting. I had no idea how to help Grandma. I didn't understand how she was feeling, how it paralyzed her. I should have asked Tom about it, his mom was a psychologist, she might have recommended something. What if Grandma couldn't continue with the trip? No way could we turn around and go back.

"I have an idea," Nick said. "You know how music can affect your mood? It can give you energy, or help you relax. Your Grandpa said they were listening to music earlier, but then it turned to static."

Kaitlyn jumped in. "We could give her one of our phones."

"Let's tell my Grandpa," I said.

We clamored back on board. Grandpa put up his hand to say stop and shushed us. "She's asleep. Let her rest a bit."

Nick grabbed his phone, and we piled back off the RV with Grandpa following, telling him our plan.

"It can't hurt," he said.

"What does she like to listen to?" Nick asked. "I'll make a playlist for her."

"She likes classical and jazz," Grandpa said.

"I've heard her listening to oldies on the radio in the kitchen," I said.

"I'll start with classical, it'll be relaxing for her when she wakes up," Nick said and began searching for songs.

"You know how music makes you remember stuff?" I said. "Like when I hear a song that was my mom or dad's favorite, it takes me right back to a time when I was with them, singing or dancing."

"Music as a time travel machine." Grandpa nodded. "She wasn't so nervous and anxious when she was younger. So, not only might we distract her, but we might even take her back to a more carefree time."

Kaitlyn hopped up and down. "Yeah, like when you hear the theme song from a movie, or like couples have songs that remind them of when they met, or they danced at their wedding."

"Do you have a song?" I asked Grandpa.

Grandpa looked blank for a moment. "You'd think I'd remember something like that, don't you? Margaret loved Rudy Vallee and Frank Sinatra, so any of their songs would be good."

Nick's fingers tapped away. "Here it is, Rudy Vallee, Frank Sinatra . . . girls were called bobby soxers? Ha! Hey, what about *Casablanca*? Did she like that movie?"

"Yes, that's a good one." Grandpa was starting to look excited now. He rubbed his hands together in anticipation.

"What about that song you danced to the other week, when I was trying on my mom's dresses. There was a saxophone?"

Grandpa smiled. "John Coltrane."

"And what about Elvis? When was he big?"

"The fifties and sixties," Kaitlyn answered.

"Well, look at you," Nick said.

"I do work at a music store, you know," Kaitlyn said.

"The King, she liked him too," Grandpa said. "Put 'You Ain't Nothing but a Hound Dog' on there. That'll get her moving."

"Howooo!" Nick howled.

We laughed and returned to the RV in much higher spirits. Grandma was still sleeping. Grandpa said he might as well start driving and asked us to keep an eye on her.

"When she starts to stir, give her some water, then slip those headphone dodads on her."

When I gave Grandma the earbuds, she gave me a crabby glare. I smiled back, knowing she was on the mend. Thirty minutes later, she was sitting up, and after a while she ventured off the bed, clutching Nick's phone, earbuds still in. Nick hopped up and held her elbow, steadying her path through the swaying RV. Pale pink color had returned to her cheeks.

"Howoo!" Nick howled again.

"What?" Grandma yelled.

"You're going to make her deaf," Nick said to me. "What'd you set the volume at?"

"I didn't touch it. It's the same as you had it," I said.

Nick cringed.

Grandma plunked down in the cockpit and handed one of the earbuds to Grandpa. "Listen to this," she yelled.

We drove the last remaining hours until we reached a campground at the edge of the Angeles National Forest.

Nick had picked up *Walden* again while Grandma had his phone. He closed the book and tossed it back to me. "For someone who believes in simplicity, his writing is far from it." He crossed his eyes. "I can't even see straight." We laughed as he fake-stumbled down the steps of the RV.

I paused on the bottom step. It was too dark to see much of the forest, but my lungs expanded as I breathed in the scent of trees. My first step back in California. A chorus of chirping frogs swelled through the night air. Kaitlyn and Nick stood with their heads tipped toward the sky. The stars were brilliant.

52

Grandma and Grandpa had arranged a surprise for me in the morning. My parents' forest-green Subaru drove up to our campsite. Stunned, I watched as the driver's door opened. My parents' friend Susan stepped out.

I ran toward her, and she wrapped her arms around me in a bear hug.

"Cara Carabiner! Wow, look at you. Your hair is so long. You look gorgeous."

I smiled, embarrassed.

She dangled the car keys in front of me. "The Subaru is yours now. I've just been taking care of her for you."

I couldn't find my voice to thank her. It didn't feel right, to have my parents' car. It made it seem so final, like they were never coming back.

"Your grandpa told me you were learning to drive. You might as well use the car until your mom and dad come back. Don't get too used to it though; they *will* come back." Her voice was light and firm at the same time.

I grinned and hugged her again.

I had been wondering how we were going to get the RV down the narrow rutted path to the cabin. I figured we'd have to park off the main road and walk, but I wasn't sure my grandparents could hike that far into the woods.

"I'm sorry, Cara. Your parents asked me to take care of the Subaru while they were away, but we left Max's van by the cabin. The fire—"

My smile disappeared and I dropped my eyes.

"I'm so sorry I couldn't save it. We . . . It's gone." She pulled me into another hug, and I let myself melt into her shoulder.

Another car drove up behind the Subaru. I pulled out of her embrace and sniffed and blinked. Susan wiped the tears at the corners of her eyes with her fingertips.

"There's my ride." She squeezed my hands, then peered closer—my rough callouses, short nails, ragged cuticles. Her lips curved into a soft smile. "Glad to see you've still been climbing. You have a big day ahead of you. Be careful."

I finally found my voice as she drove away. "Thank you!" I called out.

After breakfast, I drove Grandma and Grandpa to the cabin.

"I'll stay at the campsite with Nick," Kaitlyn had said. "It seems like something you should do with family."

In some ways I had wanted her to come. I didn't know how to talk about how I was feeling; it would have been easier just to show her. But she was right, it was something I needed to do with family.

We drove up above the tree line, wind whipping the Subaru, then down and off the main road onto a dirt side road. Dust rose from the parched earth. I drove slowly for Grandma's sake, and the car crawled over the rutted tracks.

The cabin peeked through the blackened remains of the trees ahead. The cedar-planked walls should have been hidden, tucked away in the dense forest, secluded from the road. Most of the alders were gone, disintegrated into ash. Smaller pines stood like ghostly black skeletons, stripped of their needles. Last summer I had looked into deep layers of green, brown, red. This was a gray moonscape. Pitted earth, lumps of coal, charred stumps, timber strewn in haphazard piles.

The green of Douglas firs deep in the forest beckoned, and I inched the car closer to the house. My sycamore tree had survived. Long thick branches reaching out like giant monster arms; I would climb up and sit in its embrace, disappearing behind its curtain of leaves. Now my tree was bare as winter.

I killed the engine. I knew a fire had raged through our forest, but I wasn't anticipating this desolation. In my mind, the cabin and our land had remained the same, a welcoming home. And Uncle Max's little VW van would be waiting for me.

I couldn't look at Grandma or Grandpa. We sat in quiet for a moment.

I opened my door first and trudged across the sandy, rock-strewn yard to the cabin. My heart and stomach squeezed together like a fist. My throat closed so tightly I couldn't swallow.

My cabin. My home. It was still here. Vacant, neglected, charred. The windows had blown out on one side, glass littered the ground. Someone had boarded them up, fresh new planks golden against the soot. I tripped over a hard misshapen object; our wind chimes, twisted and melted.

I glanced behind me. Grandpa and Grandma hadn't moved from the car. I didn't wait for them. I wanted to enter the cabin by myself.

One step up onto the low porch, the front door unlocked. Blood rushed in my ears. I couldn't hear. Everything was silent, still. My home. Our favorite reading chairs by the window with a view of the mountain's ridges at sunset, the futon that should have been over there but was gone. The bookcase remained, but emptied of books. The pegs on the wall for our climbing gear, a rope still coiled. The wood was blackened, the kitchen half-melted, the heat from the nearby fire had caused the most damage on that side.

Watery light spilled through the grimy windows that remained. Speckles of dust claimed the air. I was holding my breath. My throat felt parched. My eyeballs burned.

Outside, the car door shut with a bang, and I gasped.

The air grabbed the sound of my voice and held onto it, filling the empty cabin. I sank down to the floor and rested my head on my knees.

Footsteps entered the cabin and paused. I didn't look up. Grandma and Grandpa shuffled around, surveying the damage, I guess. Glass crunched underfoot. A hand paused on my head, light pressure, and then I was alone again.

When I stood up, my feet were numb. I stumbled over to our reading chairs. I curled up in my chair, dust rising around me, smelling like campfire smoke. I gazed out the hazy window at the destruction of the surrounding woods. The mountain peaks and valleys were ablaze with the yellow morning sun.

The forest was dead. Tears fell until I closed my eyes, shutting out the loss. I tried to recall the memory of our healthy forest, the way it used to look. At the sound of snapping twigs, I opened my eyes and watched Grandma and Grandpa wander past the window. They didn't come back inside.

I sat and stared out the window. And finally I noticed. The forest wasn't dead. Yes, many of the trees were definitely goners. But moss crawled over the rocks and slivers of feathery green poked out of the ground. A tiny clump of wild onion bloomed. Songbirds trilled. The forest was healing. It had been hurt, but it was growing, healing. And I realized it would take a long, long time.

Dad had talked about that poem "Diving into the Wreck." That's what I was doing here today, what he wasn't willing to do, couldn't face doing. Yet.

The cabin hadn't begun to heal. It had stayed still, damaged, but it too could be repaired. Not yet, but sometime. Uncle Max would never be here again; I didn't know if my parents would ever be here again. I looked out the window. They were out there, where there was life, growing and healing.

In my bedroom, my bulletin board of postcards dangled by one nail, the cards crinkled, warped, dusted with soot. I straightened the board on the wall, the pictures and quotes from Dad a blur. Uncle Max's rock gifts were still lined up on my windowsill. I ran my hands over their shapes and contours, and breathed easier. I rolled a cracked geode between my hands, its amethyst interior winking, then set it back down. They belonged here. But then I had another idea for just one of the rocks. Which one? I slid the slice of smooth metamorphic rock off the ledge and carried it out with me.

I closed the door on my way out and found Grandma and Grandpa waiting by the car.

We didn't need to say anything.

"You going to climb today?" Grandpa asked.

"Not today. Tomorrow."

Tomorrow, I'd be ready to climb. Tomorrow, I'd need to climb. I didn't know how to do anything else.

"Look what we found," Grandma said, holding out her hand.

"Morels." I reached out and took one of the funny shaped mushrooms, its oval top creased and ridged like a miniature brain. "Uncle Max was great at foraging, but we never found them here in our woods before."

"Those little shrooms are worth a small fortune," Grandpa said. "Looks like they're just starting to sprout up. We could gather some more for dinner."

I nodded. "Fire is actually good for some plants. The soil heats up and seeds germinate. The burnt trees release a lot of nutrients into the soil."

I handed the mushroom back to Grandma. "There's something else I need to do here," I told them. "You want to come with me? And then you can show me where the morels are hiding."

They followed me across the yard to the edge of the fire-singed woods. I found the spot I was looking for, marked with the cairn. Tahoe's tree. A majestic, big cone Douglas fir. Its thick, fire-resistant bark had protected it through the firestorm. It had been attacked by the heat, but it stood tall, where the smaller, surrounding oaks had collapsed. Its trunk was fire scarred, lower branches blackened, but it wore a crown of vibrant green.

I sat down at the base of the tree, and Grandma and Grandpa joined me. The cairn marking Tahoe's grave was blackened from smoke, but the stones held their place to form a perfectly balanced, squat tower.

"This is where we buried our dog, Tahoe."

Grandpa and Grandma nodded. We sat for a while in silence, letting the forest work its magic. I knew there were fairies out there somewhere.

I set the rock from my bedroom aside and scanned the yard for others. I began to gather them up, holding them in my hand, feeling their individual shapes, sharp and angular, smooth and rounded.

Grandpa joined me without a word, then Grandma. We each added a new stone to Tahoe's cairn, then began the work of building another. Stone by stone, gently, mindfully, balancing.

When we finished, we had created two pillars joined at the top by the smooth slice of metamorphic rock. Strokes of gold and copper melted into the stone's shallow, gray ridges. It would have made a good skipping stone, hopping and skimming the surface of a lake, alive, defying gravity, before sinking to the depths of another world.

53

It's funny how emptiness can make you feel so heavy. That night, my body felt heavy with the weight of loss, and I drifted to sleep. Sometime in the night, I woke up to see Kaitlyn slipping out of our tent. I heard her whispering and giggling with Nick. I knew I'd be happy for her tomorrow, but I was too full of that leaden weight to feel anything.

In the morning, Kaitlyn snored softly next to me, and I wondered if I had only dreamed her midnight rendezvous. I stretched my arms above my sleeping bag, the chilly air prickling my skin. The sun beat down on the top of the tent, urging me to rise. Kaitlyn stirred, murmured, and rolled over, only the crown of her head peeking out of the sleeping bag. I left her sleeping and crept out of the tent.

Grandma and Grandpa were already up, boiling water for tea. We sat around the picnic table, just like we were at home in the kitchen. I cupped my hands around the warm mug and let the steam drift into my face.

"What's your plan for the day, Carabou?" Grandpa asked.

"It's time to climb."

"We're going to go back to the cabin," Grandpa said.

"Really?"

He nodded. "Grandma wants some more morels for dinner, and I thought I'd poke around a bit more. See what can be repaired and what needs to be rebuilt."

I smiled. "That would be great. I can go back with you and help."

"Not now, it'll be a project for another time. You go on and climb today."

I scrambled atop a large boulder at the edge of the campground; twin rocky peaks in the distance, crags and canyons, and a series of dusty hills and gentle slopes to hike through and around in order to get there. The mountain landscape was like a poem, full of depth and rhythm.

Kaitlyn stood next to me. "Where are we going?"

I pointed and said, "See that speck of red on the rock over there?"

"Way out there? What is that?"

"That's a climber. That's where we're going."

"All that way? How long will it take to get there?"

"Maybe forty-five minutes, an hour. Don't worry, we'll go slow."

We divided up the climbing gear, trail mix, and water bottles, hoisted our packs, and headed for the trails. Soon, the well-marked sandy path dwindled, and we hiked along rocky ground.

"This is not a trail," Nick said. "How do you know where you're going?"

"I know," I said.

We headed down a steep slope, slippery with gravel. I knew how to keep my balance, and trotted down the hill, allowing my feet to slide with the gravel when necessary. Nick slipped and slid a few feet, cursing as he went down. Kaitlyn cautiously took miniscule steps, inching her way.

"You're filthy," she said to Nick, brushing off his backpack.

"Look at yourself," he said.

"Sorry," I said. "Should have warned you, not the best place to be wearing all black."

Nick glared and held up his hand. "I already scraped my hand and we haven't even started climbing yet."

"I brought Band-Aids and tape."

We paused for a water break when we reached the uphill part of the trek.

"Are you shittin' me?" Nick said.

"We climbed all that way down just so we could go up again?" Kaitlyn said.

"That's the only way to get there," I said.

"Buns of steel, baby." Nick swatted Kaitlyn's butt.

Kaitlyn headed uphill, pumping her arms. "This better be worth it, Cara."

"It's mostly flat after this."

"Mostly flat, my ass," Kaitlyn said as she scrambled over a boulder.

I grinned. "Sorry, forgot about this part."

We finally reached the climbing wall and dumped our gear on the ground. Kaitlyn and Nick collapsed. Nick's usually spiky hair drooped in clumps over his sweaty forehead. Fortunately, Kaitlyn hadn't worn any of her smoky eye makeup. Come to think of it, she hadn't put any on since we left Detroit. Her face was flushed pink.

"I need a nap," she said.

"I need a transfusion," Nick said.

I rolled my eyes and got to work sorting out our climbing gear. The wall was bolted so I only needed a sling with quickdraws. We were the only group of climbers there, and the quiet of the canyon calmed my mind. This was one of my favorite climbing spots with my parents and Uncle Max. We put up the routes last spring, the cliff lit with sun in the mornings. I loved to feel the warmth of the rocks against my fingertips, as if the sun was shining not just *on* me, but *within* me.

I ran my hands over the base of a route. My fingers remembered the curves and divots in the stone, the pebbly knobs, the sharp edges of a flake. John Muir wrote about currents of life that flow through the pores of the rock. It made me shiver.

"Don't laugh, but this route is named Cara's Conquest," I said.

Of course, Nick snorted and laughed, and Kaitlyn shoved him.

"My dad named it. It took me weeks to master it."

"What's it rated?" Nick asked.

"5.13c."

Nick whistled.

"Go for it, Cara," Kaitlyn said.

I tied the rope to my harness while Nick got ready to belay. Kaitlyn settled back to watch, munching on trail mix like popcorn at the theater.

The climb felt like returning home to sleep in your own bed after a long vacation. Every reach was natural, smooth. I felt strong, confident.

It was a workout, but it didn't test me. It suited my old climbing style. The new climber in me wanted to be pushed, challenged, to use every ounce of strength in me. I needed to be consumed by the climb.

In the gym, I was restricted to the routes that someone else had created. Outside, on real rock, I chose my own path. I reached the top and climbed back down, rather than being lowered. Memories were threatening to burst through, I needed to focus on the climb. I didn't want to think about anything else.

I reached the ground and looked up to find Nick studying me. "What?"

"What the hell was that?" he said.

"What are you talking about?"

"That's not how you climb in the gym."

"What was wrong with it?"

"Nothing was wrong with it. You pranced up there like it was a 5.6, and it's been almost a year since you've even climbed on real rock."

"Yeah, Cara, you rock!" Kaitlyn said.

I smiled and shrugged, proud but embarrassed. I had changed. But it wasn't my gym training that did it. It was life. Life and death, and learning where you belong.

And now it was Kaitlyn's turn. "I'm going to set up a top-rope for you over there." I pointed to a shorter wall, full of cracks and nooks and crannies. Plenty of spots for Kaitlyn to find the right fit for *both* of her hands.

"I knew you were going to make me do this," she said.

"I'm not making you do anything." I pulled my extra pair of climbing shoes out of my backpack for her.

She wrinkled up her nose. "Keep those foul things away from me." She reached into her own pack and pulled out a new pair of purple climbing shoes, the black rubber soles clean and shiny. "I brought my own."

I could not have grinned any wider. I grabbed one of her shoes and rubbed it against the rock wall. "Gotta break these things in."

Nick tied a figure eight into the rope for Kaitlyn while she tugged on her shoes. He handed her the rope and kissed her on the top of her head. "I'll belay for you."

54

We returned to the campground, dust ground into our clothes and the pores of our skin, our legs and feet achy and tired. Grandpa cooked chicken on the grill. I salivated like a dog at the first whiff of barbecue sauce.

"How'd you do?" he asked.

"Great," I said, leaning over the grill and inhaling the tangy scent. "How'd you do?"

"I don't know how to explain it, but even with all the damage, there's still a feeling of life around there."

"I know, I felt it too. You think we can fix up the cabin?"

"I do. It'll be quite a job though, and we'll have to talk to your parents about it."

I nodded. I didn't know when my parents were coming back, but surely they wouldn't object to Grandpa and me working on the cabin.

"Maybe we could come back this summer," I said.

"I'd be up for that," he said.

"Is the new cairn still standing?" I asked.

"Sure is. It sounds strange to say it, but standing near those stones, you almost feel like they're alive. The way they balance and hold together, they're not just stones anymore."

"There's an energy there."

"An energy, yes, something like that."

Grandpa let out a great big breath and wrapped an arm around my shoulder, giving me a tight squeeze. He released me and said, "One more day here in the mountains, then we head to the ocean. What would you like to do tomorrow?"

"Just climb some more," I said.

"Are you sure? Nowhere else you want to go, or anyone else you want to see?"

"Everyone I want to see is right here."

He smiled and squeezed my shoulder once more. "Go tell Grandma the chicken is almost done, okay?"

In honor of Uncle Max, I cooked his special-recipe baked beans, sweet and smoky. Grandma sautéed the baby morels in butter. We played cards until the darkness surrounded us, then Grandma and Grandpa went to bed in the RV. Moths spun around our lantern; the fire risk was too high for a campfire. Kaitlyn's face glowed with warmth. She hadn't worn any makeup all day.

"So, what does it mean really, to be goth?" I asked them.

Nick recited: "Goth unashamedly celebrates the dark recesses of the human psyche."

"I don't get it."

"Life is dark, but we're trying to find the beauty in that, you know?"

"I don't know. I like light and nature and climbing. That's all about living."

Kaitlyn smiled at me. We didn't need words. We understood.

"I'm hungry," Nick said. "Any leftovers?"

"Leftovers? You had two pieces of chicken, those fancy mushrooms, and three helpings of the special beans," Kaitlyn said.

"Good thing he has a tent all to himself," I said.

"I'll be right back," Nick said. He grabbed a flashlight and left the circle of lantern light.

I gazed up at the nighttime sky, the shadows of the forest like questions in the dark. Would daylight reveal the answers? The brightness of the stars took my breath away.

When Nick returned, he kept to the edge of the lantern light. "So you never saw anyone light a fart on fire, huh?"

The next thing I knew, the lighter flared, and a fireball pfooofed through the air.

Kaitlyn and I shrieked, and Nick collapsed on the ground in hysterics.

"Oh my god, did he just—?"

Kaitlyn groaned with disgust. "You did not just do that!"

"You are sick!"

"That's so gross!"

One of Uncle Max's jokes popped into my head. "You want some mustard with that?" I squeaked out the words before doubling over.

Kaitlyn groaned. And I was pretty sure I heard a chuckle coming from inside the RV.

Kaitlyn and I climbed in our sleeping bags after midnight. Through the mesh roof of our tent, the stars and moon gave us a celestial show.

"I'm going to be so sore tomorrow," Kaitlyn grumbled, squirming around in her sleeping bag.

"Yeah, maybe. You should have stretched before bed."

"Now you tell me."

"We'll stretch in the morning."

"You okay?" Kaitlyn asked.

"Yep, you?"

"I saw your big box of books and stuff in the RV. Are you really thinking of staying here?"

"I don't know. I thought maybe I could stay with my parents' friend Susan. Her daughter is away at college now. But it wouldn't be the same as being home at the cabin with my parents."

The sky looked so vibrant and alive compared to the low haze in Detroit. Everything was clearer out here. I hadn't worked out all the pieces yet, but I could feel the unraveling going on inside me."

"Do you want to talk about it?"

"Nah. It just feels good to be here. Especially having you here with me."

"Anytime." She rolled onto her shoulder and kissed my cheek. "Goodnight, Carabou. Indiana She-Jones."

I smiled in the dark and kissed the air. "Night-night."

A minute later, she whispered, "I can't believe I *like* him."

"So he's not gay, huh?"

"Oh no."

"Did you tell him about Eric?"

She nodded. "I told him. He took my hand, *that hand*, and kissed me. And he didn't let go."

Tears flooded my eyes.

"Don't you start crying now," she half-laughed, half-cried.

"I can't help it."

"It's probably a good thing we did all that hiking. It helped him blow off some steam. If I'd told him at home, he might have done something stupid, like drive up to East Lansing."

"Yeah, he blew off some steam, all right," I said.

"Oh disgusting, please, don't remind me."

"It's just guys. My dad and Uncle Max used to make songs out of armpit farts."

"My brother taught me how to do that!"

After a pause, Kaitlyn said, "I'm not sure I know how to be Nick's girlfriend. To be anyone's girlfriend."

"I think you're doing pretty good already."

Kaitlyn propped her head in her palm. The moonlight shone on her hair, turning it silvery purple.

A sly smile spread across her face. "Do you miss Tom?"

"I've been trying not to think about him. But I can't help it."

"You're in love!" she whispered and flopped back on her pillow.

"No, you are!" I whispered back.

Kaitlyn curled up on her opposite side to sleep, but I stayed on my back looking up at the night sky, the twinkling stars. I sent my love and wishes out into the vast universe. *Que sueñes con los angelitos.*

55

We left early the next morning for the last climb of our trip. I preferred shorter routes, but I wanted to take Kaitlyn and Nick up a multi-pitch climb. I needed to remember and understand that feeling that kept my parents climbing higher and higher. And I wanted to cement Kaitlyn's confidence.

"It's only rated a 5.4," I told them. "You can practically walk right up the thing. It's as easy as climbing a ladder."

"5.4 my ass," Nick said.

Kaitlyn stood next to him, gazing up at the mountain. "There's no way."

"It's not as bad as it looks." I raised my arm to gesture. "See, look at all the ledges. We'll take lots of breaks."

"I don't know." Kaitlyn shook her head.

Nick squeezed her shoulder. "You can do it."

"You can, you're a natural," I said. "We'll help you. I'm going to lead-climb up the first section and anchor myself. You guys will take turns climbing up after me. I'll belay you from the top."

"I don't know," Kaitlyn said again.

"We're climbing up to that ledge first," I said. "It's plenty big enough for all of us."

The sun warmed my back, the rocks still felt cool to the touch. The climb was essentially a scramble, but the rope provided extra security in case someone slipped. We followed a gulley straight up the middle. Small shrubs and roots jutted out of the rock and packed dirt, providing extra handholds and footholds. I watched Kaitlyn's every move.

"Breathe," I called down to her.

If I hadn't already known about her hand with its missing fingers, I would have never guessed from the way she steadily, even gracefully, maneuvered up, up, up, with hardly a pause.

We settled on the ledge about forty feet up, each of us anchored to a bolt in the rock.

"This is nerve-racking," Kaitlyn said.

"Just wait till you see the view from the top," I said. "It will be worth it, I promise. You can see clear to LA and the ocean."

"How many pitches are we doing?" Nick asked.

For a moment I considered dodging the question. "Four."

"Four! There's no way." Kaitlyn shook her head and crouched closer to the wall.

I spoke to her in a firm yet gentle voice, the same voice my dad had used again and again with me, inspiring confidence. "I watched you climb up the first pitch. You are a beautiful climber. I would never bring you out here if I had any doubts in your ability. You can do this."

Kaitlyn visibly straightened, and we prepared to climb the second pitch.

No one fell until the third pitch.

I led the route as usual with Kaitlyn following next. Nick watched from the ledge below.

"You look great," he called up.

I smiled. I knew she could do it, but I continued to watch her closely. This part was a little trickier than the others. I held my breath as Kaitlyn grabbed for a bulge of rock that was just beyond her reach.

"I'm gonna fall!" she yelled up to me.

"I got you! Just hang and rest for a minute."

Kaitlyn sat back in her harness and hung on the rope, her hands dangling by her sides, twirling her wrists, fingers flexing, getting the blood flowing again. After a minute, she climbed back on and found a different foothold. I tightened the rope, giving her an extra boost, and she grabbed the bulge she was going for.

"That was scary," she said, but her face glowed with triumph.

Nick began the pitch, climbing smoothly. We were surrounded

by sandstone, high up on the cliff. These mountains were gentle swells compared to the fierceness of Mount Chimborazo. The sun radiated off the rocks and left shadows, some hills brilliant with light, others doused in gray. Bits of scrub brush poked out of the rock, a few tiny purple flowers hid in the cracks. Manzanitas with their twisting branches and roots bulged out of sandy patches. In the distance, Yucca plants bloomed with tall spires of white flowers. Thoreau's words floated across my eyes. "Learn to delight in the simple pleasures which the world of nature affords."

"Faaallliiing!"

I lurched forward, sliding toward the edge of the ledge, my feet scrambling for leverage, dust and pebbles tumbling into space. Kaitlyn yelped and grabbed my harness. My mind flashed to the steep, icy slopes of Mount Chimborazo. The seam of snow splitting as the avalanche ripped Max apart from my parents, threatening to pull them after him.

The anchor jerked my harness backward, knocking the air out of my belly with a grunt. My heart thundered.

"It's okay," I gasped. "We're all clipped to the bolts. Nick?"

Kaitlyn crept next to me and peered over the edge, her hands covering her mouth. Nick swung on the rope and banged into the rock.

"Shit!"

I yelled down, "You okay?"

"Motherfucker!" Blood dripped down his leg.

"Do you need me to climb down to you?" I called.

Nick growled and kicked at the rock as he dangled on the rope. Kaitlyn didn't know how to belay; I'd have to tie myself off and climb down. He didn't look very injured, but the situation could change drastically if his habit of passing out at the sight of blood took hold. *Just don't look down at your leg, Nick.*

Nick climbed back on the rock. *That's right, just keep going, don't look down.* I pulled the rope extra tight just like I did for Kaitlyn, giving Nick a boost.

"Hey! I don't need any short-roping," he snapped.

"Okay," I said, relaxing the rope and dropping him a couple inches. "Here if you need it."

"Fuckin' pisser," he muttered, scrambling back on the wall. He pulled and pushed and hauled himself up to the ledge awkwardly, using raw strength, no finesse. But he was there.

Kaitlyn dug out the first-aid kit and tended to the gash on Nick's knee. Nick's eyes were closed as he rested the back of his head against the rock.

"Nice war wound," I said, pushing the fear out of my voice.

"That's nothing," he said, keeping his eyes closed. "Check this out." He extended his hand, palm out.

"Ooh, nice flapper." I winced. "We'll tape it up. Good thing we're almost done."

"I'm done now," he said.

Nick was right. We'd gone far enough. His fall was a reminder of how quickly things can change on a mountain, even a small one like this, how one misstep can put everyone in danger.

Kaitlyn finished cleaning and taping Nick's knee. She stood and studied my face for a minute as if reading my hesitation. I didn't say anything.

She turned back to Nick. "I'm going with Cara. You can do it. We're almost there. You have to go with me."

Nick opened his eyes, connecting with Kaitlyn's gaze. "Fine, fine, make me suffer," he said.

"Drama goth." Kaitlyn grinned and pulled out the tape for Nick's wounded hand.

The last pitch was an easy, sloping scramble again, leading up to the top of the mountain. Energy poured back into my tired muscles with each final reach and step.

"There's plenty of room to walk around, but stay anchored in," I told them. "I don't want anyone sliding off on my watch." My tone was light, but I felt the weight of responsibility for their safety.

We stood on the crest of the mountain, the wind whipping our hair and rustling our jackets. Blue, blue sky with puffs of clouds pulled apart like cotton candy.

"Wow," Kaitlyn said. "You can see the ocean. It's so, so, huge out there. Everything."

That was what always struck me too. The vastness of it all, our world, so much land, stretching for thousands of miles in all directions. Golden rolling hills dotted with chaparral. Sandstone cliffs, swooping valleys. A winding serpent river. The pencil line of a distant road. A cluster of squares, a miniature town. Rippling green ridges like a sleeping dragon. The glimmer of the Pacific Ocean.

"Those words we always use—awesome, wonderful—this makes you understand what they really mean," Kaitlyn said.

"It's different climbing out here than in the gym," Nick said. "It's like . . . primitive, primal."

Kaitlyn nodded. "It's like you, Cara. Quiet on the outside, but inside there's a wildness. Indiana She-Jones. You can just feel it out here."

I smiled. This is why my parents and Uncle Max climbed. Not to conquer the mountain, but to become the mountain. To feel its power, absorb its strength. To recognize the vastness of the world around us and how insignificant we really are. To soak up the beauty of it all. The enchantment. They had taught me this. And I could feel it, in my body, in the air I breathed. It was the only way to truly feel alive.

Kaitlyn and Nick pulled out their phones and squeezed together for a selfie. They snapped pictures of the panoramic view, but it just wasn't possible to capture the depth of this scenery.

I wandered a few steps away and sat down near the edge of the ridge. The sun had warmed the rock, but the chilly wind needled my skin. I hunched down into my jacket and rubbed my hands together. The wind howled around my ears, as if it wanted to take me, to fling me right off the edge of the mountain.

I want to stand as close to the edge as I can without going over. Out on the edge you see all the kinds of things you can't see from the center.

I remembered the breeze dancing across my face at the top of the competition wall in Ecuador, gazing out toward Mount Chimborazo, sending a wish to my parents on the waves of the wind.

Buena suerte, Mom and Dad. I hope you find what you're looking for. I hope the mountains heal you.

Maybe they were being selfish, not letting anything stand in their way, not even me. But in Michigan, with my grandparents, with Kaitlyn, I had discovered another life, another way to live. And maybe that's why my parents sent me. And maybe my mom understood that my grandparents had already lost too much. They had lost all of their babies, they had even lost my mother in a way. I was the only one left.

Kaitlyn and Nick crouched behind me.

"How can you sit so close to the edge?" Kaitlyn asked. "It freaks me out."

"When I was a kid, I used to imagine myself jumping off the cliffs," I said. "I'd take a running start, leap, and soar into the air like a bird."

"Don't even think about it," Kaitlyn said.

I had confided that to Mom once, and she said she often had that same urge, even as an adult.

And Uncle Max, was it possible that was how he felt? With his adrenaline pumping, did he feel like he was flying, soaring along with the avalanche? It was too painful to think of it any other way.

Annie Dillard had written, *I could very calmly go wild*.

"My parents have a cottage up north on Lake Michigan," Nick said. "This is how I feel when I'm there, standing at the edge of the water. It's huge like the ocean, you can't even see the other side."

"You're coming back to Michigan with us, aren't you?" Kaitlyn said.

I nodded. "For now."

"What else is she gonna do, live out here with the coyotes?" Nick said.

Kaitlyn swatted him, but smiled at me and said, "Indiana She-Jones." Then, "What coyotes?"

I smiled back. "Don't worry."

How I wanted to hold on with my animal instinct like Annie Dillard's weasel, to not let go. Hold on to the cabin, to the mountains, to my wilderness, to my wildness. *We can live any way we want*. We can hold on and let go at the same time.

My fingers swirled the sand in the rocky ridges and pried loose chunks of stone. I felt their irregular edges, smooth, angular, rounded, sharp, then handed one each to Kaitlyn and Nick. We stood and took one last look, drinking in the dangerous beauty.

I pulled my arm back, clutching the stone like a baseball. My body twisted and heaved the chunk of rock, sending it sailing over the edge into the vastness.

Nick wound up like a pitcher and followed, releasing his rock with a grunt.

"I'm keeping mine," Kaitlyn said, tucking her stone into her pocket.

I nodded. "Ready for some rappelling?"

"What?" Kaitlyn said.

"How did you think we were getting back down?" I grinned.

PART IV: HOME

I left the woods for as good a reason as I went there. Perhaps it seemed to me that I had several more lives to live.

—Henry David Thoreau, *Walden*

56

I followed Grandma around the yard, admiring the daffodils and crocuses and hyacinth that had sprung to life. She pointed to a cluster of green stalks surrounding the maple tree. "Those are tulips, they'll bloom next."

I joined Grandpa as he poked along the edge of the backyard, pulling up the strangling vines of ivy, searching for spring wildflowers.

"There's the trillium. And here's the wild columbine and geranium shooting up. No morels here." He nudged the spongy soil with his foot and sneezed. Then sneezed again and again.

"Bless you!" I backed away.

Grandma shared her tentative gardening plans: strawberries, cherry tomatoes, basil. It was as if she'd been hibernating for the past year, and now she was venturing out, step by step.

We planted petunias in the flower boxes and pots on the porch. I left Grandma to dress the goose in her flowered spring dress and bonnet, while I went in to get ready for Tom.

I peeked at Grandma's angel figurines inside their glass case. Kaitlyn was right, this was a curio case of memories. Five babies. Three had died before they were born, the fourth one grew up to become my mom, and I was baby number five. I smiled at the thought of a rock-climbing angel.

There was still a mystery left to solve, and while Grandma and Grandpa were busy outside, I searched for scraps of paper that Grandpa had written on. A grocery list, a phone message. I never paid much attention to his handwriting. His reading glasses rested on the Sunday crossword puzzle in the *Detroit Free Press*. Just as I suspected—perfectly neat, block printing, in black pen. An engineer's handwriting, like Tom had said. Grandpa had access to my notebooks and textbooks, and he knew about my past climbing life. But why?

"You found me out, huh?" Grandpa stood in the doorway, grinning. He held a shoe box at his side.

"The handwriting matches," I said. "Time to fess up."

"Confession, Grandma and I saw two of the other notes someone had sent you. We weren't spying, I promise, one was out in the open when Grandma gathered up your dirty clothes, and one was in your jeans pocket. You know, she usually checks before she tosses pants in the washer. Then we overheard you talking to Kaitlyn about it on the phone. And I was talking to Jake at the climbing gym one day when I picked you up, and the kid confessed everything to me. But swore me to secrecy. Your grandma loves a good mystery. You've seen all her Agatha Christies in here."

"Those are Grandma's? I thought they were Mom's. I've never seen Grandma read anything but magazines."

"You're right. That's one of the things that changed when she stopped going out. She didn't go to the library for books anymore. Maybe that will start to change now. And your mom read all those Agatha Christies too, that's why they're in here now."

"So your Grandma loves mysteries, and she thought we could add to your mysterious notes, make it even more challenging to solve."

"It was *Grandma's* idea?"

"She remembered the *Mystery of the Orient Express*, where every passenger is a suspect and has a secret. In your case, there'd be so many different people involved with the notes, it'd be hard to sort out." Grandpa looked a little sheepish. "I guess we get a little bored staying home all day, especially cooped up all winter."

"But how'd you know I had gone to all those places? You even knew the names of the climbing routes."

"I wanted to remind you of your climbing history and special times with your parents." He held out the shoe box to me, and I took it. "I've been saving this for you, adding to it every year. Truth be told,

I've always been afraid something would happen to your parents. I'm glad I'm not giving you the box in those circumstances."

He smiled and turned to go. "Have fun with Tom," he called.

I opened the lid of the box. It was stuffed full of letters. Letters on notebook paper, stationary, e-mail printouts. Letters from my mom, telling Grandma and Grandpa all about me, for years and years.

I closed the box and sighed. *Wow. Michigan's a mystery novel.* I'd return to the letters later, when I could savor them. They would last me a long time.

My big box of books and magazines was back in my closet. I opened the flaps and reached inside, my hands brushing something soft. I pulled out red yarn, and kept pulling and pulling—a scarf. I gathered it into a ball, my fingers twined in the loops, and held it under my chin. *Kaitlyn.* She'd crocheted me a going-away gift. Or was it a coming-home present? I hung it around my neck and reached back into the box.

I pulled out Annie Dillard and Mary Oliver and stacked them next to Thoreau on my desk. Maybe I'd take Grandpa up on his offer to build me a bookcase. We could do it together.

I sat on the front porch waiting for Tom. I drank in the blue, blue sky and remembered a moment with Mom and Dad when I was younger. We sat at the base of a cliff, resting after a climb. The sky was blue like today with trailing wisps of clouds. My dad had picked up a stick and was slowly waving it in the air in twirls and figure eights.

"What are you doing?" I asked.

"I'm stirring the sky."

That's exactly what it looked like. He was stirring the clouds, blending and swirling them into the blue.

"It's magic," Mom had said.

Thoreau wrote, *Not till we are lost, in other words, not till we have lost the world, do we begin to find ourselves, and realize where we are and the infinite extent of our relations.* Before, I thought Thoreau was talking about getting lost in nature, leaving the busy world behind and discovering yourself out in the woods. But now I wonder if he meant more than that. Last year, I lost the only world I had ever known—life with my parents in the mountains. We had lost the world that held Uncle Max. And now, we were finding our way in a new world.

Grandma and Grandpa strolled across the yard, their shadows trailing behind them. I used to play a game with Dad when I was little, trying to fit inside his shadow as we walked. I liked to be hidden, safely absorbed by his shadow, then stick out an arm, wiggle my fingers, kick a foot. I remembered how free I felt competing in Ecuador, on my own, outside of my parents' shadow.

I felt it strongly now, a stab in my ribs; I had to keep climbing. Somehow, my climbing would keep them going too. It seemed interconnected. I couldn't just sit home and wait. It was time for me to call Coach Mel.

A horn honked, and I looked up to see Kaitlyn and Nick waving from Kaitlyn's beast of a car. I trotted down the walk.

"We're going to work, but wanted to show you my new do." Kaitlyn tossed her head from side to side and flipped her hair. "What do you think?"

Her hair had been cut to just above her shoulders and streaked maroon-red.

"I love it!"

"And she came up with a new name to go with the hair," Nick said.

Kaitlyn opened her jean jacket, revealing a black T-shirt with a picture of a silver-whiskered grinning cat.

"Kat!" she said with a squeal. "That's my new nickname."

"I get it. I love it!"

"And it's even better because her mom got a dog," Nick said.

"Not a chocolate Lab named Cocoa?" I said.

Kaitlyn scrunched up her nose. "It's a Chihuahua mixed with a Dachshund. Who does that?"

Nick couldn't hold back his laughter. "It's a Chiweenie!"

I slapped my hand over my gaping mouth.

"It's a real thing!" Kaitlyn said. "That's what they're actually called." She shook her head.

Another horn beeped behind us. Tom pulled up in his sun-faded silver Escort wagon.

"What are you and Tom doing?" Kaitlyn asked.

"I don't know," I said. "It's a sunny day surprise."

"I was rich, if not in money, in sunny hours and summer days, and spent them lavishly," Nick recited with grandiose gestures like he was on stage.

"Ha!" I pointed my finger at him. "You've been reading Thoreau!"

Nick crossed his eyes. "Someday I'll write my own manifesto, in plain, *simple*, language."

Kaitlyn and Nick leaned out the window and yelled hi to Tom. "We gotta go. Have fun."

"Bye Kat!" I said and waved.

Tom hopped out of the car and met me on the sidewalk. He held out a card in his hand. "Ta-da! I've got my license, whoop-de-do!" And he did a hip swiveling, jump shot victory dance.

I laughed and studied the picture. "Nice mug shot."

Grandma and Grandpa came around from the backyard, the knees of their pants stained with dirt.

"Nice car," Grandpa said.

"Ha-ha. I wish," Tom said.

Grandpa chuckled. "Your time will come. You've checked this one out? The tires, oil, gassed up?"

"All set. It's ugly, but safe."

"Bring Cara back in time for dinner, and you can eat with us," Grandma said.

We waved good-bye and headed out to enjoy the glorious day.

"So what's this surprise?" I asked.

"You'll see when we get there."

We sped onto the highway, in the opposite direction that I had taken with Grandpa toward downtown Detroit. This time, we were heading north out of the city, through the layers of suburbs, until the subdivisions almost disappeared, replaced by trees and open space. Tom looked more relaxed driving than I had ever seen him. His car was a stick shift, and he smoothly switched the gears. He was still a careful driver, fifty-five miles per hour, cruising in the right lane.

He noticed my smile. "What's so funny?"

"Nothing. You. You're driving great!"

"Thanks. I've been practicing. For you." He took his eyes off the road just long enough to glance at me and smile. "It took me a while to get the hang of a stick, but I think it makes me less nervous. I have to concentrate on shifting."

"Kensington Metro Park," he said, reading the highway exit sign. "I thought about going down to Belle-Isle in Detroit, but I know my way around here better."

"What's Belle-Isle?"

"A big park along the Detroit River. It's really pretty. Not what people expect when they hear Detroit."

"Next time."

He reached over and squeezed my hand.

We drove along the curving roads inside the park, passing green lawns, signs for hiking and biking trails, a sparkling lake.

"Have you ever been to Lake Michigan?" I asked.

"Sure. Sleeping Bear Dunes, Petoskey stones, pasties."

"Pasties?"

"Little pies stuffed with meat and veggies. Yum."

"Pupusas and pasties. I've been missing out. Nick said we could all go to his cottage on Lake Michigan this summer."

"You're gonna love it." Tom pulled in a parking lot and grabbed his backpack out of the backseat.

"What do you have in there?" I asked.

"Picnic essentials. You up for a little hike?"

"Sure."

A magnolia tree, bursting with blooms, marked the entrance to a trail. We passed through the sweet, spring perfume and followed the dirt path, up a sloping hill.

"I can't believe we're the only ones here," I said.

"It'll be more crowded in the summer, but it's so big, you can still find your own private spot."

We walked a little further until the path leveled out.

"This way." Tom slipped his hand into mine and led me off the trail, over to a small gathering of pine trees.

"Is this the perfect picnic spot or what?"

I sat down on a blanket of pine needles, always surprised at how soft they are. I leaned back on my forearms, gazing up at the canopy of trees encircling us. The branches were like outstretched arms, the sun glittering through the fingers.

"Mmm, this would make a great campsite."

Tom lay down next to me, propped up on his elbow.

"It's *sylvan*. Ha, SAT word."

His sandy, hazel eyes were more green than usual; spring was showing up everywhere.

"I wanted us to get away before basketball camp starts up. I won't have as much free time then."

He pulled a rolled-up magazine out of his backpack. "Jake asked me to give this to you. He marked a page for you to look at."

I sat up and spread the magazine across my lap. It was the May edition of *Climbing* opened to the listing of competitions and rankings. Jake had highlighted one name in several of the junior competitions.

"Becky!" I blurted.

"That's how he said you'd react."

"I can't believe it! Third place, second place," I scanned the list. "First place!"

"So what's her story?" Tom said.

"She's . . . she's just not that good!" I sputtered. "At least she never used to be. She's not in tune with nature, like I bet it would never occur to her to think there's energy in rocks." I tossed the magazine over my head. "Her family creeps me out. They just want the spotlight."

"Looks like she's got the spotlight now."

"Worse, she's taken my place on the podium," I said.

"You gonna take it back?"

I looked at him for a moment without answering. "What did Jake say?"

"He said you're going to kick some butt. And he wants to go with you."

I grinned and pushed his shoulder.

"I want to focus on outdoor climbs though, the bouldering comps, putting up new routes. I need to get Jake out on real rocks. Then he's gonna be unstoppable. I think he can get some sponsors, at least get his gear and some travel expenses paid."

"You really think he's ready?" Tom asked.

"Oh yeah, definitely. I'm going to steal away your hoops protégé."

We were quiet for a minute, and I leaned back on my forearms again, closing my eyes. A whisper of breeze tiptoed across my face. After the winter gloom, everything felt fresh and new. Alive.

Jake and I had already started planning a bake sale at Planet Granite to fund our travel, and Grandma had agreed to help us make her amazing cookies. If I could get her out of the house to help us sell the cookies too, with all those climbers praising her baking skills —it'd be a win-win.

"So I guess you'll be busy this summer too, if you're traveling to cliffs and competing again," Tom said.

I nodded. "I don't think I could ever play a sport like basketball. It's so loud. I couldn't concentrate. Climbing is quiet. It's all you can think about."

"Actually, basketball's the same way. You have to keep your head in the game. One tiny distraction and you've lost the ball. That's one reason why I never had a girlfriend before. Ann-Marie and her friends would come to the game yelling my name and expecting me to look over and wave or something. But you can't do that. They don't understand."

I did. I squeezed his hand. "What's the other reason? For never having a girlfriend."

"There wasn't anyone I liked enough. Until now."

A wavy lock of hair flopped over his eyes as he looked down into my face, his grin so irresistible. He trailed his fingertips up my forearm.

"Back in middle school, everyone started dating. My friends were asking girls out, and then they'd break up a week later. It was so stupid. Finally, in seventh grade, they bugged me enough about this one girl, and I asked her out. It was so weird. We broke up a month later, and she wouldn't even look at me after that."

His fingertip plucked the beaded bracelets on my wrist and stroked along the inside of my elbow. "I liked you so much, but I didn't want things to ever get weird between us."

"You're already thinking of breaking up with me?"

"No! I didn't mean it that way. I don't know, I think my parents' divorce kind of messed me up."

"Do they still talk to each other?"

"Barely. My dad picks me up on Wednesdays and waits in the car for me to come out."

"Wednesdays at the pupusaria?"

"He's working in South America for a whole month. No pupusas for a while."

"You could take me instead."

"All right, yeah, this Wednesday. It's a date. You have to speak español though."

"What? Seriously?"

"Nah. Everyone else will though. It's a bunch of Latino guys eating at folding tables in this Salvadoran lady's garage."

"The pupusaria is at someone's house?"

"So *delicioso*." Tom rubbed his belly, then laughed.

"What?"

"Just picturing you there with all the dark-haired hombres. Kind of like you hanging out with the goth crowd at school. How did that even happen?"

I shrugged. "I don't know. Kaitlyn and I joked that it was destiny."

"After Adam's accident, it was like the earth had tilted. Everything was just a little bit off. I didn't feel like the same person. But then, you know, time goes by, I was busy with school and basketball and everything. And then you showed up, and the earth tilted again."

I had felt it flipped upside down.

"You looked so lost. Your shiny gold hair, and your deep, dark, sad eyes. Sitting at the goth table. You were like . . ." Tom paused and grinned. He continued in a dramatic, deep, slow voice, "The Angel of Darkness."

"Angel of Darkness!" I squealed.

We cracked up, and I shoved him onto his back. I jumped on top of him, pinning his arms.

"I am the Angel of Darkness, and I will haunt you forever!"

"Have mercy," Tom cried, struggling to free himself. "Damn, you're strong."

He stopped struggling, and I relaxed my hold.

"I was worried you wouldn't come back from California," he said.

"Me too."

"I'm so glad you decided to come home."

"Me too."

I brushed my fingertip over the scar on his lip, then leaned down and kissed him. A deep, lingering, blood-cell-bursting kiss. Our lips parted, and he whispered, "Have mercy."

In one swift movement, he flipped me onto my back and pinned me. "Ha! Gotcha!"

His eyes locked with mine, and our lips met again, hungry and searching. The Earth tilted.

ACKNOWLEDGMENTS

A mountain of gratitude to:

My editor, Jotham Burrello, for ushering my book out into the world. For sharing my vision and for having confidence in my writing and what I have to say.

This manuscript rode a wave of luck and landed in the inbox of a fellow rock climber, Amanda Hurley. Your enthusiastic embrace of Cara's story was so rewarding, as was that of the three judges of the Helen Sheehan YA Book Prize, Kelly Jensen, Anne Rouyer, and Meghan Dietsche Goel.

The rest of the team at Elephant Rock Books: Joe Giasullo, Anne McPeak, Jessica Powers, Christopher Morris and Grace Glander. Fisheye Graphic Services crew: Lee Nagan, Dan Prazer, and designer Amanda Schwarz. I couldn't have dreamed of a more perfect cover.

Carrie Pestritto, my energetic and exuberant literary agent whose emails are always filled with exclamation points!

The Society of Children's Book Writers and Illustrators and the kid-lit writing and blogging communities. Especially my longtime critique partners and mentors, Tracy Bilen, Lisa Chottiner, Laura Handy, and Nan Cappo, who have been there from the beginning. I couldn't have grown as a writer and persevered without your support year after year.

An extra shout out to Lisa for teaching me Yiddish. And Gladys Venegas for correcting my Spanish.

Edite Kroll: you were the first publishing professional to believe in this novel. In memory of Heather McManus: this manuscript benefited from her hours of careful reading alongside Edite.

My first teen reader, Elena. Sorry you had to read the super sad early draft.

Carolyn Coman at the Highlights Foundation Whole Novel Workshop, for rescuing me from the dead-parents canon of YA literature.

Tim Wynne-Jones for a year of cranky first-draft critiquing / missed deadlines on a different novel via Humber College. Lessons learned.

Bri Kinney at Planet Rock for answering my questions about the intricacies of teen competition climbing. Any mistakes are my own or a purposeful altering to better suit the story.

Kathy Gardner, my first rock climbing compadre.

Cherie and Gerry for sharing their Ecuador travel experience and enduring my picky questions. "So, the market was colorful, but what did you smell? What did you touch?"

My friends and family who continued to ask about my writing year after year, even when I had little progress to show beyond my own computer files. You are here in my neighborhood, spread across the country, and even overseas. You know who you are, and I'm sending each of you a super squeeze hug.

An extra hug for my Ecuadorian friend Martha for making sure I got it right.

Mom and Dad, for always being there and believing in me. For letting me read any book whenever and wherever I wanted.

My brother, Jason, for all things computer related. You awesome nerd.

My patient husband, Bob, who marvels that I somehow chose the two worst-paying careers—social work and writing. We have years of memories of camping, climbing, and traveling, and many more adventures ahead of us.

My daughter, Maya, most of all.

THE ART OF
Holding
On
AND
Letting
Go

Kristin Bartley Lenz

ELEPHANT
ROCK
BOOKS
YA

Elephant Rock's Amanda Hurley discusses the writing of *The Art of Holding On and Letting Go* with author Kristin Bartley Lenz. Learn more about Kristin at kristinbartleylenz.com.

Amanda Hurley: How did *The Art of Holding On and Letting Go* come to be?

Kristin Bartley Lenz: I moved from Michigan to Atlanta, Georgia, in my midtwenties and discovered a new world of outdoor enthusiasm in the mountains of Georgia, Tennessee, and North Carolina: hiking, backpacking, white-water kayaking, climbing. My husband and I followed the careers of well-known mountaineers, and one by one, each of these climbers died attempting epic summits. These were men with wives and children at home. Around the same time, a famous female mountaineer, Alison Hargreaves, died on K2, and she—unlike her male counterparts—was criticized for leaving her children behind. I began to wonder what it would be like to be the child of a famous mountaineer. How would that child's upbringing be different? And what if both of her parents were extreme mountaineers, not just one? How would this shape her world?

AH: So these essential questions are triggered by a tragedy you observed. Then how soon after did you realize Cara would be the young hero to sort it all out?

KBL: I sat with these questions for several years and wrote a different novel based on my social work experience. That first novel hasn't been published, but it was the practice I needed to understand how to write Cara's story. An article in *Outside* magazine about families left behind by the deaths of mountaineers brought me back to those earlier questions, and Cara was born.

AH: You have several different locales for this tale: the mountains of Ecuador, the suburbs of Detroit, the wilderness of California. Why did you choose these settings for Cara's story?

KBL: My husband and I lived in California for four years, and the Angeles National Forest was our rock climbing playground for the first year. I could clearly picture Cara and her family living there. I would love to go to Ecuador one day, but for this story I had to rely on research. I wanted Cara's parents' expedition to be somewhere other than the Himalayas. Everest has become overrun by commercial operations, and many of the truly dedicated mountaineers are seeking other remote mountains. Chimborazo is unique in that it rivals Everest in height because of its location at the bulging equator—just like Cara's dad explains in the story. There really was a World Youth Championship near Quito several years ago, and around that same time I had friends who traveled to Ecuador. They took notes during their trip and shared photos and descriptions. And metro Detroit is my home. It's where I grew up and where I eventually returned to raise my daughter. Through Cara's story, I wanted to explore this idea of home and what it means to each of us.

AH: To quote the dust jacket copy—"discovering that home can be far from where you started." This is the major theme of the novel. It resonated with the Sheehan judges and subsequent readers. My previous question was about place, but Cara learns that the idea of home transcends a physical place.

KBL: "Home is where the heart is" has become a cliché, but it only tells part of the story. Cara's heart is in California, but it's also in Michigan, and there's a piece left behind in Ecuador too. Home can be what you make it, wherever and whenever you need it to be.

AH: Cara's is a soul divided. Between the mountains and the city. Between her old life and new. Why did you structure the novel this way? What is it about Cara's struggle that makes her story universal?

KBL: I wrote Cara's story a few years after I moved from California back home to Michigan. I was struggling with this transition and the losses that came with it: I had left my job, friendships, and a beautiful climate with daily access to nature. I was a new mom, feeling isolated and uncertain in a new environment, trying to raise my daughter. My grandmother died suddenly. I think everyone can relate to this feeling of loss during times of transition. Children and teens especially experience so many transitions as a normal part of growing up: changing schools, changing friends, even their own changing bodies. Even if you haven't yet experienced the loss of a loved one, I think everyone can connect in some way to Cara's struggle.

AH: Cara relies heavily on the wisdom of nature writers. What is your connection to these writers and works? How do you think these works shape or mimic Cara's journey?

KBL: I'm not sure when I first discovered some of these nature writers. A friend gave me one of Rick Bass's books many years ago, and I've long been a fan of Barbara Kingsolver. But it was Annie Dillard's *Pilgrim at Tinker Creek* that really made me want to incorporate these themes into a young adult novel. Dillard was influenced by Thoreau, and I stumbled upon an old copy of *Walden* at a used bookstore. When I refer to *Walden* in Cara's story, it's my own beat-up copy that I'm describing— the yellowed pages, the cover that's held on with tape. These writings have been a respite during stressful or lonely times, especially when I've been unable to be out in nature myself. Many of these books are about seeking—either the author or her characters are looking for something, something they've lost or something they need to find—in order to heal, to feel complete, content. They're a window into the peace and depth of wilderness. They're about discovery and asking big questions. In this way, they were perfect guides for Cara.

AH: What importance does Cara's back-to-nature journey have in our current environment of kids and teens who are glued to their iDevices?

KBL: I didn't intend to write a book urging teens to unplug, but as the story developed, this theme emerged—how differently Cara's worldview has been shaped by her immersion in nature rather than electronics. The powerful effects of nature on healing and learning are increasingly researched and reported, and I hope more kids and adults find slices of nature whenever they can, whether it's a trip to a national park or a simple stroll through their neighborhood park.

AH: You chose to root a good portion of the story in the arena of competitive rock climbing.

KBL: I learned to rock climb on an outdoor cliff in Tennessee. Indoor rock climbing gyms existed but weren't as popular as they are now. I never became a competitive climber, but I've climbed around the United States and in Europe.

AH: Was researching this aspect of Cara's life difficult?

KBL: I had been immersed in the sport for many years when I wrote the first draft of this story, but I still needed to research the competition aspects. There are different types of competition climbing, levels, age groups, et cetera, and I simplified all of it for this story because ultimately Cara's journey is about much more than climbing.

AH: The climbing sequences are incredibly vivid. The scene of Cara climbing under the viaduct is a personal favorite. Have you ever done that sort of urban climbing?

KBL: When you become a climber, you see the potential everywhere—brick buildings, stone walls. There have been times when I couldn't resist reaching out and climbing on, but I've never sought out urban climbing beyond the climbing gym. It's a popular movement that's gaining momentum right now. It might seem at odds with traditional climbing in the wilderness, but urban climbing has its pluses—it brings accessibility and diversity to the sport.

AH: Did your background as a social worker inform your treatment of Cara's coming of age?

KBL: I've always worked with children and teens as a social worker. When adults talk about teens, it's often in disparaging or dismaying terms—how difficult they are and how parents have to suffer through these trying years. Yes, it's a time of great growth and upheaval, which is challenging, but people tend to underestimate the resilience, capacity for empathy, and intellectual depth of teens. My own daughter and her friends amaze me on a regular basis, and I continue to be inspired by the teens I worked with as a social worker years ago.

AH: How does Kaitlyn's journey of self-discovery mirror Cara's? Did you mean for the two girls to be foils of each other?

KBL: I guess I did create Cara and Kaitlyn as opposites in many ways without putting a lot of thought into it initially—that came later through revision. I didn't want Cara to easily fall in with athletic peers; she needed to learn from someone different from her. And she needed to take some actions rather than simply reacting to everything thrown at her. The most obvious action would have been running away back to California. But I've seen this in many other stories, and it would have been unrealistic for Cara. I decided that she needed to think outside of herself and help someone else. She could teach someone to climb, someone who would especially benefit from the mental and physical strength that climbing brings. Who would climbing be especially difficult for?

Kristin Bartley Lenz

AH: Kaitlyn.

KBL: Exactly. A character who is missing fingers and has experienced a major rejection that knocked the confidence out of her.

AH: Were you trying to make a statement about femininity, feminism, and woman power in sports with the dichotomy of Cara and Becky?

KBL: I knew I wanted Cara to be a strong female protagonist, but Becky's character didn't get more fully developed until later drafts at the urging of my editor. I needed to ask myself what her purpose in the story was. For Becky, climbing is a trendy sport to be used for fame; she makes the most of her sexuality and physical allure to make a name for herself. It's about how she looks, which is the message that girls are bombarded with from a young age. Cara doesn't care how she looks getting up that wall, so long as she's got the strength and stamina to do it. For her, climbing is about the challenge, the balance of strength and skill, finesse and focus, as well as being connected to nature and the greater world around her. But at the same time, she's becoming more aware of her own evolving sexuality, beauty, and strength throughout the course of the novel.

AH: For me, Cara and Becky represent two different "ideals" of women in sports. I felt a little bad for Becky, almost like she's resorted to this version of acceptance because her sexuality is what's been touted to her as her biggest asset. Does having a daughter of your own bring this struggle of the "feminine ideal" to the forefront of your mind?

KBL: I had always hoped my daughter would find a sport to grow her strength and confidence. It didn't turn out to be climbing, but she's played soccer since she was five. The girls play aggressively, and in Michigan they're often playing in challenging conditions: it's cold, wet, muddy. (It's great to see the US women's soccer team using their power to fight for equal pay.) For some girls it could be music or robotics or the arts; however they succeed and find a way to express themselves.

My hope for girls is that even though they're exposed to all of those sexy images that surround us in the media, they'll be able to focus on their strength and health and what's right for them without trying to live up to unrealistic ideals.

AH: What was the revision process for *The Art of Holding on and Letting Go*?

KBL: This story was rewritten several times over several years. In the first draft, Cara's parents died, and Uncle Max was later found. I brought the manuscript to the Highlights Foundation Whole Novel Workshop, where I worked with award-winning author Carolyn Coman. She suspected that I wanted to explore loss, not major grief, and asked me to consider keeping Cara's parents alive. She was right, and I completely rewrote the story. The Ecuador section didn't exist in the early drafts; the story started in Michigan, and the reader learned what had happened in flashbacks. I also experimented with different ways of telling the story and wrote one version with alternating past/present, Ecuador/Michigan chapters. After I won the Sheehan prize, and Elephant Rock acquired the novel, I spent four months of intensive revising with my editor, Jotham Burrello. He pushed me to look deeper, hear Cara's voice, show emotions, add specific details, and cut lines and repetitive scenes that didn't advance the story. Writing is something that you learn by doing. I am a slow learner. I wish my process went faster, but with each story, with each draft, I continue to grow as a writer.

AH: How'd you know it was capital D "Done"?

KBL: I don't think it will ever be done! This story has lived with me for so many years, but at some point I had to trust that I'd shared enough of Cara's journey for readers to understand and make it their own.

O

QUESTIONS AND TOPICS FOR DISCUSSION

How do the writings of naturalists such as John Muir, Henry David Thoreau, and Annie Dillard shape Cara's worldview?

Cara is deeply affected by the death of her uncle Max. In what ways does she mourn and celebrate his memory?

The contrast between Cara's climbing life and her suburban life are in conflict throughout the novel. How does she make peace with these competing landscapes?

Cara feels most free when she's climbing. What activity in your life brings you this kind of joy and liberation?

Did you notice the lack of technology in Cara's life? What are the effects of Cara not having her nose buried in a cell phone 24-7? What is she able to experience more fully?

How does being an outsider on the climbing team and in school shape Cara's identity?

How does Kaitlyn's experience and growth throughout the novel mirror Cara's? How do these friends help each other?

How does Cara's relationship with her free-spirited parents evolve over the course of the novel? What does Cara understand about her parents at the end of the book that she didn't at the beginning?

Compare and contrast the three different settings of the novel. How do these environments contribute to the action and meaning of the book?

Cara spends the first two-thirds of the novel wanting to return to California. What does she realize about the meaning of home during her time with Nick, Kaitlyn, and her grandparents?

ALSO BY ELEPHANT ROCK BOOKS

The Carnival at Bray
by **Jessie Ann Foley**

"Powerfully Evocative!"
– *Kirkus Reviews*, Starred Review

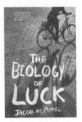

The Biology of Luck
by **Jacob M. Appel**

"Clever, vigorously written, intently observed, and richly emotional."
–*Booklist*

Briefly Knocked Unconscious by a Low-Flying Duck: Stories from 2nd Story

"This collection will demand, and receive, return trips from its readers."
–*Publishers Weekly*, Starred Review

The Temple of Air
by **Patricia Ann McNair**

"This is a beautiful book, intense and original."
–Audrey Niffenegger